A Man Like That

ALISON HENDERSON

This is a work of fiction. Names, characters, places, and incidents either are the product of the author's imagination or are used fictitiously, and any resemblance to actual persons living or dead, business establishments, events, or locales, is entirely coincidental.

A Man Like That

COPYRIGHT 2018 by Alison Henderson

All rights reserved. No part of this book may be used or reproduced in any manner whatsoever without written permission of the author except in the case of brief quotations embodied in critical articles or reviews.

Cover Art by *Creative Author Services*

Publishing History
Originally published by The Wild Rose Press, Adams Basin, NY, 2011
Second Edition published by Alison Henderson 2018

Published in the United States of America

ISBN-13: 978-1-0910-7920-5

DEDICATION

To my wonderful husband Michael, without whom I could never have written this book.

And to my parents, whose enthusiasm and support for my writing career has never waned.

Chapter One

Weston, Missouri
October 1866

Clusters of yellow chrysanthemums glowed on the altar. Organ music piped in the background. Wedding guests murmured in the sanctuary. Every detail was perfect, except one.

Hoops swaying beneath her ivory silk gown, Jessamine Randall paced the length of the tiny anteroom of the Weston Baptist Church, clutching the mass of limp threads that had once been her favorite lace handkerchief. Every few steps, she paused to bat at the lone copper curl that escaped its pin and dangled in front of her nose.

Back and forth, Jessy marched past the other two occupants of the room without acknowledging their presence. She caught her lower lip between her teeth and turned her head toward the door. The muffled din of the guests in the sanctuary had grown to a jabbering chorus. She stopped pacing.

Where in heaven's name is Morgan?

Her mother fluttered about like a trapped moth. "Oh, Jessamine, whatever shall we do if your young man doesn't arrive soon? We've kept the guests waiting so long as it is. I'm afraid everyone will begin to leave."

"Oh, bother the guests." Jessy waved away her mother's concern with the remnants of her handkerchief, barely noting the look of shocked horror on her mother's face. Annabelle Randall treated social obligations like the Ten Commandments—carved in stone. Right now, Jessy had more serious concerns.

Lisa Tanner, her oldest childhood friend, reached for her arm. "I'm sure Morgan will be here any minute."

"He should have been here an hour ago. When he arrives, I don't know whether to kiss him or kick him."

Lisa's dark brows drew together. "I can only imagine how I would have felt if Jared had been late for our wedding. Would you like me to ask him to check the boarding house to make sure Morgan is all right?"

Jessy bit her lip, her indignation forgotten. Three weeks had passed since Morgan had saved her life in the fire at her school, but the doctor had assured her he'd fully recovered from the effects of the smoke inhalation. What if he'd suffered a relapse?

She flashed Lisa a look of gratitude. "That would be wonderful."

Lisa nodded and slipped from the room in search of her husband.

"Oh, dear," Annabelle fussed. "I do hope he hasn't come down with the ague. One can never be too careful."

"Mama, he was perfectly healthy yesterday. I'm sure he's fine." A tiny shiver shook her shoulders.

Morgan had tried to see her that morning, but she'd sent him away. At the time, she'd been anticipating his expression when she walked down the aisle on her father's arm. Now, she regretted her decision.

Her mother wrung her small hands in their lace mitts. "I feared Morgan wouldn't turn out to be the reliable sort."

Jessy choked and tried to cover it with a cough.

Reliable. What would her proper mother say if she knew her future son-in-law had once ridden with Jesse James?

"Mama, I'm not marrying Morgan because he's reliable. That would bore me in a week. I'm marrying him because he's exciting."

But excitement was only part of the attraction Morgan held for her. Jessy didn't have the patience to unravel the complex tangle of her emotions right now. Besides, she doubted her mother could understand the tingling thrill that raced through her when Morgan held her in his arms. She was sure Annabelle Randall had never tingled in her life.

"Jessamine, I can't imagine where you get such ridiculous notions. A good husband is stable and dependable, like your father. Exciting indeed! Do you think it's exciting to fail to appear for one's own wedding?"

Jessy refused to waste time arguing with her mother, who, as the wife of the local judge, was a scion of society in the small western Missouri river town and a paragon of propriety. She resumed her pacing. Her father popped in and out several times, his face growing redder with each visit.

After what seemed like an eternity, Lisa returned, and Jessy pounced on her. "Did Jared see Morgan? Is he all right? Will he be here soon?"

Lisa swallowed and glanced at her shoes.

"Well, tell me. What did Jared find out?"

"I'm afraid he didn't see Morgan."

"Morgan wasn't there?"

"No." Lisa continued to avoid Jessy's gaze. "But he left this for you." She held out a folded piece of paper.

Jessy snatched the note and scanned the words twice before crushing the paper in her fist.

Distress crept across Annabelle's features. "What is it, dear?"

"Of all the misguided, wrong-headed...I can't believe he wrote me a note. He couldn't even bring himself to tell me to my face."

"What's happened?" Her mother's brows pinched together in alarm.

Jessy threw the crumpled paper to the floor. "He's gone, left town. He says he can't marry me because we're too different, because he has nothing to offer me. What nonsense!"

"Now, dear, Morgan's circumstances are somewhat uncertain, despite the position your father arranged for him at the mercantile. Perhaps he decided a man should be able to properly provide for his bride before he marries." Her mother's tone left no doubt as to her opinion on the subject.

"Mama, I am not marrying Morgan for his money."

"Obviously not, dear."

Jessy shot her mother a sharp look but held her tongue. An argument now wouldn't help anything.

Her mother patted her arm. "I'm afraid if the man has left town, you won't be able to marry him at all."

That bald-faced statement of truth deflated Jessy. Not marry Morgan? Unthinkable. For the past three weeks, since nearly losing him in the fire, she had plunged body and soul into her plans to marry Morgan. She could no longer imagine a future without him. A sudden inspiration burst into her mind. She drew herself up to her full five feet two inches and squared her shoulders.

"I will just have to go after him."

Her mother gasped and clutched one hand to her well-corseted bosom. "Jessamine, you'll give me palpitations. You mustn't even consider such a thing. For whatever reason, Mr. Bigham has changed his mind about marrying you. It would be shameless, not to mention dangerous, to go chasing after a man who doesn't want you. I won't hear of it."

Jessy forced her expression to remain confident, but her stomach knotted, recoiling from the blow of her mother's words. What if Morgan really didn't want her?

Had she read too much into the blaze in his eyes that singed her soul whenever they were alone? Although she'd endeavored to overlook the fact, he'd never come right out and said he loved her. She'd chalked it up to natural reticence. The man was stingier with words than a miser with pennies.

But he needed her. She knew it. And since her school closed, he was the only one who did. Her parents loved her, but they didn't need her. Her father buried himself in his work, and her mother flitted from one social event to the next. Morgan might not be a big talker, but he had a way of looking at her that made her feel like the center of the universe, his universe.

She refused to let doubts sneak in and cloud her thinking. Action was the answer. Action would put all doubts and confusion to rest. Morgan was simply— albeit wrongly—trying to be noble. She would go after him, find him, and force him to admit how much he loved her. Then they would come back to Weston and settle down.

It was a very tidy plan, and she clung to it with single-minded tenacity.

"Mama, I am not a child. I'm a grown woman of twenty-one, and I know what I want from life. I love Morgan, and I am going to marry him. You can't stop me."

"Oh, Jessamine, why do you have to be so stubborn? Can't you see you're throwing your life away on a no-account drifter?"

"Mama…"

Annabelle dropped her hand from her throat. "I'm going to get your father. He'll know what to do." She swept out of the room, leaving Jessy alone with Lisa.

"Jessy, you aren't serious, are you?"

"Of course, I am." Jessy was rapidly warming to the idea. "It's the only thing to do."

Lisa shook her head. "Jessamine Randall, in all the years I've known you, this is without a doubt the most harebrained scheme you've ever hatched."

Jessy didn't reply as her thoughts jumped ahead to her search for Morgan. The adventure had already assumed the proportions of an epic quest, and she found herself anticipating it with relish.

"I bet I know where he's gone," she murmured, more to herself than to Lisa.

"Jessy, be reasonable. He could have gone anywhere. Does he have any family?"

Jessy nodded. "He has family in the Ozarks, and he hasn't seen them since the war ended. I'm sure that's where he's gone."

Lisa frowned and shook her head. "You don't know that, and even if you did, you can't go after him alone. This whole thing is idiotic. I bet you don't even know where the Ozark Mountains are."

"Of course, I do. I am a teacher, remember. The Ozarks are in southern Missouri, and I know which direction is south. Besides, I'm sure I'll catch up with him before I have to worry about that."

Lisa puffed out a breath. "Jessy, be serious. Morgan has spent the last several years on the back of a horse, and he knows where he's going."

Jessy lifted her chin. "I'll remind you I'm an experienced traveler. I have been to Philadelphia and back."

"Yes, on a train."

The door crashed open. Her father stormed through and glowered. "I've called off this charade and sent everyone home. I understand Bingham skipped town, and you think you're going after him."

"Papa, he hasn't skipped town, as you put it."

He raised his hand to dismiss her protest. "No point splitting hairs. To my mind, you're well rid of the man. Now let's go home." He ran one beefy hand down the fine worsted fabric covering his portly midsection. "It's almost six o'clock, and I want my supper."

Secure in her plans, Jessy nodded. "Of course, Papa." It wouldn't do to further aggravate her father. If he accepted the explanation in the note she planned to leave, he might not come looking for her for a day or two. That should be all the time she needed.

During supper, no one mentioned her plan to follow Morgan. Her father announced his satisfaction that she seemed to have recovered from her hysterical notions. Her parents were solicitous when she retired to her room early, pleading exhaustion and a headache. She hoped they would follow her lead and fall asleep early. She had preparations to make if she hoped to leave by midnight.

Her nimble mind had been churning for hours and bubbled with plans to catch up to her errant fiancé and bring him back where he belonged. Morgan didn't have more than a day's head start, and he wouldn't expect her to follow him. If she made good time, she could find him and persuade him to return before anyone realized what had happened. By this time next week, she would be Mrs. Morgan Bingham, as planned.

She laid out her dark blue serge riding habit and boots and stuffed a few necessary items, along with the money her father had given her as a wedding present, into a large carpetbag. She thought about what she would say to Morgan when she found him. She could picture the whole scene in her mind. He would be surprised to see her and maybe a little angry at first. But her tenderness and eloquence would persuade him of the depth of her emotions. Finally, he would capitulate and declare his undying love. They would return to Weston and be married, only a few days late. She refused to allow the slightest qualm to threaten the romantic picture.

When she had dressed and finished packing, Jessy wrote a letter to her parents explaining that she had gone to spend a few days with Lisa at her farm to "recover from the heartbreak and shame" of the cancelled wedding. She begged them to leave her in peace until she overcame her "devastation." Then she sprinkled it with a few drops of water for effect. Her mother would never question such a response from a jilted bride, and with luck, no one would come looking for her. She turned out the kerosene lamp next to her bed and sat down to wait.

As soon as she was sure the household had sunk into imperturbable slumber, she picked up her bag and tiptoed into the hallway, careful not to make a sound on the polished wood floor. The cold, bright light of a full moon shone through the arched window on the landing above the stairs, casting a pattern of elongated rectangles across her skirt and the floor.

She made her way down to the kitchen where the housemaid had packed the large pantry with the food intended for the wedding supper. Peeking into various containers, Jessy helped herself to sliced smoked ham, half a loaf of tangy rye bread, and a large wedge of peach pie. She only intended to be gone a few days, and she and Morgan could buy more food for the journey home.

Fully provisioned, she slipped from the house and lugged her bag across the moonlit backyard to the carriage house where her horse Princess was stabled. Princess nickered softly when she pushed open the door of the darkened building. Minutes later they emerged together with Jessy seated atop her custom-made English sidesaddle with her bag strapped on behind.

She hadn't exaggerated her knowledge of geography to Lisa by much. She had a vague idea where the Ozarks were. When she and Princess reached the outskirts of town, she nudged her mare to the right, and they headed south down the deserted dirt road. With luck, she would meet someone who had seen Morgan by the time she reached Independence the next day. If not, she might have to buy a map.

By the time the sun rose the next morning, Jessy began to have second thoughts about her plan. In her excitement, she had forgotten how penetrating the cold of a clear October night could be. The thin wool jacket of her stylish riding habit offered scant protection against the frosty night air. She had also neglected to consider the physical effects of several hours perched on the rock-hard sidesaddle.

By seven-thirty, according to the small watch pinned to her jacket above her left breast, her back screamed, her eyes stung, and her stomach growled. She drew Princess to a halt next to a small stream and dismounted stiffly. Through the skirt of her habit and layers of petticoats, she massaged her aching backside while the horse guzzled the cold, clear water. Until now, the longest ride either of them had taken was a pleasant morning's canter through the neighboring fields. It occurred to Jessy that Princess was no more accustomed to the ordeal of a long, hard trip than her mistress.

She patted the horse's flank. "I'm sorry, girl. It won't be much longer." Morgan would have had no reason to ride through the night. They must be gaining ground on him with every mile.

As she watched Princess graze, her stomach rumbled again with greater insistence. She marched over to the carpetbag on the ground and rummaged for the parcel of food. Ignoring the bread and ham, she went straight for the peach pie.

The battered condition of the pastry did nothing to diminish its delectable flavor. Savoring the first sweet, flaky mouthful, she reveled in the defiant gesture. She would never have dared eat peach pie for breakfast at home, but doing so now renewed her sense of independence and adventure. By the time she finished the whole piece, her spirits had rebounded. She washed her hands and face in the icy stream, took a good, long drink, and prepared to mount.

The next ten hours took a bruising toll on her body and spirits. By the time she and Princess dragged themselves into Independence, they had been on the road for almost a day without rest. Poor Princess was hobbling, and Jessy struggled to hold herself upright in the saddle. The sun had set when she reined in at a small hotel on the courthouse square. She ordered a bath and a meal sent up to her room and a bag of oats and a good rubdown for Princess in the livery stable out back.

After the hot bath banished the chill from her bones and the cook's chicken pie filled the hollow in her stomach, she climbed into the warm bed, pulled the covers up to her chin, and tried to fall asleep. She should have dropped right off after everything she'd been through during the past thirty-six hours, but her mind refused to relax.

Thoughts of Morgan rushed in to torment her. Where was he? What was he thinking? Did he miss her as much as she missed him? Why had he run off like that? He was no coward. Perhaps some deep, hidden secret prevented him from marrying her. Maybe he had another wife somewhere.

She frowned and cursed her runaway imagination. Whatever the answers, tomorrow she would know. Tomorrow she would find him. It had to be soon. She wasn't sure how much more she and Princess could take.

A few hours' sleep and a hot breakfast went a long way toward restoring her energy and determination. She decided to start the next day off right—she went shopping. At the nearby mercantile, she dabbed at some very convincing tears with her handkerchief while telling the owner how she was moving west with her young brother after the tragic death of their parents. She would need a full suit of warm, sturdy clothes for the boy, who was about her size. She also needed a couple of warm blankets and a revolver with ammunition. She didn't want to worry about being accosted on the trip.

The elderly proprietor frowned while he filled her order. "Missy, I hope you and your brother don't have no notion to travel out west by yourselves. There's all manner of riffraff around since the war ended. The trail's no place for a young lady and a boy travelin' alone."

Jessy widened her eyes in a fashion guaranteed to pry information from the most close-mouthed male. "Why no, sir. I've arranged for a guide. Perhaps you've seen him—a tall, lean man, cleanshaven, with sandy hair and hazel eyes. He goes by the name of Bingham, Morgan Bingham."

The man stopped to consider, stroking his tobacco-stained, white-stubbled chin. "Seems to me we had a feller through here yesterday answerin' to that description, but he weren't headed west. If I recollect, he said he were goin' home, somewhere in the mountains, down around Springfield, I think. Must not have been your man."

"No, I don't suppose so."

So, Morgan was here yesterday. A giddy sensation rushed to her head. She was on the right track. Now, if only she could make up some time...

She accepted the brown paper-wrapped package. "I must be on my way. Thank you."

"You're welcome, missy. You and that brother of yours be careful, y' hear?"

Jessy smiled and hurried out of the store. She walked back to the livery stable as fast as her high-heeled boots and numerous petticoats would allow. When she stepped into the dark, dusty barn, she was relieved to discover the owner was not on duty. Instead, she encountered a dull-eyed young man who nodded sleepily at her request to trade her custom-made sidesaddle with the beautiful hand-tooled leather for a worn, plain saddle she pointed out hanging from a nail in the wall. She thanked him and led Princess into the frosty morning sunlight.

She mounted and squirmed, trying to find some decent way to accommodate the unaccustomed shape of the saddle to the skirts of her riding habit. She finally hooked her right knee around the horn and held on for dear life. Directing Princess to the street, she rode south very slowly, like a Bedouin maiden on a swaying camel.

As soon as they left the outskirts of town, she steered Princess to a thicket of walnut and oak trees beside the road. She slid to the ground and untied the parcel from the mercantile. After tugging and jerking on hooks, tapes, and buttons, she transformed herself from a stylish young lady into a small, nondescript boy.

Jessy grinned with satisfaction and tucked her long hair under the shapeless brown hat, completing the metamorphosis. She felt better already. Even though she had retained her restrictive stays and other feminine undergarments, the thick wool pants, heavy socks and boots, flannel shirt, and fleecy woolen coat warded off the chilly air much better than her own clothes. They also gave her a heady new sense of freedom. She felt so unrestrained. She bundled her riding habit and tied it behind the saddle. Then, thrusting her left foot into the stirrup, she vaulted into the saddle the way she had watched men do all her life.

It took a moment to adjust to the strange sensation. The width of the horse's back forced her legs apart in an unfamiliar way, and the heat of the animal's body warmed her flesh through the pants. She gave Princess an experimental nudge with her heels, and the horse moved forward obediently.

Mindful of the importance of speed, she kicked Princess's sides a bit harder. The well-trained horse switched to a trot. With a little more encouragement, she shifted to a canter, and then to a full, uninhibited gallop.

Jessy let out a whoop of sheer joy. She had never felt anything like it, racing along with the wind, moving as one with the sleek animal beneath her. She was off on the adventure of her life—off to find the man she loved.

****

Morgan Bingham allowed his roan gelding to set its own pace down the worn wagon ruts that passed for a road. He knew he should be making tracks, but the long shadows of the trees reminded him of the waning daylight, and he needed time to think— about where he'd been and where he was headed. He didn't want to think about Jessy. He'd tried hard not to think about her ever since he'd left Weston, and as a result, she'd been on his mind every step of the way.

No doubt she'd been as mad as a wet cat when he hadn't turned up for the fancy wedding she'd planned.

But, dammit, she had to accept the fact that they had no future together. She was the cosseted only daughter of a wealthy judge, and he was the eldest son of a foul-tempered, half-pickled mountain man who was long dead and never missed. He'd done things during the war that still tormented his dreams. Hell, he'd even spent a few months as a bank robber.

Now, those months had come back to haunt him. Two days ago, he'd gotten wind of a Pinkerton man sniffing around asking questions. When he hadn't been able to talk Jessy out of the wedding, he'd taken the only remaining course of action. He'd left town. He was used to watching his back, but Jessy wasn't, and he couldn't condemn her to that kind of living hell just because she was too stubborn to know what was good for her.

Besides, how was he supposed to support her? He couldn't imagine standing behind the counter in a store all day like her father had planned. He doubted he could even walk behind a plow since he'd taken a Yankee bullet to the knee at Centralia. And he didn't know how to do much else, leastwise not on the right side of the law. He hadn't even been able to read and write until she taught him.

After breathing in all that smoke carrying her out of her burning school, he'd been stuck in bed at the doc's coughing like a consumptive coyote for three weeks. When his lungs healed enough so he could get three words out in a row, he'd tried to make her listen to the truth, but once she got hold of an idea, she held on like a thirsty leech. She seemed to think he'd be willing to live off her father's charity for the rest of his life. How could she understand so little about him?

Morgan let his mind drift back over the months he'd spent with Jessy, starting with the first time he saw her at her friend Lisa's house. Jessamine Randall's fiery beauty, with her translucent white skin, bouncing red curls, and snapping green eyes, had hit him like a bullet between the eyes. It was the first time he'd been in the presence of such a fine lady, and when she asked him to escort her to her buggy, he'd found himself tongue-tied.

He should have seen it coming that first day, right from the start. Jessy had charged into his life and taken over before he had time to figure out what was going on. Her fashionable exterior hid a feisty little spitfire, a reformer committed first to abolition and then to the education of the freed slaves. Looking back, she must have viewed him as an exciting challenge, a dangerous outlaw ready and waiting to be reformed.

To be truthful, he had quit riding with the James gang after meeting Jessy, but that hadn't been just for her. He'd had more than his fill of the outlaw life.

In spite of—or because of—everything she knew about him, Jessy was fool enough to think she loved him. She had insisted he marry her and refused to listen to any reasons to the contrary.

He could have tried harder to stop her. Should have.

He could tell himself it was because he was weak from the smoke, but that was only half-true. His will was even weaker than his body. The idea that he might deserve a woman like Jessy tempted him beyond reason. If it hadn't been for the Pinkerton man, he might have given in and married her against whatever sense he had left. As if any decent woman in her right mind would want a man like him.

Despite his certainty, a deep ache stabbed his chest when he thought about Jessy. He rubbed, wishing he could make the pain disappear. In a few short months, she'd brought new light and color and meaning into his life. But he didn't love her. He couldn't love her. He wasn't even sure what the word meant. Love had never had any place in the dark, tangled mess of his life.

But he wanted her. Lord, how he wanted her. The few times he'd broken down and touched her, Jessy had responded with an innocent fire that stirred him even now. Thank God he'd always managed to keep his head at the last minute. It sure as hell hadn't been easy.

In fact, nothing about Jessy was easy, but he'd done what he had to do. He always did.

Morgan rode until nightfall, when he stopped next to a thick clump of trees and brush and made camp. He hunkered down next to the fire, wrapped in a blanket to ward off the chill while he waited for the coffee to boil. With the pot in one hand and a cup in the other, he heard a soft rustling in the long grass several yards away. He peered into the darkness, but the light from the fire blotted out everything beyond its reach. He listened carefully. There it was again. A snake? He set his cup down and reached for his revolver.

"Drop it." A high-pitched voice rang out from the darkness.

He flinched in surprise but kept his grip on his gun as he scanned the perimeter of the light circle.

"I said, drop it," the small voice commanded again.

"Show yourself."

"Drop your gun first."

"Like hell."

The figure of a small boy materialized in the semi-darkness at the edge of the light, leading a horse and holding a large pistol, pointed straight at Morgan's midsection. "I said, drop the gun."

He stared, incredulous. His eyes must be playing tricks on him. He squinted in the faint light. "What in the name of heaven? Jessy, is that you?"

Chapter Two

The boy lowered his pistol and reached up and pulled off his hat. A cascade of flaming curls framed a familiar impish grin. "Of course, it's me. Now put that thing down."

Morgan slid his gun into its holster and started toward her. "You little fool! What do you think you're doing, sneaking up on me in the dark with a gun? Don't you know I might have killed you?" He was shouting by the time he reached her and grabbed her shoulders.

"I had the gun precisely so you wouldn't shoot me. I couldn't very well ride up on you unannounced in the dark, could I?"

He dropped his hands, stepped back, and ran his gaze over her from head to foot and back. "Not in that get-up. You look like a damned boy. What are you doing, dressed like that?"

"I thought it would be safer than my own clothes, and it's warmer and more comfortable."

"You look ridiculous, and it could have gotten you killed."

"You wouldn't have shot me. I had my pistol pointed at you. Remember?"

With a snort, he dismissed the idea that she posed a serious threat. "What I can't figure out is what you're doing here in the first place."

"I came after you."

"I figured that, but why?"

"To bring you back."

He steeled himself against the invitation in her smile. "I thought I spelled things out in my letter."

"The letter was clear enough. It was just wrong, the product of faulty logic. I'm sure you'll agree when you've had more time to think about it." Jessy took a step forward and slid her arms beneath his jacket and around his waist. "Now aren't you going to kiss me?"

He grabbed her wrists and threw her hands off him as if she harbored a dread disease.

"Are you sure you don't want to kiss me?" she persisted. "Aren't you glad to see me?" Her seductive tone was pure torture.

Morgan scowled and didn't answer. He had no intention of answering the first question and wasn't sure about the second. At the moment, it required every ounce of strength and resolve he had to keep from jerking her into his arms and taking everything she offered and more.

He stared down at her face in the flickering firelight. Her sparkling eyes beckoned him. Her moist lips parted in invitation. But the same fresh innocence that had always stopped him held him back again.

He could take what he wanted. He knew it. There was no one around to stop him, and Jessy wouldn't resist. She was crazy enough to think she loved him. Talk about faulty logic.

It would be so easy to give in, so easy to forget the past and the future for a few sweet hours in her arms, to forget their differences and lose himself in the generosity of her love. But he couldn't do it. To take her and leave her would be to steal something more precious than her virginity. He would be stealing the bright fire that formed the essence of her, the fire that had drawn him from the beginning. As much as he wanted her, he prayed for the strength to resist her.

"Go home, Jessy." His voice was as cold as the lonely core of his heart.

"I will not. Not without you."

He forced himself to remain calm and implacable. "You have to face the truth. I'm not coming with you, and I'm not going to marry you."

"But I love you, and I know you love me."

"You only think you love me. You'll get over it."

"Stop talking to me as if I were a wayward child. I know how I feel, and I won't get over it."

****

Tears of frustration burned in Jessy's eyes, but she refused to cry. Why was he being so stubborn? Why couldn't he admit he loved her and come home where he belonged?

Morgan remained implacable. "You don't love me. You can't love me."

The remaining shreds of her control gave way, and hysteria threatened to overcome her. She was cold and tired, and this whole encounter was not going according to plan. "Who are you to tell me I can't love you? I know what I feel."

She took a step toward him and poked a finger at the center of his chest. "Of course, there are times—like now—when you can be infuriatingly stubborn, but you are also strong and brave and selfless." She accentuated her recital of his attributes with short jabs of her finger.

He shook his head, a look of stark pain in his green-gold eyes. "You don't know me. I'm none of those things."

The hoarse tone of his voice haunted her. She swallowed the lump forming in her throat at the signs of his suffering. "I know you better than you know yourself. You forget, I've seen you in action."

When he didn't respond, she went on. "You risked your life to protect me in the fire at the school, and don't try to deny it. Everybody in town knows what you did. If that isn't bravery, I don't know what is."

His lips quirked up in a tiny, self-deprecating smile, but his eyes still held the deep sadness that aged him beyond his years. "It's not hard to be brave when it doesn't matter if you live or die."

Her mouth dropped open. "How dare you say that? It matters to me."

"Jessy, we have no future together. I've told you time and again, but you refuse to listen. I'm not the right man for you. I can't give you the kind of life you should have, the kind of life you're used to."

"I don't care about any of that." She reached for him. "I love you."

He shrugged off her hand. "No, you don't." Hard anger replaced the sadness in his voice. "You've got some little-girl infatuation with a big, bad outlaw. You think you can tame me and make me into something I'm not. Well, you can't. I am what I am, and you can't change it. Nobody can."

Her anger rushed to meet his. "You're talking like I dreamed this whole thing up on my own. Not three days ago you wanted to marry me."

His eyes narrowed, and he leaned down until scant inches separated their faces. "Did I? Think back. When did I ever ask you to marry me? When did I ever agree to marry you? You decided all by yourself that was what you wanted. Well, one of these days you're going to have to grow up and face the fact that your papa's money won't buy you everything you want."

A sudden, horrible suspicion dawned in her mind. Bile tickled the back of her throat. She swallowed hard. "Did my father have anything to do with this?"

"What are you talking about?"

Outrage made her bolder. "He did, didn't he? He paid you to leave me."

He didn't respond, but his eyes blazed.

His anger didn't frighten her. The idea that her father might have done such a thing and that Morgan might have accepted the offer pushed her to the edge. "How much did it cost him? How much was I worth?"

His arms rose as if he meant to grab her then dropped to his sides. "Dammit, Jessy. Do you think any man on earth has enough money to keep me away if I decide I want you?"

She searched his eyes then shook her head in silence.

He leaned close, until his face loomed over hers in the darkness. She closed her eyes against the ferocity of his burning gaze.

Now. Now he's finally going to kiss me. Then he won't be able to lie about not loving me anymore. His kiss will tell the truth.

His hot breath fanned her lips, and she let them part, waiting, waiting....

Abruptly, he turned away. He walked back to his gear and picked up his discarded cup. She stared at his stiff back.

Why did he fight so hard when they were so good together? Did he think she couldn't hear the passion in his voice and feel it in his touch? He might be angry and resentful, but he wasn't indifferent to her.

"So now I'm supposed to believe you don't want me?"

He didn't glance up from the coffee pot in his hand. "That's about the size of it."

She marched over and stood beside him with her hands on her hips. "That's a lie."

"I've shot men for saying less." A tiny muscle worked in his jaw, belying his soft tone.

"Then go ahead and shoot me, big, bad outlaw."

His features relaxed. "You always did have a sassy mouth."

"So, what are you going to do about it?"

He looked her over, as if considering his options, and a lazy smile appeared on his face. "Not a thing. Not a dad-blamed thing. You're not my problem. Go on home and find some other poor fool to devil."

"I told you before; I am not going home."

"That's your business then. You're not my problem."

He reached for his saddlebags and fished out a hunk of cornbread. Squatting by the fire, he poured a cup of coffee.

The sight of food and the smell of coffee reminded Jessy's stomach how long it had been since she'd eaten. She pressed her hand to her middle to quiet the insistent gurgle, but one glance at Morgan's face told her the effort was wasted. He kept his gaze on the flames in front of him, but the corner of his mouth twitched in amusement.

She stalked back to where Princess stood nibbling the scrubby grass and yanked the ties holding her bag. It fell open, and she reached inside. Unfortunately, two days of travel had taken their toll on her provisions. The ham was suspiciously slimy and the bread hard and stale. She wrinkled her nose, but they would have to do for tonight. She refused to ask Morgan to share his food.

She dragged her blanket to the fire and draped it around her shoulders. While she ate, she watched him.

He could be difficult and stubborn when he had a mind to be. What was it about him that drew her so strongly? He wasn't handsome, not with that craggy face, thick sandy hair, and deep-set eyes. Perhaps it wasn't the whole, but the separate parts that gave her that sharp, hollow feeling high in the pit of her stomach when she looked at him.

Maybe it was his mouth. She loved his mouth with its well-defined upper lip and full lower one. She loved to kiss that mouth and tug on the lower lip with her teeth. He had taught her that. He had taught her the thrilling sensation of tongues twining. He had opened her eyes to the wonder and mystery of the relationship between men and women, and she wanted more.

Maybe his appeal lay in his eyes, hazel with flecks of green and amber. With every glance, they burned into her from beneath the ridge of his brow. Sometimes his look was lazy and sensual like a well-fed cat, sometimes sharp and hard like splintered granite, and sometimes—rarely, and just for a moment—wounded and vulnerable like a bird with a broken wing.

Maybe it was that hint of vulnerability. He was so strong and tough on the outside and so seldom allowed more than a tantalizing glimpse of the man inside. But that glimpse was enough for her. Morgan needed her, and she knew it. Nothing drew Jessy as much as knowing she was needed.

And now he wanted to deny everything, to deny her and himself.

The bread tasted like sawdust, and she shivered in spite of the heat from the fire and the thick folds of the blanket. By the time she'd choked down all the food she could stomach, the heavenly aroma of Morgan's coffee had driven her to the brink.

Hang her pride. She had to have a cup.

"Do you think you could spare a cup of that coffee?" She tried to keep the question casual, but it came out tainted with the sharp bite of sarcasm.

"I suppose. Got your own cup?"

Drat. Something else she'd forgotten. "No."

"I guess you can use mine."

She rose and walked around the fire to where he sat. He handed her a fresh cup of coffee and watched while she sipped the piping-hot brew.

"Want some more?" He offered the pot when she'd finished.

She returned the cup. "No, I'd better not if I want to sleep tonight."

"Were you planning to sleep here?"

She gritted her teeth. She wanted to grab him and shake this infuriating mood out of him. She much preferred the fire of Morgan riled to this laconic indifference.

"Were you planning to turn me out alone in the dark?"

"I suppose tomorrow's soon enough for you to start back. You might as well stay."

"Thank you so much." She stomped back to her own side of the fire. Then she unsaddled Princess and tied her reins to a sturdy sapling near Morgan's roan.

Wrapped in her blanket, she lay down with her back to the fire, and to him.

****

Morgan glanced at her as he settled his gear for the night. So, Jessy had followed him. He should have expected it; she didn't have a cautious bone in her tempting little body. Life had always been easy and kind to her. As a result, she was too innocent to have a healthy fear of things that were truly dangerous, things like ex-outlaws with nothing to lose.

The firelight cast a warm glow, igniting her soft, tangled curls and illuminating the delectable curve of her back, waist, and hip. He could walk over there right now. His body hardened at the thought. He could do it. He could take her and give himself some much-needed relief, but he wouldn't. Tomorrow he had to send her back, and he wanted to be able to do it without guilt, without regrets, and without wondering whether or not there might be a baby as a result.

God knew there were too many bastards in the world already.

****

Jessy awoke early the next morning, just before dawn. At first, she couldn't feel anything. She tried to straighten her cramped legs and realized she'd never been so cold or so sore in her life. Every inch of her hurt, from the roots of her hair to the heels of her feet in their heavy boots. She had never slept on the ground before, and she swore she'd never do it again, even if she had to ride straight through the night, dragging Morgan behind her all the way home. She tried to roll over, and a groan escaped her lips.

"You all right?" a husky, morning male voice asked.

"No."

Blankets rustled and footsteps crunched across the grass behind her back. A hand touched her side, and painful needles speared her flesh.

"What's the matter? Sore?"

She winced. "And cold."

"We can't have that." He punctuated his observation with a light swat on her backside before rising to his feet.

"Aaaaah!"

He laughed, and she heard the sounds of him tending the fire. Soon the popping and hissing tempted her with thoughts of blissful warmth.

"Don't worry. You'll be all right. We'll have you back on your horse and on your way home in no time."

She released a soft, lady-like snort. "I doubt it. I can't even move."

"Then I'll have to move you, won't I?"

He knelt behind her and drew the blanket aside. Jessy shivered hard and groaned again. She felt his hands on her body, both of them this time, and his touch was neither playful nor sharp. It was strong and slow and infinitely tender. Starting at the back of her neck, he massaged the stiff, painful muscles and sent the circulation rushing back to her chilled flesh.

When she could move her neck again, he slid his hands to her shoulders and worked them with slow, sure strokes until she arched into his touch like a cat. His hands moved down her back until he encountered the thick, stiff edge of her stays beneath her shirt and hesitated.

"What the...what have you got on under here?"

"My stays."

"You slept all night on the hard ground trussed up like a rabbit on a spit?"

"Not exactly. I'm sure the rabbit would have been much warmer." She tentatively straightened her legs.

"Take that infernal thing off."

"I can't."

"What do you mean you can't? You sure don't need to worry about the way these clothes fit you."

She winced. She should have changed into her riding habit when she saw his campfire last night instead of appearing dressed like this. No man would be overcome with love at the sight of his fiancée dressed like a shabby boy. But last night she hadn't been sure it was Morgan until it was too late.

She tried to roll onto her back, and the movement brought an involuntary grunt of pain. "I can't take it off because I can't sit up."

His single-word response expressed his feelings succinctly, but his hands were strong and gentle as he lifted her into a sitting position. He began to unbutton her shirt.

"I can do that myself." She slapped him away, but her fingers were too stiff with cold to work the small bone buttons through their holes.

"I'll do it." Morgan's gruff reply was at odds with his tender touch. He brushed her hands aside and finished the job.

When he slipped the warm flannel shirt off her shoulders and down her arms, violent shivers wracked her body. He swore again and pulled out his knife. With one quick motion, he sliced through the laces of the corset all the way up the back until the offending garment split open like a clamshell. He dragged the blanket around her quaking shoulders and pulled her into his arms and onto his lap.

Snuggling into his surrounding warmth, Jessy began to thaw, and her teeth stopped chattering. He adjusted her position and reached one hand under the blanket.

"What were you thinking, taking off on a trip like this alone?"

His rough voice contrasted with the magic of his fingers working their way down the cold, stiff muscles of her back to her waist.

She gave a soft moan of agonized pleasure. "I...I didn't..."

"You didn't think at all." His strong hand kneaded the life back into her. "You just got some wild idea and set off on a big adventure without giving a second thought to the consequences, didn't you?"

She didn't reply. His assessment was painfully close to the truth.

"What if you hadn't found me? What if you'd stumbled into some stranger's camp? What do you think would have happened then?" His voice rose with his temper. "Even if you didn't get robbed, or raped, or murdered, you don't have adequate provisions and equipment for the trail. A girl like you doesn't have any experience camping out in the open."

She wanted to defend herself but couldn't. She was still too cold to speak, and unfortunately, he was right. Any number of awful things might have happened if she hadn't found him when she did.

His hand continued to work the muscles at the top of her hips. "I ought to turn you over my knee right now for this escapade and paddle some sense into you. If your father had done it years ago, none of this would have happened."

Then the wonderful, pleasure-giving hand was gone. He rose to his feet, pulling her with him. Clutching the blanket, Jessy sent him a questioning look.

"You ought to be able to travel now. Get dressed." He thrust her shirt into her hands, stalked over to his saddlebags, and unpacked the fixings for breakfast.

She stared after him. His behavior was a jumble of contradictions, solicitous one minute and angry the next. His hands soothed and excited, in sharp contrast to his hard and uncaring words. One thing she knew — indifference had no place in his feelings for her. She just had to find the key to the lock he kept on his emotions.

Dressed in warm clothes once more, she became aware of a pressing need she had been trying to ignore since the night before. She glanced around the campsite trying to figure out what to do about the problem. Traveling alone, privacy hadn't been an issue, but with Morgan not ten feet away, it was another matter altogether.

There were several clumps of bushes near the trees where the horses were tethered, if she could just slip away. Morgan was busy with the skillet, so she wouldn't have to bother with excuses. She hurried toward the beckoning concealment of the bushes.

"While you're at it, you'd better fill your canteen at the creek and water your horse before you set off," he called after her, amusement ringing in his voice.

She muttered the most unladylike word she knew and disappeared into the brush.

She returned refreshed. After taking care of her most urgent business, she had taken his advice and splashed icy water on her face and filled her canteen while Princess drank from the stream. By the time she returned to the campfire, all she needed was hot food and she would be ready to travel again. She had no intention of making the return trip to Weston alone but saw no need to mention that before breakfast.

She strolled over to Morgan, determined to show no more than a casual interest in his food. The aroma of bacon and coffee in the crisp morning air brought tears to her eyes.

"What have you got—" A loud gurgle from her stomach interrupted her.

His hazel eyes danced with laughter, but the rest of his expression remained neutral. "Want some breakfast?"

"Yes, thank you." She plopped down next to him.

He regarded her with a smile as cold as the creek water. "Help yourself, Miss Randall. I don't see any servants around here, do you?"

Jessy resisted the urge to stick her tongue out at him and clambered to her feet. Using the two-pronged fork, she speared the last two slices of bacon from the cast iron skillet but wasn't sure what to do with them. Morgan had a tin plate and fork but made no offer to share.

After a moment, she plucked the bacon off the fork with her thumb and forefinger and held the strips gingerly, trying not to burn herself. Hunger overcame a lifetime of drilling in proper table manners, and she wolfed down the bacon, savoring every greasy bite. When she finished, she wiped her fingers on her pants and turned to her reluctant host. She was thirsty and running out of patience.

"How about some coffee?" She didn't bother softening her tone.

He regarded her over the rim of his cup and took his time draining the last of his own coffee. When he finished, he passed the cup to her and stood. He began packing his gear while she downed one quick cup of the steaming brew. Minutes later, the fire was doused, the coffeepot and cup rinsed and packed, and both horses saddled and ready.

"You'd better get going if you want to make it back to Independence by nightfall." He thrust his left boot into the stirrup and swung into the saddle.

She mounted Princess and faced him with a glare. "I've already told you, I'm not going anywhere without you."

"And I've already told you, I'm not going back to Weston."

She lifted her chin. "Then I'll just have to go with you, wherever you are going."

He exploded. "You sure as hell will not. You're not coming anywhere with me." He nudged his horse forward to within two feet of her. "I don't know how to make it any plainer. Go home. Leave me alone. I don't want you." His anger had disappeared, leaving his voice hard and flat.

His blunt words brought a sharp, physical pain to the center of her chest. She tried to tell herself he was just being noble. He didn't mean it. His touch told her he wanted her; his eyes told her he needed her. Even if want and need weren't quite love, they must be the next best things. Her love could be enough for both of them.

"I don't believe you, and I'm coming with you to prove you wrong."

He regarded her with a steady gaze. "You are without a doubt the most hard-headed woman I've ever met. I pity the man who winds up saddled with you for a wife. From now on, what you do and where you go are your own business." He jerked his reins, wheeled his horse around, and headed down the trail without another word.

She blinked back treacherous tears, nudged Princess with her heels, and followed behind.

Chapter Three

Morgan heard the plodding hoofbeats and occasional snuffle of Jessy's horse several yards behind him but refused to turn his head or acknowledge her presence. If he ignored her, she was bound to give up and go home sooner or later. How long could a soft, town-bred girl last riding across rough, open country? In another day, they would reach the dense forests and steep hills marking the beginning of Ozark country. The rugged terrain had turned back many a rider more experienced than Jessy.

The sky had scarcely brightened since daybreak, and a flat, thick layer of pasty gray clouds dashed any hope of the sun breaking through. He turned his collar up against the penetrating chill and thought about the woman riding behind him. In spite of her heavy clothing, she had to be uncomfortable. He knew for a fact she wasn't wearing long underwear beneath the shirt and pants, and her lacy camisole and drawers couldn't keep out the cold like a stout pair of woolen long johns. He tried to convince himself that was just what he wanted — for her to be miserable enough to give up and go home — but it didn't work.

He hated the thought of her suffering, even if she had brought it on herself. She was as stubborn as a mule in clover. Why couldn't she have let him go? She would have forgotten him in no time and moved on with her life. And he? It didn't matter what happened to him. He had already lost his soul.

****

A light drizzle began around midday, adding to Jessy's discomfort. When they reached the banks of a shallow creek, Morgan reined in his horse and dismounted. Without a word or glance in her direction, he refilled his canteen and allowed his horse to drink. As soon as the horse raised his head, Morgan mounted, pulled a couple of sticks of beef jerky from his saddlebags, and set off again, gnawing the tough brown strips as he rode.

She stared at his back, fuming. If he thought bad manners and worse weather would discourage her, he had a lot to learn about Jessamine Randall.

Given his leisurely pace, she could afford a brief stop. In this weather, he wasn't likely to gallop off the second she was out of sight. She climbed down and led Princess to the creek, where she followed Morgan's example and refilled her canteen. Cold water held none of the appeal of hot coffee, but that would have to wait until they stopped for the night.

Once he saw she couldn't be discouraged, he would have to accept her as a traveling companion and give up this ridiculous farce of pretending she didn't exist. She took advantage of his absence to answer nature's call before setting off once more.

Over the course of the afternoon, the drizzle progressed to a cold, steady rain and finally to a downpour. Morgan stopped and pulled a black oilcloth poncho over his head. Jessy watched its protective folds spread out to cover both man and horse and was struck by a surge of jealousy for the horse. It had to be warmer and drier than she was.

By late afternoon, her frozen hands could no longer hold the reins. The rain had soaked her gloves as thoroughly as the rest of her, and she had no strength left. Even the tips of her ears were numb. Her nose dripped like a leaky faucet, and her sodden handkerchief failed to stem the flow.

Without warning, Morgan pulled to a halt beneath the leafy brown canopy of an enormous oak. He climbed down, whipped his reins around a nearby sapling, and marched over to where she wobbled in her saddle.

"Get down," he ordered.

"I...c-c-can't." Her teeth chattered with the effort to speak, and violent chills shook her slender frame.

He swore a vicious oath and reached up to pluck her from the saddle. The moment his hands released her weight, she collapsed. Her legs refused to support her, and she was too miserable to care.

He squatted, slid his arms around and under her, and straightened, as if she weighed no more than a child. He carried her to a spot near the trunk of the tree where the thickness of the leaves sheltered the grass and set her down before returning to his horse.

His hands jerked the strings tying his bedroll to the back of the saddle. "Dammit, Jessy. Look at what your pigheadedness has done to you this time. You're near frozen and half dead. We'll be lucky if you don't come down with lung fever."

"I d-d-didn't—"

"Don't try to talk. Wrap this around you, and I'll see if I can find enough dry wood to make a fire." He draped a dry blanket around her shoulders then stripped off his poncho and dropped it over her head.

The relief was immediate. Besides keeping the rain out, the waterproof coating on the fabric had trapped his body heat inside. In minutes, warmth swathed her in a protective cocoon. She bent her head and stuck her frozen nose through the wide neck hole. The warm man-smell mingled with the scent of wet wool from her clothing. She closed her eyes and inhaled. If she tried hard enough, she could pretend she was warm and dry, wrapped in the safety and comfort of his arms.

Moments later, he reappeared with an armful of small, dry branches and two good-sized logs. He tossed his load to the ground and began to arrange the wood in a careful pattern. She watched his competent hands make quick work of the task. Soon a puny yellow flame snaked up from the pile.

He poked the wood with a long stick. "It may be a little smoky, but it's the driest wood I could find."

She nodded, unable to summon the energy to speak. She desperately needed the meager heat emanating from the ever-growing blaze but couldn't move to get near it.

He glanced over his shoulder. "What are you waiting for?"

She remained mute.

He dropped the stick and strode to where she sat huddled under the blanket and poncho. "I ought to drag you over there by your hair."

In spite of the threat, his arms were gentle as he lifted her and carried her to the fire. "I'll make coffee as quick as I can." He set her down near the flames.

Jessy swayed toward the fire, drawn by its seductive warmth. She closed her eyes and basked in it, trying to store up heat like a lizard sunning on a flat rock. It was impossible to get too close, impossible to get too warm. The prospect of death by burning lost its fearsome power. In fact, it seemed a welcome alternative to the life-stealing cold that still gripped her limbs.

"Get away from that fire!" Morgan dropped the coffeepot, raced over, and yanked her away. "What are you trying to do, cook yourself?"

In a daze, she glanced down and saw the front of the poncho smoking. The acrid scent assailed her nose and brought tears to her eyes.

"Are you completely helpless? Can't I leave you alone for five seconds without you getting into trouble?"

"I was cold." Although determined to defend herself against his unfair attack, she could barely hear her voice above the snap and hiss of the wood on the fire.

"That's your own fault, and you know it. You had no business coming after me, especially this time of year. If you'd stayed home where you belong, you'd be in warm, dry clothes, in a warm, dry house instead of soaking wet and freezing in the woods."

He refilled the pot and set it on the fire to boil. Jessy didn't have the strength to argue. She pulled herself into a tight little ball inside the blanket and waited.

When the coffee was ready, he filled the tin cup and offered it to her. "Drink this. It'll warm you from the inside."

She accepted the steaming cup and brought it to her icy lips. The first gulp scalded her tongue, but she adjusted and switched to tiny sips. The rich, nutty aroma revitalized her. She savored each mouthful as it rolled down her throat carrying much-needed heat to her frigid core. When she had drained the cup, she handed it back.

"Better?" He poured a cup for himself.

"Yes, thank you."

Morgan drank his coffee, observing her through the steam. "What am I going to do with you?" he asked, more to himself than to her.

"Come back with me?" She offered a small, lopsided smile.

He didn't return it. "We've been through that."

He regarded her a moment longer while he finished his coffee. When he set the cup aside, a look of resolution settled over his face. "First thing we have to do is get you out of those wet clothes."

She tightened her grip on the blanket. "But I'll freeze."

"You'll surely freeze if you spend the night in them. Let me help you." He reached for the poncho.

"I can do it myself." In spite of her dependence on him in these rustic circumstances, she wanted to retain a shred of dignity, if possible.

His gaze narrowed. "Suit yourself. I'll try to rig up some sort of clothesline near the fire. I'll also need that oilcloth to make a tent for the night."

With one hand, she pulled the poncho over her head and handed it to him. She set about the challenge of undressing inside the blanket while he busied himself with a length of rope. After wriggling like a contortionist, she managed to remove her damp clothing. Clasping the blanket together with one hand, she offered the sodden lump to Morgan with the other.

He had strung a piece of rope between two trees and draped the oilcloth over it, holding the long side down with several large rocks to form a makeshift tent. Another smaller piece, which had covered his bedroll, served as the floor.

He took her wet clothes and gestured toward the tent. "Get in. I've got to tend to the horses."

She scooted under the shelter, for although it was no longer raining heavily, the huge, fat drops dripping from the wet leaves overhead had almost the same effect. Morgan made two trips with their saddles and gear, tucking everything under the low side of the tarp where it would stay as dry as possible. When he had finished, he slid his rifle from its long holster on his saddle and picked up his cartridge bag.

"What are you doing with that?" Jessy asked.

"I'm going hunting. You need hot food."

A hot dinner sounded too good to be true, but she wondered what kind of game he expected to find. She hadn't seen a single animal all day. Besides, it was almost dark. "How can you hunt now? You can barely see your hand in front of your face."

His teeth slashed white in the dim light. "I know where to look. Didn't I ever tell you I'm part mountain lion? I can see in the dark."

She shivered. He did remind her of a mountain lion, with his tawny hair and gold-green eyes. "What are you planning to hunt?"

"Whatever I can find: birds, rabbits, squirrels."

Her hollow stomach turned over. "I can't eat a squirrel!"

He gave her a humorless smile. "You will if you're hungry enough. Now wait here." Without another word, he strode out of the circle of light cast by the fire and disappeared in the dusky twilight.

Jessy pulled the blanket tighter around her shoulders. She hoped he would find game quickly, whether it was something she could eat or not. She didn't want to be alone one second longer than necessary. What if something happened to him? What if he didn't come back? Suppose he encountered a bear in the woods. She had no idea if there were bears in the vicinity and no desire to find out.

She shivered, despite the fact that Morgan had been right—she was warmer without her damp clothes. She couldn't relax. It was too loud.

The profusion of night noises disturbed her senses. She strained to pick out the sounds of man or beast from the rustling going on all around her. Since the rain stopped, the wind picked up, and gusts ruffled the tattered leaves overhead. Tall, dry grasses whooshed and swayed. Somewhere deeper in the woods, an owl called out. The total effect of the country sounds on her frayed nerves was anything but peaceful.

She switched her thoughts to Morgan and his enterprise. Although her family lived in a small town surrounded by woods and fields, Jessy's father never went hunting. All the meat in the Randall house came from McGonigle's Butcher Shop. There was something primitively satisfying about having a man go out to bring back food he'd captured with his own hands. She just prayed it wouldn't be squirrel.

A pair of rifle shots cracked in the distance. That must be Morgan. He would be back any minute with supper.

She waited. And waited. And waited. How far had he gone?

Then another thought occurred to her. What if he couldn't find his way back in the dark?

That did it. She crawled out of the tent and struggled to her feet. She couldn't wait any longer worrying and wondering. She had to do something. She had to find him.

Still clutching the blanket, she shuffled over to the remaining pile of brush beside the fire. She selected a long, sturdy stick and wound a length of dried wild grapevine around one end. It wasn't much of a torch, and she didn't know how long it would burn but hoped it would last long enough to find Morgan.

With her blanket wrapped around her like a misshapen toga, she lit the torch and set out in the direction of the shots.

****

Morgan's chest swelled with proud satisfaction as he strolled into the camp swinging a plump pheasant by the feet. No squirrel for Jessy tonight. He'd never admit it to her, but it had been a piece of luck to hit the bird at this time of day. He stepped into the fire lit circle and glanced at the tent. It was empty. His eyes took a quick inventory. Her horse still grazed next to his. Her clothes still hung from the line. She couldn't have gone far, probably just into the bushes for a few minutes of privacy.

He hunkered next to the fire to pluck and clean the pheasant, burying the refuse so as not to attract predators during the night. When he had finished and she still hadn't returned, he felt a surge of fear mixed with anger. He hadn't heard a sound from the direction of the camp while he'd been hunting. Of course, the wind carried sounds away quickly in open country. If thieves had attacked, they would have stolen the horses, and there were no signs of a struggle. She had to be somewhere out in the dark alone. Why would she do such a stupid thing? Why couldn't she ever do as she was told?

He hung the pheasant by its ankles in a tree and prayed it would still be there when he got back. Picking up his rifle, he set out hunting again.

****

Jessy had no idea how far she'd walked. She wasn't even sure of the direction. Things had a way of getting turned around in the dark. Her torch was burning low, and she doubted she'd have much success finding anything dry enough to burn if it went out.

She'd had no luck finding Morgan. She stopped every few feet and called his name. When there was no response, she walked a short distance and called again. Finally, she was forced to accept the fact that if she didn't find him soon, she would have to go back to the camp alone and try again in the morning.

One last time. I'll give him one last chance. She took a deep breath. "Morgaaaan!"

"What the hell are you doing?" a furious, deep voice behind her demanded.

"Aaaaaah!"

She screamed and spun around, dropping her torch. The flames sputtered out in the wet grass and leaves, plunging her into darkness. For a few long seconds, she crouched like a frightened rabbit, her heart fluttering. She trained her ears, trying to pick up the slightest sound—the rustle of grass, the snap of a twig. Out of the darkness, a big hand clamped around her arm with an iron grip and hauled her to her feet.

"Dammit, Jessy. What are you doing here? I told you to wait back at camp."

She tried to make out his features, but there was no question who held her. Her breath came out in a rush. "Morgan."

"Were you expecting someone else?"

She ignored his disapproving tone and sagged against him in relief. "No. I was looking for you. I heard the shots, and I waited, but you didn't come back. I thought something had happened to you."

"Nothing happened to me, but God knows what will happen to you if you pull a stunt like this again." He reached for her discarded blanket with one hand, keeping a firm grip on her arm with the other. "Put this back on, even though it's probably wet by now."

She struggled with the blanket until he snatched it from her hands and roughly wrapped it around her.

"Now come on. We still have to cook supper."

He half-dragged her through the brush back to camp. Stumbling along in the dark behind him, she couldn't see the bushes and saplings that whipped against her sides or the roots and sticks that snagged her feet. Morgan had no such problems. He forged through the inky darkness without hesitation, displaying an uncanny sense of direction. Maybe he was right. Maybe he was part mountain lion.

When they reached camp, he thrust her toward the fire. "Try to get that blanket dry. It's the only one we've got for tonight. Yours is still soaked because you didn't have the sense to protect your gear with a waterproof covering."

She wanted to snap back at him, but he was right. She had come on this trip woefully unprepared. But she was tougher than he thought, and she learned fast. She was determined to prove she could meet any challenge he threw at her.

She decided the best way to dry the blanket and warm herself in the bargain was to stand next to the fire, wearing it like a cigar store Indian. Every few minutes, she turned like a piece of toast.

While she dried, he rigged a spit over the fire, took down the naked carcass of a large bird from the tree, and skewered it on the spit. Her stomach rebelled at the sight of its pale, goose-pimpled skin and bloody, vacant cavity. She swallowed hard. She was hungry, but was she hungry enough to eat that?

As the bird roasted, a heavenly smell filled the air. The ugly, white skin took on a deep amber color, and her mouth began to water. "What is that?"

Morgan didn't look up from his cooking. "Pheasant."

"It smells wonderful."

He turned his head and flashed her a rare grin. "Thanks. I thought you'd find it tastier than squirrel."

Her heart leapt at the first real smile she'd seen from him in days. She made a playful face at his mention of squirrel, and he laughed out loud.

The pheasant tasted even better than it smelled, and the atmosphere around the fire was much lighter than the night before. Morgan sat beside her as they ate with their fingers and passed the single cup back and forth. He seemed relaxed, almost content. She hoped if she waited for the right moment, she could convince him to return with her in the morning.

After they finished eating, he stood and stretched. "You about dry?"

She checked the blanket. "I think so."

"Good. As soon as we clean up here, we'd better bed down for the night. I want to get an early start in the morning."

Now was her chance. "Where are we headed?"

"Home."

She grinned in elation. He was coming home with her, and she didn't even have to work to persuade him. She threw her arms around his waist and hugged him, letting her blanket fall to the ground. "I'm so happy. You won't be sorry."

He disengaged himself and retrieved the blanket. "I hope not." He draped the blanket around her shoulders again. He wasn't smiling.

After banking the fire, he knelt inside the makeshift tent. "Hand me that blanket."

Her brows knit in confusion. "But mine's still wet, and so are my clothes. I'll freeze without it."

"We'll both freeze without it. Now hand it over."

Then it dawned on her; he was making a bed for both of them—a bed to share. How wonderful. How romantic.

Except for a few impassioned kisses, Morgan had always maintained a respectful distance. Now they would sleep together, really together. Now she would know the truth of his feelings.

What could be more perfect, alone in the wilderness with the man she loved? What harm could there be if they anticipated their marriage by a few days? She stripped off the blanket and thrust it at him.

She rubbed her bare arms and shivered, as much from anticipation as from the cold night air, and watched him arrange the blanket on the waterproof fabric.

"All right," he said. "Take your boots off and get in."

Butterflies danced in her stomach as she complied. She burrowed under the blanket and watched him sit beside her and tug off his boots before climbing in and tucking the blanket around them.

Now, she thought, cuddling against him. He didn't respond, so she wiggled again, with more vigor.

"You cold?"

"No." She wasn't cold — she was frustrated. What did it take to dent the man's armor, anyway?

"Then settle down and go to sleep."

Morgan lay on his side with his back toward her and his head pillowed on one arm so she couldn't see his face. She poked him in the shoulder, and he turned his head.

"What is it?"

"This isn't right at all."

"What isn't right?"

"Don't you even want to kiss me?"

He rolled onto his back and looked at her. "That isn't a good idea. We both know where it's likely to lead."

"Would that be so awful? I love you, and I know you love me."

"It won't work, Jessy. Now go to sleep." He rolled back over.

"What won't work?"

"Any of it."

She touched his rigid shoulder. "You want to kiss me. I know you do."

Her fingers began a delicate dance across the hard muscles. The flesh beneath his shirt rippled under her touch. Emboldened by his reflexive response, she drew her nails down the line of his spine until she reached the stiff leather of his belt. She followed the line of the leather around his waist to the front, and her hand began to massage the ridged muscles above his belt buckle.

Suddenly he growled and rolled backward, taking her with him until she lay flat on her back, trapped beneath the weight of his body. His hands pinned hers to the blanket on either side of her head, and he held her legs captive with his. His body shook with need. His eyes blazed with it.

"You little fool. You never know when to stop, do you? This time you've gone too far."

His mouth ground into hers, pressing her soft inner lips into her teeth. He seemed determined to punish her for her boldness. She moaned and squirmed.

He lifted his head just enough to separate their lips. "What's the matter?" The heat of his breath fanned against her mouth. "You don't like it? Too bad. You crossed the line this time. That's what happens when you play with fire—sometimes you get burned." He dropped his head again.

She turned just as his lips came down, and they caught the side of her jaw. He made no attempt to find her mouth. Instead, he nibbled along the line of her jaw to her ear and down the side of her neck. His bristly chin abraded her tender flesh, then his lips followed, soothing and arousing at once.

She moaned and turned, seeking his lips.

He lifted his head and gazed into her eyes. "Oh, God, Jessy, why do you do this to me?" Rough anguish shook his voice.

He released her hands and brought his own to frame her face, brushing the curls back from her temples with his thumbs. She smiled, parted her lips, and closed her eyes. This time when his mouth returned to hers, his kiss tasted of tenderness as well as desire.

He kissed her with a thoroughness he'd never shown before, as if he had all the time in the world to test, to sample, to arouse. She grew restless as his patience fanned the embers burning inside her. She sought his mouth again and again.

Abruptly, he rolled off. His chest heaved as he struggled to control his breathing.

She stared in dazed disbelief.

"That's enough."

He sounded angry, but she had no doubt his arousal was as intense as her own. "Why?"

"Because I don't want to make you pregnant."

She stroked his chest. "That doesn't matter. We'll be married in a few days. No one will know."

Morgan scowled. "We'll talk about that in the morning. Now go to sleep." He rolled over, making it plain the conversation was finished.

She glared at his back, then rolled to her side, rammed her backside into his for good measure, and tried to go to sleep.

The pale glow of dawn barely lit the interior of the makeshift tent when a sharp slap on the posterior awakened Jessy.

"Get up. Breakfast is ready, and we need to be on our way."

She sniffed the air. Besides the strong aroma of coffee, she smelled the mouth-watering fragrance of frying fish. Her stomach growled.

"Put these on." Morgan tossed her clothes onto her lap in a heap. "I need to pack the blanket."

She struggled into her shirt, pants, and jacket and shivered. The heavy garments were still damp and stole every glimmer of heat from her sleep-warmed skin. She hurried to stand by the fire.

Her stomach gurgled again at the sight and smell of the fish, sizzling crusty and golden in the skillet. "Where did you get those?"

"The Osage River is just over the next hill. I got up early and went fishing."

A river. She glanced at her grubby hands, glad she couldn't see her face. She'd hate to have to check into the hotel in Independence looking like this. "Do you think we could fetch enough water from the river to heat and wash with?"

"No. It's too muddy. Besides I don't have anything bigger than the coffeepot to carry or heat water in. You'll have to wait 'til we get home."

She grimaced. "But that will take three days."

He glanced up from the fish. "I figure if we ride hard, we can get there by tomorrow evening."

"We can't possibly ride all the way to Weston in two days."

He straightened. "I never said I was taking you to Weston. I said I was taking you home, my home."

"What?" She balled her fists. "Morgan Bingham, you deliberately misled me."

"I told you I wasn't going back there. It's not my fault you chose not to believe me. Now that I've seen how unprepared you are to survive on your own, I can't let you go back by yourself. I have no choice. I have to take you with me and figure out some way to get you back to your father later."

"You talk about me as if I were some piece of unwanted baggage."

"You said it, I didn't." He forked two pieces of fish onto the tin plate and shoved it at her. "Now get busy and eat, or you'll have to ride on an empty stomach."

She snatched the plate and plopped down in a huff in front of the fire. Heat flamed her cheeks. How dare he talk to her like that, as if she were an incompetent child? She'd show him. She'd ride back to Weston by herself without so much as a backward glance.

So much for you, Mr. Morgan Bingham.

Then she remembered last night, lying in his arms, his hungry mouth devouring her alive. He needed her as much as he wanted her, no matter how he denied it. And she wasn't ready to give up without a fight. Morgan loved her. She knew he did. Maybe going home with him would be the best way to prove it.

They rode all day in silence. As the terrain changed, Jessy marveled at the unfolding beauty of the land. The hills grew higher and closer together, their sides glowing with the brilliant red, orange, and yellow hues of maple, walnut, hickory, and oak. The faint trail wound mostly through the trees, but from time to time they broke into a clearing on a ridge. The views of the neighboring hills across the narrow valleys took her breath away. Surely everything would go right for her in this magical place.

The sun burst forth at last, bringing with it the surprising warmth of Indian summer and filling her with a corresponding glow. She couldn't find it in her heart to be unhappy or worried on a day like this. She took off her hat and turned her face to the sun, basking in its precious heat. A day like this was a gift, meant to be cherished. One never knew when it might be the last before the dreary damp of winter set in.

They held a steady pace through the rugged terrain, stopping only to water the horses. For lunch, Morgan provided beef jerky to be eaten in the saddle and washed down with cold water, but she didn't mind. The land spoke to her. Its rocky hills and winding valleys sang of ancient days and ancient ways and a time before man arrived to make his mark. An occasional plume of smoke rising above the treetops in the distance was the only reminder that they were not the first humans ever to see this glorious place.

That night, they camped by a small, swift stream and ate fish again for supper. Morgan remained silent and brooding, but Jessy's spirits were buoyed by her natural optimism and fed by the wild beauty around her. She refused to let him dampen her enthusiasm.

"Are we close to your home?" she asked while they ate.

"We should be there by suppertime tomorrow."

"What's it like?"

"It's like nothing you've ever seen." His voice was hard and flat.

She gave him a little frown. "Aren't you even a little excited? I'm sure your family will be thrilled to see you."

He shifted his gaze to his boots. "Don't count on it."

He might be trying to sound as if he didn't care, but he couldn't mask the pain in his voice. Apprehension crept in to crowd her positive outlook, and she wondered what they would find when they arrived at the Bingham homestead the next day. Perhaps there was some problem with his family, and that was the reason he hadn't gone home after the war. If so, why had he decided to go home now?

Those questions, and more, troubled her deep into the night. Soon she would learn the answers, whether she wanted to or not.

Chapter Four

The next morning, a thick fog swirled through the hollows between the hills. Camped on high ground, Jessy and Morgan escaped the worst, but the eerie curls of mist sent gooseflesh racing up her arms. The fog ebbed and surged with a life of its own, and the landscape, akin to paradise only the day before, now seemed to bubble and boil with malevolent purpose.

Jessy shivered and hugged her coat tighter. The damp cold penetrated her soul even as it worked its way through her clothes. She had suffered the chill of Morgan's steady withdrawal since the night before. He rebuffed all efforts at conversation and made no move to rebuild the cozy little tent. Instead, he spread his bedroll in front of the fire several feet from her and lay down alone.

Before first light, he disappeared with his saddlebags and returned wearing a supple buckskin shirt the color of pale cornmeal and dark leather britches. She had never seen him dressed that way. He looked unfamiliar, wilder and more dangerous. Even when she'd known he was an outlaw, she had never been afraid of him, but this transformation made her uneasy. The shell around him seemed to harden before her eyes, as if he were girding himself for a dreaded confrontation.

After breaking camp, they packed their gear and mounted up. Only the soft creaks of leather and clinks of metal broke the strained silence. She wanted to ask how much farther they had to travel, but the barrier of his self-imposed isolation kept her quiet.

Even poor Princess fell victim to the crackling tension. She stamped her feet and snorted, blowing small clouds of vapor into the still morning air. Jessy reached down and patted her horse's shoulder with more assurance than she felt.

In the hollow, fog as thick as day-old porridge condensed in tiny droplets on her cheeks. She could barely make out the ghostly outline of horse and rider in front of her. Every now and then, Morgan moved farther ahead, and the fog surged between them, swallowing him whole. She kicked her heels until Princess fell in line nose-to-tail behind his roan. The last thing she wanted was to become separated from him. The woods reminded her too much of the spooky forests from the fairy tales her father had read to her when she was young. It didn't take much imagination to picture a witch or an ogre popping out of the underbrush.

For hours, Morgan picked his way along the banks of a rushing river with huge limestone bluffs looming overhead in the mist until they came to a quiet pool formed by a natural rock dam.

"We'll cross here," he said, his first words since the night before.

The gray afternoon light had already begun to dim, and Jessy felt hollow, physically and emotionally. She had been running on sheer nerves since daybreak. "Are we close?"

He turned to glance at her. "The farm is about three miles away, but we'll have to cross the river again before we get there."

"Why? Is the land too rough?"

"This is McTaggart land."

"I see." She didn't.

"No Bingham has set foot on McTaggart land in my lifetime."

Her growing anxiety about seeing his home and meeting his family surged into a lump in her throat. She wouldn't cry. She refused. She just wanted to get it over with. She needed a hot bath and a soft bed and couldn't see a single logical reason to make the trip longer than necessary.

"But we won't do them any harm, and besides, these McTaggarts are your neighbors. What would they do, shoot us?"

"Maybe."

She glanced at him looking for a sign of teasing humor but found none. He must be serious. While Weston had its share of loners and curmudgeons, most people had figured out how to coexist without bloodshed. Apparently, that was not the case around here. "Morgan, that's barbaric. These people must know you."

He gave a short laugh. "Oh, they know me all right."

A frisson of suspicion and fear raced up her spine and down her arms. "What did you do before the war?"

"It wasn't so much anything I did..."

He seemed willing to let it go at that, but she needed to know more about what she was getting into. "What are you trying to say? Are you responsible for this feud in some way?"

His lips twisted in a small, ironic smile. "I guess you could say I'm responsible. I committed a great crime twenty-seven years ago. I was born a Bingham."

"What do you mean, you were born? That doesn't make any sense."

He turned away, but not before she noticed a muscle flex in his temple.

"You don't know anything about life in these hills. Things are different here. We've got our own code, and people don't always live by the rules you're used to."

"But—"

"Drop it, Jessy." His tone brooked no resistance. "The sooner we get going, the sooner we'll be there." He urged his horse forward, leaving her to follow.

Princess picked her way across the rocky ford behind Morgan's roan. Jessy didn't want to be left alone in such inhospitable country where your nearest neighbors couldn't wait to shoot you if they got the chance.

Darkness threatened by the time he led the way back across the river and headed up the side of a gently sloping hill. Following the rough path through the brush and across patches of open ground, they reached an area where the trees had been cleared, leaving a forest of stumps. Around and between the stumps, the stubble of dried and flattened corn stalks gave stark witness to meager efforts to coax subsistence from the stony hillside. Jessy thought she heard a muttered oath from the man in front of her, but the sound mingled with the rustling of the corn shocks and disappeared.

After passing through a narrow band of trees, they rode into another clearing, this one free of stumps. Several ramshackle wooden buildings of varying sizes squatted haphazardly around the property, the rough log walls blending with the trees beyond. A covered passageway connected two buildings, each leaning against a tall stone chimney, and twin plumes of smoke curled into the evening sky. The larger house had a long, covered front porch. Missing shingles speckled every roof.

Something about the place threw her off balance. She tilted her head for a second look. Not a single wall stood plumb and true. Each building sprouted from the ground at its own peculiar angle, and the result provoked an unsettling sensation of vertigo. None of it seemed to disturb the inhabitants of the farmyard, however. A few bedraggled chickens pecked listlessly in the dirt, and a bony hog with tiny red eyes stopped rooting in a garbage pile long enough to glare at the newcomers.

They rode to the front porch of the main house, and Morgan dismounted, wrapping his reins around the railing. He started up the rickety steps then turned. "This is it. You coming in?"

She wasn't sure how to answer. She had to dismount and walk to the steps—there was nothing else to do—but she wasn't sure she could. The whole place had such a dismal and unwelcoming air. She experienced a momentary stab of fear that she had made a dreadful mistake coming here. What if the family inside was no more congenial than their farmstead?

She gave herself a mental shake and remembered this was Morgan's home. Whatever else, it was part of what had made him the man he was, the man she loved.

"Of course." She forced a determined smile and climbed down.

He paused at the sagging door, drew a slow, deep breath, and squared his shoulders. He raised his fist and knocked once before opening the door.

She peeked around his shoulder at the inside of the cabin. It was a single large room with a long table and benches of rough-hewn planks, a couple of hand-carved wooden chairs, and a double bed pushed against one wall. Cooking utensils cluttered the large stone hearth at one end of the room, and a ladder against the opposite wall led to a sleeping loft under the rafters.

An old woman sat at the end of the table eating from a battered wooden bowl with an old pewter spoon. Two young women, a young man, and a small boy joined her. At the sound of the door opening, all heads turned.

The faded brown eyes of the small, gray-haired woman widened. The color drained from her face. Her mouth moved soundlessly, and she clasped a gnarled hand to her throat. "Morgan, son, is that you?" Her voice creaked.

Morgan remained just inside the doorway, as if uncertain of his reception. "It's me, Ma. I'm home."

His voice was thick, and his Adam's apple bobbed. Jessy's throat tightened in response. She squeezed his arm.

The old woman struggled to rise, and he took a step toward her. Then another. By the time he reached her, the woman's chest shook. Her gnarled hands reached out and clawed at his shirt as she peered into his face.

"Where've you been, son? It's been ten years." Her voice dropped to a broken whisper. "Ten years. We thought you was dead."

"Yeah, big brother. Where have you been? To hell and back?" The harsh words came from the handsome, black-haired man who remained seated.

Morgan's mother shuddered. "Ethan."

The single word was both admonishment and plea.

Ethan slammed his fist on the surface of the table. "Dammit, Ma! How can you welcome him back now, after ten years, after what he did?"

"He's your brother."

"He's a ba—"

"Shut up, little brother," Morgan ordered, "and finish your supper while you've still got teeth."

Ethan's eyes blazed blue fury, and a tight muscle worked in his jaw. "Don't think you can tell me what to do. You're nothing but a murderer, a murderer and a coward."

Morgan's hands balled into fists, but he held steady against the barrage of hateful words.

"You took off, didn't you?" Ethan continued, seemingly too angry to recognize the threat, or care. "Well, I stayed here to take care of Ma and Sally."

"Ethan, you know—" Morgan began.

But Ethan wouldn't be stopped. He waved an angry hand at his brother. "Hell, I know the place is falling down around our ears, but I done my best. At least I didn't run out. And this place isn't the only thing that's changed, big brother, not by a long shot."

He swung around on the bench and threw off the ragged blanket covering his lap. Jessy's gaze fell to his legs, to his leg, rather. Where the other should have been there was only a stump inside a cut-off, rolled-up pant leg. Her hand flew to her mouth.

Morgan's face paled beneath his tan, and he took a step toward his younger brother.

"That's right," Ethan raged. "Stare at the cripple. Stare all you want!"

"Ethan, I—"

"Shut up! I don't want any of your damned pity. Just keep out of my way." He picked up a pair of crude crutches lying on the floor behind his bench and struggled to stand. "Come on, Corrine, we're going home. And I'd better find a fresh bottle in the cupboard or there'll be hell to pay."

He stumped toward the door, and the young woman who had been seated next to him stood. From the plain gold ring on her finger, Jessy assumed she was Ethan's wife. Large, wary eyes peered out of a thin, pale face. She clung to the hand of the small dark-haired boy who stared silently at Morgan. As soon as Corrine stood, Jessy's attention was drawn to the bulging mound of her belly beneath the threadbare calico dress before returning to her face. Corrine was so young, much too young to bear the burden of an angry, crippled husband, a small son, and another baby on the way.

The worry and sorrow in Corrine's hollow-cheeked face tugged at the strings of Jessy's heart, kindling a familiar spark. The need and suffering of others always energized her, and here were people who needed help.

Ethan's angry words had shocked her. Palpable currents of pain and unhappiness flooded the cabin. She was determined to find a way to knit the family back together.

She stepped out of the doorway, and Ethan stormed past her followed by his wife and son. Lost in her misery, Corrine seemed not to notice Jessy, but the little boy regarded her with large, curious eyes as his mother dragged him behind her.

Morgan spared a brief glance at the other young woman before turning to his mother. "Ma, what...?"

Rachel Bingham looked as thin and brittle as a dried oak leaf. "It's been bad here, son, awful bad. With both you and Caleb gone, Ethan had to be the man in the family, but he was too young."

Jessy stole a look at Morgan's face in the firelight. His expression was stony, but his eyes betrayed the guilt and pain caused by his mother's words.

Rachel stared into the fire for a moment before she continued. "After Ethan married Corrine and had Samuel right away, we had two more mouths to feed. I was a'feared the baby wouldn't make it for a while. By the time things were starting to look up, the war had begun. Ethan didn't want to go, but soldiers came and took him. They sent him home after he lost his leg, but it was too late." Her voice broke. "He'd changed so much I almost didn't know him."

Rachel paused, as if to gather her composure and allow her mind to return to the present. "The worst thing is, his spirit is crippled worse than his body. I hate to say it, but sometimes he puts me in mind of Caleb these days."

The sadness and resignation in her voice moved Jessy, but her main concern was for Morgan. How must he feel to hear such an account of his family's suffering? His narrowed eyes and granite jaw gave little away. Nothing prepared her for the violent anger and revulsion that swept his face at the mention of the name Caleb. The look disappeared as quickly as it came but left Jessy shaken.

"Has Ethan raised his hand to you or Sally?" Morgan demanded.

Rachel shook her head. "No, no...but I couldn't say for sure about Corrine and Samuel. I haven't seen anything, mind you, but they've both got a look about them."

He swore and slammed his fist on the table. "I should have been here."

His mother reached out to cover his hand. "That's no never mind. You're home now, and that's what matters."

"I'm home." Iron determination resounded in his quiet words.

The woman sighed and dropped her hand. Turning from Morgan, her gaze fell on Jessy for the first time. Her face lost all expression except for a slight narrowing of the eyes. Jessy flushed with the acute embarrassment of an intruder who has witnessed the most intimate of family dramas.

"Have you brought someone with you, son?"

Morgan glanced over his shoulder as if he had forgotten he wasn't alone. "That's hard to explain. Jessy, come here."

She smiled, trying to bolster her flagging confidence. These were hardly the circumstances she would have chosen to meet her future in-laws. Conscious of her bizarre appearance in her boy's clothing, she walked forward until she stood next to Morgan. She plucked off her hat, and down spilled a tumble of curls.

Across the room, the young dark-haired girl stood frozen like a statue with a stack of dirty dishes in her hands. Suddenly she came to life. With eyes as round as the plates she held, she gasped and squealed, "He's a girl!"

Jessy tried to ignore the outburst. She thrust her hand into Rachel's. "It's a pleasure to meet you, Mrs. Bingham. I'm Jessamine Randall, Morgan's fiancée."

The older woman stared. With a shudder, her knees gave way, and she sank to the bench behind her. Questioning brown eyes rose to Morgan. "Son, do you truly mean to wed this...this..."

Morgan shot Jessy a hard look, as if daring her to contradict him. "No, I'm not going to marry her."

She rose to the challenge. "Now, just one moment—"

"Not now," he commanded.

"Son, if you're not going to marry her, then who is she? Why did you bring her here? And why is she dressed like that?"

He drew a slow breath and let it out in a rush. "It's a long story, Ma."

The older woman glanced from Jessy to Morgan, and her thin lips tightened. "You've brought a woman with you who isn't your betrothed and isn't your wife. This isn't seemly. What will her people say?"

"I can just imagine," Morgan muttered, keeping his gaze on Jessy. "Don't worry about it, Ma. I'll take care of everything...somehow."

Heat rose in Jessy's cheeks again, but this time not from embarrassment. She'd had enough of being discussed as if she were an inanimate object. She'd never had trouble speaking for herself, and she didn't intend to start now.

"I promise I won't be any trouble, Mrs. Bingham. I'm sure there are plenty of ways I can help during my visit."

Morgan's mother looked skeptical.

"Don't worry about it, Ma. She won't be here long."

Jessy opened her mouth to reply.

"Morgan, have you forgotten your manners?" The pretty young girl's importuning voice interrupted.

Morgan turned, and his expression eased until he almost smiled. "I suppose so, but you've been so quiet I couldn't be sure who you were. Jessy, I think this little girl is my sister Sally."

Sally pouted. "Little girl! I'll have you know I'm a woman grown. I'm seventeen."

Morgan's smile widened. "Maybe so, but I haven't seen you since you were seven, and you don't look all that different to me."

Jessy wasn't certain how a young girl might take such comments from an older brother, especially one who had been absent for so long. In an effort to avoid further sibling warfare, she stepped in.

"Stop teasing, Morgan." Turning to Sally, she was relieved to see a twinkle in the girl's blue eyes. "It's a pleasure to meet such a lovely young lady." She offered Morgan's sister a smile. "I hope we can become friends."

Sally glanced from Jessy to Morgan and back. "I think I'd like that."

Morgan sent his sister one more amused glance before turning back to his mother. "Ma, Jessy and I could use some food, if there's any to spare. I'll bring in the gear and put the horses in the barn."

He gave Jessy a long look then walked out the door, leaving her alone with his disapproving mother and Sally, who appeared to find her fascinating. The young girl couldn't seem to take her eyes off her brother's *maybe* fiancée.

Sally hurried to the table and pulled out one of the benches. "You can sit here, and I'll dish up a couple of plates. Have you been riding long? We didn't even know Morgan was alive all these years, much less that he would show up so suddenly, and with an intended bride. This is so exciting." She kept up a steady stream of chatter while she bustled around the room. Jessy smiled to see how the girl's shyness disappeared in her brothers' absence.

She was already seated when Morgan returned and took his place beside her. She glanced up from the mysterious gray chunks in her bowl to see his face drawn in grim lines.

"There's a lot of work to do around the place," he said between bites, glancing across the table at his mother. "Not a single building's got a decent roof, the barn's about to collapse, and the holes in the hen house are big enough for an army of foxes to sneak in."

"Ethan's done what he could."

Guilt flashed across Morgan's craggy features, and pressure squeezed Jessy's chest.

"Well, I'm back now. I'll get everything fixed up before winter sets in. If you tell me what you need, I'll ride into town in the morning for supplies."

His mother slowly shook her head. "Son, there's no money, hasn't been for years. And even if there was, the stores in Camdenton don't have anything to buy. Having two armies camped around here for so long pretty near cleaned everyone out. I don't know how we would have held body and soul together while Ethan was gone if Peter Bennett hadn't been so generous with flour from his mill."

Jessy stole another glance at Morgan's face, and the pressure in her chest tightened further. He was so proud, and now to learn his family had been forced to rely on handouts from a neighbor to survive...

"I've got money enough to take care of this family." Morgan's voice was gruff with emotion. "I don't want you to worry anymore, Ma. And I'll pay Bennett back. Binghams don't take charity from anyone."

The energy drained from his body, and pain overlay the exhaustion in his face. He stood and walked to the front door. As he bent to lift his saddlebags, his movements were reminiscent of an old man.

"I've got to get some rest. I'm going to sleep in the barn." His tired eyes focused on Jessy. "Ma, if you could find some place for Jessy, I'd be obliged." Soul-deep weariness filled his voice. "I'll sort this out tomorrow."

He started to walk away, and panic gripped Jessy at the thought of being separated from him. With the possible exception of Sally, the other members of his family obviously didn't want her here. His mother refused to speak to her and had made it clear she was an unwelcome intruder.

The feeling of being unwanted was new, and she didn't like it. On the trail, she had depended on Morgan's strength, but now the sudden urge to cling to him disturbed her. She knew he would reject such an effort, so she took refuge behind her best weapon, her sharp tongue.

He opened the door to leave, and she called out, "Wait just a minute, Morgan Bingham. I am your intended wife, and I'll have you know I will not be sorted out like a pile of mismatched socks."

Before she could continue her scolding, Sally stepped forward and slipped a restraining arm around her. "Don't worry, Morgan, I'll take good care of her. She can sleep in my bed in the loft, and I'll sleep down here with Ma."

"Thanks." He gave Jessy one last glance then stepped through the doorway.

Jessy turned to her rescuer. "You didn't have to do that. I was just getting started."

Sally didn't smile at her lighthearted tone. "That's what I was afraid of."

A wary note in the younger woman's voice caught Jessy's attention. As she studied the face of Morgan's younger sister, her smile faded. Sally's gaze remained pinned to the closed door, her shoulders hunched with tension. Jessy frowned. Morgan might be tired and a little grumpy, but he wasn't frightening.

"It's all right," Jessy said. "Morgan gets annoyed with me all the time."

Sally continued to stare at the door, as if a raging beast might burst through at any moment. "It's best not to rile men. A man's anger can be a fearsome thing."

"Morgan's your brother, not a wild animal."

The tension in Sally's shoulders eased a fraction, and she turned. "With some men, there's not much difference."

"Morgan's not that way," Jessy assured her. "I know you haven't seen him in years, but you have nothing to be afraid of. I've never known a man with more self-control."

Sally relented and offered a tiny smile. "I hope you're right. It would be a blessing. If you follow me, I'll show you where you can sleep."

"Thank you." Jessy pondered Sally's reaction, wondering what had caused the girl to be so fearful of men. Of course, if Ethan's behavior tonight was common, his sister had cause to be skittish. Jessy could never live in the same house with a man who had such a violent disposition. Morgan's taciturnity might drive her crazy sometimes, but at least he never scared her.

Before turning in, she wanted to make one more effort to leave a better impression with his mother. She might not look like a lady, but at least she could act like one. "Good night, Mrs. Bingham. Thank you for supper. I appreciate your hospitality."

Rachel slowly raised her eyes. "I've never yet turned away a traveler in need, but if you're going to stay, I hope you've got a dress in that bag. I don't cotton to having a woman dressed in men's clothes in my house."

A dull heat crept up Jessy's throat to her face. She had worn the clothes only to be warm and comfortable, but Morgan's mother seemed to think she was unnatural. She would have to prove to the woman how feminine she really was and what a good wife she would make her son. "I did bring a couple of dresses, but I'm afraid they're rather wrinkled by now."

"We don't have much, but we've got an iron."

"Yes, of course." Jessy had never meant to imply the Binghams lacked basic household necessities, despite their obvious circumstances. "I'll take care of it in the morning. Good night."

Rachel didn't reply. Hefting her bag with a sigh, Jessy followed Sally up the ladder to the sleeping loft.

The low roof timbers grazed her back as she stepped onto the small platform. The dim firelight from the main room below struggled to reach the loft. It was dark, cold, damp, and dismal. She took a couple of tentative steps in the shadowy darkness and banged her shin into something hard. "Ouch!"

"Hold still while I get you a candle. I forgot you wouldn't know your way around in the dark up here like I do."

Sally scampered down the ladder and returned with a flickering candle. The tiny flame sputtered and flared, sending glowing yellow light and sharp shadows through the small space under the rafters. She set the candle in its protective globe on a small table next to a hand-hewn single bed covered with a red and white patterned quilt. A simple chest and chair completed the furnishings. It was a far cry from Jessy's large, bright bedroom at home with its matching mahogany four-poster, dresser, and wardrobe.

Sally pulled open a drawer and removed her nightdress.

"I'm sorry to be putting you out of your bed."

"Oh, that's all right. I don't mind." Morgan's sister bundled her gown under one arm and started toward the ladder. "Sleep well. I'll see you in the morning."

"Thank you."

Jessy hauled her bag to the bed where she could see to unpack and spread the contents out. The riding habit, day dress, underclothes, and few toiletries that had seemed like plenty when she left home would be inadequate for a long stay. She would need to ride to town with Morgan in the morning and purchase several additional items. Despite Rachel's comment on the state of the shops, she hoped there would be a competent dressmaker. She didn't even have a nightdress.

She undressed to her chemise and drawers and slipped beneath the covers. The cornhusks inside the thin mattress crackled under her weight, and the rough muslin sheets lay icy against her skin. She shivered and curled into a tight little ball.

She tried to sleep, but thoughts of Morgan drifted through her mind. She remembered his strong, competent hands preparing food when she was cold and hungry on the trail. She remembered the warmth of his body wrapped around hers, warding off the chill of the night air. It would be so easy to lay life's burdens at his feet.

But what were her burdens compared to those of his family? She could see how desperately they needed him. She would have to help him do his duty to his family before they could return to Weston and be married.

What a devastating homecoming it must have been for him to be greeted with such anger and hatred by his own brother. And what did Ethan mean when he called Morgan a murderer and a coward? Morgan was the bravest man she knew. Whatever ugliness lay behind the accusation, it could never change her feelings. Tomorrow Morgan wouldn't be the only one to sort things out.

Chapter Five

Clanging pots woke Jessy long before the first hint of dawn. She sat up, wrapped the quilt around her shoulders, and scooted to the side of the bed to peer over the edge of the loft platform. Below her, Rachel and Sally had begun their morning chores. The older woman poked small sticks of kindling into the fire, and her daughter stood by the front door tying a fringed woolen shawl over her head.

"I'll be back in a few minutes with the water, Ma." Sally shouldered a carved wooden yoke with a bucket dangling from each end. Rachel Bingham nodded and continued her work.

Jessy knew she should get dressed and help, but she hated the thought of leaving the toasty comfort of her quilt. The cabin was so cold she was sure she could see her breath if there were enough light. That thought led to another problem—how to get dressed. If she lit the candle, she would be illuminated for anyone who walked through the front door, including Morgan or Ethan. If she didn't, she wasn't sure she could manage the complicated fastenings on her clothes.

While she pondered her dilemma, the door creaked on its hinges. She peeked down again, and Morgan stepped into the cabin wearing his buckskins from the day before. That settled it. She would have to do her best to dress in the dark. She couldn't stand on display in front of his mother and sister in nothing but her underwear.

"I'll leave for town as soon as it's light," he said to Rachel. "I worked on the old buckboard in the barn the best I could last night, and I think it will hold together until I can get the tools and materials to fix it."

Jessy listened with one ear while she struggled into her green twill day dress with black braid trim, along with the two petticoats she'd brought. She intended to ride to town with him as soon as he was ready.

"Ma, there's no cow in the barn—no mules nor horses either."

"Soldiers took 'em all." Rachel's voice was matter-of-fact. Crockery clattered on the table.

"But Samuel needs milk, and Corrine's got another baby coming."

"We've done the best we could, son. I told you how it was.

"But how did you get the corn in?"

"We took turns with the plow—me, Sally, and Corrine."

"By God, that will never happen again as long as I live. I swear it!"

His words pierced Jessy's heart. He'd already faced so much. To learn his mother, sister, and pregnant sister-in-law had worked like draught animals in the field during his absence must be a shame beyond bearing.

"We do what we must," Rachel said. "But as for the animals, I told you there's no money."

"And as for money, I told you not to worry about it."

Jessy heard Rachel sigh. "I'm glad you're home, son. You always were a good boy."

"I was no such thing, and you know it, but I aim to make it up to you."

As presentable as she could make herself without light or a mirror, Jessy stepped onto the ladder. She searched for each rung with her smooth-soled shoes. She could imagine the impression she'd make if she slid down the ladder and landed in a heap on the floor. When both feet rested safely on solid ground, she turned to face Morgan and his mother with a nervous smile.

"Good morning, Mrs. Bingham. What can I do to help?"

Rachel's gaze traveled the full length of Jessy from head to toe, as if looking for something to fault. "Hmph. I see you can look decent when you've a mind to."

The hairs on the back of Jessy's neck bristled. She had always been the most fashionable girl in Weston and was not used to having her appearance faulted. She caught a glimpse of Morgan's mocking hazel eyes and knew her feelings must have shown on her face. She held her tongue and sent him a bland little smile.

"If you're looking for something to do," Rachel continued, "I guess you can gather eggs. Samuel usually does it, so you might see him down at the hen house. Here's a basket."

Jessy took the basket and made her escape. The minute she stepped onto the porch, the damp cold penetrated straight to her bones. *Bother!* The boy's rough jacket was the only coat she had, and she had forgotten it on her way out. Rather than face Rachel Bingham's disapproval again, she clenched her teeth to stop their chattering and picked her way across the muddy yard to the hen house.

A surprising warmth, laced with a pungent, eyewatering smell, assaulted her at the door. Someone, probably Morgan, had nailed a board across a gaping hole in the side of the small, low-roofed building. It wasn't pretty, but it served as an effective barrier to keep the chickens in and predators out.

She stepped inside, and half a dozen chickens squawked, flapping their wings and flying at her. She screamed, dropping the basket, and threw her arms over her head to shield herself from the storm of sharp beaks and claws.

The door flew open, and Morgan burst into the maelstrom. He wrapped one arm around her and tossed a handful of dried corn on the ground with the other hand. The hens descended on their breakfast in a clamorous flutter, now oblivious to the intruders.

Still in shock from the sudden attack and Morgan's swift rescue, Jessy closed her eyes and struggled to catch her breath. She expected him to release her immediately and was surprised when he turned her in his embrace instead. His free hand came up to cradle her head against the solid wall of his chest, and he tightened his grip around her waist. She sighed and relaxed against his body while her racing heart slowed its beat.

His hand spanned the width of her head, reminding her of his greater size and power. Strong fingers caressed her hair, and she succumbed to the urge to snuggle against him. She relished the assurance of his protection, however fleeting.

"You okay?" His voice rumbled in his chest.

She nodded, reluctant to break the contact. It seemed like ages since he'd held her like this, fighting neither anger nor desire. She wanted to stretch the moment, make it last forever. But she knew better.

He dropped his arms, and she stepped back. Raising her eyes, she saw none of the tenderness she'd felt in his touch. Instead, his eyes taunted her.

"Can't you even gather eggs without causing a disturbance?"

She glared at him, angrier at his withdrawal than his mocking question. "Those chickens attacked me!"

"A four-year-old child can do it, but I guess that would be too much to expect from a girl like you."

"What do you mean a girl like me?"

"You've never had to do anything for yourself, have you?"

She was in no mood to be castigated for her upbringing. She poked a finger into his chest. "I'd like to remind you, Morgan Bingham, that I am a fully qualified teacher. In fact, I'm the one who taught you to read, in case you've forgotten."

"I'll grant you've got plenty of book learning, but you won't find that too useful around here."

"Knowledge is always useful."

He leaned down and plucked the basket off the ground. "Then you'll be all set as soon as you find a book about chickens, won't you?"

"Give me that." She snatched the basket from his fingers. "I'll be back in the house with the eggs in five minutes, and I'll be ready to ride as soon as you are."

His eyes narrowed. "Who said anything about you riding into town?"

She collected eggs in the basket while the chickens concentrated on their breakfast. "This is the only dress I brought besides my riding habit, so I'll need a few more, as well as some other personal items." She turned and held out her basket in triumph. "And don't worry. I brought plenty of my own money. Now let's get going. I'm hungry." She brushed past Morgan and out the door.

Back in the main house, she set her eggs on the table with pride.

"I poured some hot water for you, if you want to wash." Sally pointed to a chipped china basin.

"Thank you. That was very kind."

Dipping the warm rag Sally gave her into the basin, Jessy scrubbed her hands and face, allowing the water to warm her chilled flesh. She craved a full bath but wasn't sure how to go about asking. The rest of the family seemed clean, so they must bathe, but the one-room cabin offered none of the privacy to which she was accustomed.

When breakfast was ready, Corrine and Samuel arrived. The bruised-looking hollows beneath Corrine's eyes were an even deeper shade of purple than the night before.

"Where's Ethan?" Sally asked.

"He's got a bad head this morning. Says he can't eat."

No one commented further on Ethan's absence. Rachel said grace, and the family ate in silence. As soon as Morgan finished, he stood and announced he was leaving for town.

"Wait for me." Jessy stuffed the last spoonful of grits in her mouth.

He didn't reply and headed toward the door. She raced for the ladder to the loft and scurried up. She found her money and hurried back down.

"Good-bye, Mrs. Bingham, and Sally." She grabbed her rough wool jacket from its peg and bolted out the door.

By the time she reached the barn, Morgan had hitched his roan to the sorriest looking wagon she'd ever seen. She wondered how the vehicle would make it down the hill, much less all the way to town.

He eyed her from the narrow plank seat. "Well, climb on up."

She scanned the buckboard. "I'm not sure it can take the extra weight."

A hint of a smile hovered around his lips. "I think it can take it. You're no bigger than a mite." Without warning, he reached down, grasped her beneath the arms, and swung her onto the hard seat with a thump. The air rushed from her lungs.

"Well!" she said, unable to think of anything else. She was grateful her petticoats had helped absorb some of the shock.

"Yeah, well." Morgan snapped the reins and the horse strained against the unaccustomed load.

They drove down the hill the same way they'd come the night before, through the cornfield and toward the river.

Jessy flew up then came down hard when the wagon hit a deep rut. "Is it very far to town?"

Morgan kept his gaze on the rough ground ahead, trying to steer around the worst patches. "It'll take most of the morning, if we manage not to lose a wheel."

She held her breath and clutched the sides of the wagon as they clattered down a steep, rocky section leading to the river. One misstep and they'd end up soaked to the skin. After they reached the ford safely, she exhaled in a huff.

He glanced at her. "Worried?"

Annoyed by the hint of amusement in his tone, she released her hold on the wagon, sat up and straightened her jacket. "Not a bit."

"Good. I've been thinking—while we're in town, you can send a wire to your folks, telling them where you are. I'm sure your father can afford to send someone to take you back."

She snapped her head around. "I will do no such thing. I told you before—I will not go back without you."

He jerked the reins, and she had to grab the wagon again to keep from being thrown out. Stormy hazel eyes burning beneath the ridge of lowered brows met her glare.

"What was that for?" she demanded.

"We've got to get something straight here and now."

"Oh? And what might that be?" As if she didn't know. He never took it well when she refused to do as he told her.

She opened her mouth, but he cut her off. "Hold it right there. Before you get started and talk me into the ground, I'm going to say what I have to say."

She clamped her mouth shut and crossed her arms.

He shifted his gaze to the reins in his hands. His thumbs rubbed the rough, worn leather. "You've seen the place, such as it is, and you've met my family." His voice crackled with anger...or was it pain?

She fought the urge to throw her arms around him, to absorb some of the pain. He wouldn't welcome her comfort now. His pride had taken too many blows.

He glanced up, and the raw plea in his eyes startled her. "You can't stay here, Jessy. Even someone as stubborn as you should see that. You have to go home as soon as possible." He raised his hand to head off her objections. "I know you're going to argue, but it's no use, so you might as well save your breath."

"Are you finished?"

He shifted his weight on the board seat, refusing to meet her direct gaze. "I guess that's it in a nutshell."

She placed a hand on his forearm. "I'm not leaving without you. I understand you can't leave your family now. They need you."

"Yes."

"Well, they need me, too."

His expression told her what he thought of that statement. "How do you figure?"

"You said it yourself, there's a lot of work to do. I'm sure you could use an extra pair of hands."

His brows shot up. "To do what? I know you can't cook. You probably can't sew or clean either. Unless you've been hiding a great skill with a hammer or saw all this time, there's nothing you can do to help."

She dropped her hand. He always knew what to say to deflate her confidence. "I'll have you know I can too sew."

"Jessy, we don't need fancy embroidery here" His voice was gentler than before. "Life in the hills is hard, too hard for a woman like you."

"I'm stronger than you realize."

He shook his head. "No."

She took a deep breath. "Even if I can't plow a field or mend a roof, I can give the rest of your family what I gave you. I can teach them to read and write."

"What good would that do? The only book in the house is the family Bible."

She pushed harder. "Think what a comfort it would be for them to be able to read it for themselves. Samuel might be a little young, but I'm sure he'd enjoy having stories read to him."

Morgan's expression hardened. "We can do without your meddling. The Bingham family is not another charity case."

Why did he have to be so mule-headed? She let out a short puff of exasperation. "Of course not. How could you suggest such a thing? I just want to do what I can to help."

He turned away and snapped the reins. "Then mind your own business and wire your father to come get you."

If she'd been holding anything heavier than her reticule, she would have been tempted to knock some sense into his hard head. No one's life ever improved because they chose to remain ignorant. She could make a difference. She knew it.

As soon as they reached the main street of Camdenton, she revised her hopes for their shopping excursion. The town appeared to have once been a thriving center for the surrounding area with a number of charming brick homes, shops on both sides of the main street, and even a town square. Now, the devastation of the war blighted every view. Boarded-up and derelict buildings dotted the main street. The few people out in the middle of the day looked as gaunt and miserable as the horses tied in front of Boone's Mercantile.

After Morgan dismounted and tied his horse next to the others, he turned. "This looks like the only store left in town that's still open. Are you coming in?"

She made no move to alight. "A gentleman would help a lady down."

His lazy gaze swept the wooden sidewalks. "I don't see any gentlemen here. Do you?"

She crossed her arms, and her remaining patience evaporated. "Morgan Bingham, you put me up in this contraption, now you get me down."

He laughed before he reached, lifted her off the seat, and swung her to the ground. Offering his elbow with mock gentility, he escorted her up the steps to the boardwalk and into the shabby wooden building.

A grizzled old man no taller than Jessy stood behind the counter. "Howdy, folks. What can I do for you?"

"Hello, Hiram. I need everything from bacon to nails. I hope you can help me."

The old man squinted. "Morgan? Morgan Bingham? Is that you?"

Morgan smiled and walked toward the counter. "Sure is, old man. How've you been?"

Hiram chuckled. "Well, now, that's a long story. But just look at you—I barely recognized you. How long's it been since you left, ten years? Last time I saw you, you were just a lad. Now you're a man. What brings you back?"

"It was time to come home."

Hiram nodded. "I was sorry about what happened with Caleb. Bad business, that."

"It's in the past now."

The old man brightened. "That it is. It's good to have you home, son." His gaze shifted to Jessy. "And who's this lovely lady?"

Before Morgan had a chance to answer, Jessy smiled and offered her hand. "I'm Jessamine Randall, Morgan's fiancée."

Hiram grinned. "Hoo-ee. So, you got yourself a fee-an-cee, do you? Well, she's a mighty fine-looking gal. Pleased to meet you, little lady. I'm Hiram Boone." He stuck out a wiry palm and pumped Jessy's hand with enthusiasm.

"Miss Randall needs to send a telegram." Morgan kept his gaze on Jessy, daring her to contradict him.

Hiram clucked. "I'm afraid the lines are down. Actually, the lines have been down for the last three years. Both the Union boys and the Confederates kept cutting them until it seemed easier just to leave them down. Since the war ended, the company hasn't gotten around to stringing them back up." He looked hopeful and added, "If you want to write a letter, one of my boys could ride over to Waynesville and get it on the stage to St. Louis."

Morgan frowned. "It could take weeks to get back across the state to Weston, but it sounds like that's the best we can do."

"I got a pencil and paper right here," Hiram offered.

Jessy hesitated. She'd already made her position clear and refused to be bullied. "I—"

"Write the letter, Jessy." Morgan pushed the paper and pencil across the counter in front of her.

She smiled around clamped teeth. "Of course. Why don't you go ahead and take care of the rest of the supplies?"

She picked up the pencil and gripped it so tight it almost snapped. Oh, she'd write a letter all right, but she wasn't about to let him read it over her shoulder.

He cast her a sharp glance but moved off with Hiram to inspect the small stock of building materials.

She bit the end of the pencil as she tried to decide what to say to her parents. Even if it took several weeks for the letter to reach them, she couldn't be sure when she and Morgan would be ready to leave.

She settled on telling them she was safe, happily married, and planned to return to Weston with her new husband in the spring. She couldn't describe the location of the Bingham farm if she wanted to, so even if her father sent out a posse, it would be difficult to track her down in such a remote area without more specific clues.

Feeling much better, she sealed the letter then busied herself with the dry goods while Morgan and Hiram loaded the wagon with foodstuffs, tools, nails, and paint. The half-bare shelves held few bolts of fabric, but she found a couple of sturdy calicos and some soft muslin for undergarments.

She was about to carry her selections to the counter to be measured when a thickset, black-haired man pushed through the front door of the shop. He strode over to where Morgan stood with Hiram Boone.

"So, it's true. I heard you was back."

His words were as much an accusation as a statement of fact.

Morgan turned. His right hand slid to his hip out of instinct or habit but encountered only the smooth leather of his breeches. "News travels fast," he answered in an even voice.

"You've got a hell of a nerve showing your face around here again, after what you done to my brother."

"I always did." Morgan's eyes glittered like a big cat ready to strike.

"Well, you can turn around and go back where you came from. We don't want you here." The man's solid face reddened, and his fists clenched.

Jessy glanced at Morgan in alarm. She knew he could take care of himself in a fight, but the other man had the build of a blacksmith and a demonic gleam in his eyes.

"Sorry, I can't do that. This is my home, and I mean to stay."

Hiram stepped forward and raised his arms to separate the two before they came to blows. "Now, Thomas, Morgan, I don't want any trouble here."

Morgan glanced at Jessy. "There won't be any trouble, Hiram. Miss Randall and I were just leaving. Weren't we, Jessy?"

"Oh...yes. I just need some lengths cut off this cloth."

Morgan took the bolts of fabric from her arms and handed them to Hiram. "We'll take the whole pile. Just wrap them up."

"Sure." Hiram tied the cloth in brown paper and hurried out the door to load it in the wagon with the other purchases.

Morgan took Jessy by the arm and touched the brim of his hat, keeping his eyes trained on the angry black-haired man. "We'll be going now. Nice to see you again, Uncle Thomas."

Uncle Thomas?

It was all Jessy could do to hold her questions until they were outside and in the wagon. She bade Hiram good-bye as politely as she could and held her tongue until he disappeared inside.

"Morgan, who was that man? Is he really your uncle? Why was he so angry, and what was all that about his brother?"

Morgan's tough confidence drained away. He hunched forward on the seat with the reins dangling in his hands.

"Morgan, answer me."

"You don't want to know."

"I certainly do, or I wouldn't have asked. Ever since we arrived, people have been making all sorts of strange comments. I think you owe me an explanation."

He turned, and the blaze in his eyes knocked her back. "I don't owe you a damned thing. I didn't ask you to follow me, and all I'm concerned about now is how fast I can send you home. So, keep your questions to yourself."

Jessy's heart contracted. At first, his rejections had fueled her determination, but she wasn't sure how much more she could take. Knowing the obstacles he faced, she knew he needed her more than ever. She also knew the greater his need, the stronger he would fight it. She could help him, but only if he let her.

"I want to help."

"You can't help me. Nobody can." His answer was hard and final and bitterly lonely.

Not a word passed between them on the long drive home. By the time they pulled into the yard, the sun had slipped behind the mountain, and deep shadows streaked across the rutted mud. Morgan stopped the wagon next to the front porch and lifted her down before she could speak. He unloaded the sacks of food and carried them inside. With her paper-wrapped parcel in her arms, she followed him up the steps. Sally and Rachel were preparing supper, and Morgan set the bags next to the table.

"I'll take these out to the dry shed tomorrow, once I've had a chance to repair the leaks. I bought some tools and plenty of nails, so I can start work on the rest of the place. I promise you, Ma, by the time winter's here, I'll have everything tight and dry."

Rachel nodded. "Thank you, son. Now go wash up. Supper will be ready soon."

Jessy carried her package to a chair in front of the fire and tore open the brown paper. As she examined the fabrics in the firelight, she caught a whiff of burnt biscuits and glanced over. The pan sat unattended on the fire while Sally peered over her shoulder. Considering the well-worn condition of the girl's dress, Jessy wasn't surprised she was interested in the bright new material.

This might be the perfect opportunity to get closer to Morgan's younger sister. Since he had insisted on buying three whole bolts, there was much more than Jessy needed. And since he had also insisted on paying for it, it seemed only right that his sister should have a new dress, too.

"Sally, when those biscuits are done, I wonder if you could give me some advice about this fabric. I need a couple of new dresses, but I've never sewed one by myself before. I think there's much more material here than I need."

Sally started, then yanked the darkening biscuits off the fire with a sheepish grin. "Of course, I'd be glad to help."

Rachel's sharp voice broke in. "Sally, you've got those potatoes to tend to."

"Oh, Ma, I know, but this will only take a few minutes. You should see what she bought."

"Supper won't cook itself. Mind your chores."

"But, Ma—"

The last thing Jessy wanted was to cause more friction in the household. The place was already like a powder keg. "There will be plenty of time after supper."

A few minutes later, Morgan returned from the barn, washed at the basin, and took his seat at the table next to Jessy.

Rachel set a platter of ham and a steaming bowl of boiled potatoes on the table. "Sally, go tell Ethan and Corrine supper's ready."

Before Sally could respond, the connecting door to the smaller adjacent cabin banged opened, and Ethan stumped into the room followed by his wife and son. His gait on his crutches was even more unsteady than the night before, and his bloodshot eyes kept blinking. When he passed beside her, the raw smell of corn liquor stung Jessy's nostrils.

Corrine's blue eyes were red, too, and streaky tracks marred her pale cheeks. One hand rested on her belly while the other clutched her son's small hand. Samuel's thin four-year-old face was as solemn as ever. Silently, he took his place at the table next to his mother.

Rachel glanced at her younger son and his family, sighed, then said grace and passed the food.

"I went to town today...bought some tools and a keg of nails," Morgan said while the rest of the family ate with heads bent and eyes on their food. "Thought I'd get started tomorrow with some of the repairs. Thought maybe I'd start with your roof, Ethan, and any other projects you've got that need doing."

Ethan's head snapped up, and he clutched his fork like a dagger. "Keep away from my house. We don't need help from you. We don't need anything from you."

Distress pinched Corrine's features. "But Ethan…the roof…"

"Shut up, woman!" He flung his plate to the floor where it clattered and sent potatoes flying. "I said we won't take anything from that bastard, and I meant it."

Corrine flinched as if she'd been struck, and fresh tears welled in her eyes. Jessy stared at Ethan in horror then glanced at Morgan. He had to do something. The poor woman was terrified of her bullying, drunken husband. Jessy didn't care if the man was his brother.

Morgan pushed back from the table and stood. "Ethan, go home. Go home, and go to bed. You're drunk and acting like a fool."

"I don't have to do what you say," Ethan slurred. "You're nothing but a low-down killer. You're nothing…" His voice trailed off as he worked to focus reddened eyes on his brother.

"Are you going home under your own steam, or do I have to throw you out?" Morgan took a step closer.

Ethan reached for his crutches and struggled to stand.

"No!" his mother cried. "No more fighting in this house. Not brother against brother, not here." She sank back, and tears slid down her lined cheeks.

Ethan stared at her. "Aw, Ma…"

"Do like he says, Ethan. Go home." Rachel covered her eyes with one hand and gave a weak wave with the other.

Corrine stood and slid one arm around her husband's waist. "Come on, Ethan. I'll help you."

The poignant mixture of love and pain in Corrine's voice amazed Jessy. How could the woman continue to love a man who treated her the way Ethan did, who behaved the way Ethan did? Was Corrine weak or stupid? Maybe in her present condition, she felt she had no choice.

She studied Corrine's face, looking for answers. She saw love, but nothing as simple as the adoration she'd seen on the faces of her friends when they were enamored of a new beau. Corrine's tortured blue eyes shone with a love of maturity and depth that belied her years. It glowed through the tears, profound, tempered to unyielding strength by her suffering, a love deep enough to see under the ugly surface to the hurting man beneath.

Jessy shifted her gaze to Morgan. She knew he had been an outlaw, but she'd never allowed herself to consider what that meant. His brother and uncle had accused him of murder, and he'd hinted he'd done awful things, things that would make her hate him. She'd always brushed his warnings aside and assured him her love was strong enough to overlook anything in his past. But was it? She wondered if she had Corrine's strength.

In one respect, Morgan was right. She was untested. She wouldn't dispute that her parents had given her an easy life, but her privileged upbringing didn't make her weak or incompetent. The Bingham family might not be aware of it, but they presented a challenge, one she was determined to meet.

When the door closed behind Ethan, Corrine, and Samuel, Morgan approached his mother and rested a hand on her shoulder in a gentle caress. "Has he been like this ever since he came home from the war?"

Rachel Bingham shook her head. "He was bitter when he came back, but the drinking's been getting worse, especially since he found out Corrine's expecting another baby. And it's worse now that you're back. I don't know where the liquor comes from—Lord knows there's no extra money. I'm afraid he may have set up Caleb's old still somewhere, but I haven't been able to find it." Her tired eyes implored Morgan. "Can you help him?"

"I don't know, Ma. I think there's more wrong with Ethan than just the drink. If I find the still and smash it, he's bound to be angry. He might take it out on Corrine and Samuel."

He rubbed his hand along his jaw. "I guess we could try to move them over here, but I'm not sure Corrine would come. Besides, if I take his family away from him, Ethan will only get worse. I'll have to think about it."

A tiny waver in Morgan's voice betrayed his fatigue, both physical and emotional, and Jessy's heart went out to him. He was a strong man, but the weight of the burden he carried was enough to crush anyone. Her parents had never needed anything from her—they had always taken care of her—and she had no brothers or sisters. Morgan had only been home two days, yet his family had already turned to him to solve all the problems that had accumulated in his absence.

It wasn't fair, but he seemed to accept it as his duty. She wanted him to know he wasn't alone in his struggle, that she would stand by him. If this was to be the test of her love, it would be the most important test of her life.

Later that evening, as Rachel and Sally settled down for the night, Jessy pulled on her jacket. Making the excuse of a visit to the necessary, she slipped out the door and made her way down the porch steps. The night was cold and dark, lit only by a silvery sliver of moon, partially obscured by thin, drifting clouds. She hoped she could cross the yard to the barn without running into a rock or stepping in a hole and breaking her ankle. She wanted to talk to Morgan, and, more important, she wanted to force him to really talk to her.

The hulking outline of the barn loomed ahead. She reached out and patted the solid wall until her fingers touched the handle of the door. Grabbing it with both hands, she pulled hard until the heavy door rolled aside far enough for her to step into the darkened barn.

Once inside, she blinked and stared, waiting for her eyes to adjust to the loss of the pale moonlight. They didn't. Not a single silhouette separated itself from the impenetrable gloom. She heard a faint fluttering in the rafters and shuddered. If Morgan was in here, he would have to come to her. She couldn't see as far as the end of her nose and didn't want to risk coming face to face with a bat.

"Morgan," she whispered into the blackness, unwilling to disturb any night creatures. "Are you here?"

Chapter Six

Morgan had lost track of time since coming out to the barn after supper. He hadn't even bothered to light the lamp, just stretched out, fully dressed, and threw a blanket over himself while he pondered the problems with Ethan. Round and round, his tired mind whirled, trying to devise a solution, some way to save his younger brother from the quicksand of his misery. There had to be a way out for Ethan, but at the moment he couldn't see it.

The trip to town had brought even more unwelcome surprises. Now, he had the added complication of Jessy stirring things up for God knew how long. It might be months before her father received the letter and made arrangements to return her to Weston. Now that he'd seen how things were for his family, there was no way he could consider taking her back himself.

And she couldn't stay. Sweet mercy, she couldn't stay.

She'd managed to hide her disgust at the miserable condition of the farm, but no matter how hard he worked, he could never turn it into the kind of place she deserved, the kind of place where she could be comfortable, the kind of place where she could stay forever.

In spite of her sassy mouth and brash ways, Jessy was a lady. She deserved the best of everything—silk dresses, a home filled with fine furniture and carpets. Even if he could afford to give her those things, they had no place in the hills. And since coming home, he knew he belonged in these hills. He'd been away too long. He never intended to leave again.

If only he hadn't run into Thomas Bingham. He'd worked so hard to suppress the ugly memories of that fateful night, but Thomas's accusations had brought them flooding back. Ten years' worth of defenses crumbled in minutes.

"Morgan...pssst, Morgan..."

He shot up from his cot in the hayloft, heart pounding.

"Morgan...Morgan, I need to talk to you."

Even if he hadn't recognized the voice, he could guess its owner. Only one person would seek him out in the darkened barn. He leaned over the edge of the loft and peered down. Pale, silvery moonlight outlined a familiar silhouette in the open doorway.

He tried to ignore the burgeoning ache deep in his chest. How he longed to drag her into the barn and up to his cot. Tonight, more than ever, he needed the comfort of her open and generous affection. He needed to sink into her softness and let her absorb the pain and confusion gnawing at his vitals. He suppressed a groan as his body responded to the image.

But he couldn't do that to her. He couldn't dump his burden on her. It was his to bear, his alone. Although it would be a relief to share the load, he couldn't bring himself to do it. It wouldn't be fair. It wouldn't be right. Ethan's problems were private problems, family problems. And whatever else she was, Jessy was an outsider. It went against the unspoken code of the hills to allow an outsider to be privy to family matters. To keep on the safe side, he'd better climb down and send her back to the house as fast as her well-bred little feet could carry her.

"I'm coming down."

****

Jessy sucked in a sharp breath. "Oh, Morgan, you startled me. It was so dark and quiet, I wasn't sure you were here. Why don't you have a light?"

He stepped off the final rung of the ladder and faced her. "I've got one of the new kerosene lamps we bought in town, but I didn't light it. I didn't expect company. What do you want?"

She strained her eyes but could barely make out his shadowy form. "I want to talk to you. Can we go outside? I can't see anything in here."

"Fine."

He reached for her elbow and steered her back outside, stopping just beyond the doorway. "What do you want to talk about?"

She peered up at his face. The light from the quarter moon cast shadows across the blunt planes of his nose and cheekbones. Frowning at her in the moonlight, he looked every inch the dangerous outlaw. She swallowed, reminding herself how important this was.

"Let's take a walk."

His frown deepened. "It's cold out here, and I've got a lot on my mind."

"Come on, just for a few minutes" She reached for his hand. He hesitated, then acquiesced.

With a firm grip, she led him across the yard and through the trees toward the cornfield. As soon as they were out of earshot of the house, she said, "I want to talk about Ethan."

Morgan stopped dead. "He shocked you." It was a statement, not a question.

"Well, I've never known anyone with his...um, problems before."

"And he disgusts you."

"No. At least not the way you mean. But I am worried about him, and Corrine and Samuel, too."

He glanced away, across the stubbly remnants of the corn. "They're not your problem."

"They're your problem, so they're my problem, too." She remembered Corrine's haunted eyes and Samuel's unnatural stillness. "Besides, I'd be concerned even if they were no relation."

"I'll take care of it." His voice lacked its usual conviction.

"Come sit down." She led him to a pair of stumps. She perched on one and turned expectant eyes on Morgan until he gave in and sat atop the other, stretching his long legs in front of him.

"Tell me about Ethan," she prodded. "It's been ten years since you've seen him. What was he like as a boy?"

Morgan stared at his boots, crossing then re-crossing his ankles. "He was fourteen when I left, and I guess he was pretty much like any other boy that age, wanting desperately to be a man but not sure how."

"Did you get along?"

He shook his head. "Not really. Ever since he was a little boy, Ethan was always trying to prove something—that he could run as fast as me, that he could shoot as straight or swim as far. But he never could. I was three years older. It always made him mad."

"Lots of little boys want to emulate their big brothers. I wonder why Ethan felt so competitive."

"Probably because of Caleb."

Caleb again. Ever since she arrived, Jessy had heard mysterious and sinister references to someone named Caleb. His name seemed to be woven into the fabric of distress that bound the Bingham family. If she was ever going to understand them, she had to find out more about him.

"Tell me about Caleb."

Morgan pulled his legs in and stood. He paced in front of her, stopping from time to time to kick the pale, crumpled cornstalks with the toe of his boot. Finally, he stopped and faced her. "All right, you asked for it. But when I tell you, you'll wish I hadn't."

She simply waited.

His eyes shifted to focus on some point beyond Jessy, both in time and place. "Caleb Bingham was my father…and not my father."

"What?" Instead of understanding more, she understood less.

"He was my mother's husband. I thought he was my father. And I killed him."

"Oh, Morgan!" Her horror echoed in her words. What a burden to carry all these years.

Returning his focus to her face, his smile was so hard the pain almost didn't show through. "I told you there were things about me you'd rather not know, but you wouldn't listen."

She had to do something to ease his searing pain. She slid off the stump.

He took a step back. "Don't touch me. I told you what I am. I'm a murderer."

His confession failed to sway her. Whoever Caleb Bingham was, she couldn't believe Morgan had killed him in cold blood. "You said you thought he was your father."

"After I killed him, Ma told me he wasn't really my father, that she'd been carrying me when she married him. It explained a lot."

"Tell me. I want to know. I want to know everything."

He didn't answer at first, then when he did, his eyes fixed on the barren field in front of him. "Caleb Bingham was a drunk, a mean, vicious drunk. I doubt he ever did an honest day's work in his life. I came to see that as I grew up. But when I was little, I thought he was my pa, and I never understood why he couldn't stand the sight of me."

Morgan might never admit he needed a father's love, but Jessy's heart ached for the lonely little boy he'd been, the same boy whose voice she heard now.

"It wasn't much consolation that he didn't have any use for Ethan or Sally, either. Whenever one of us displeased him, he beat us. As we got older and bigger, his drinking and the beatings got worse."

He paused, raising his eyes to the wedge of moon. "One night, when I was seventeen, he came home liquored up and lit into Sally. One of his cronies had seen her playing with Will McTaggart. They were only about seven and weren't doing any harm."

Anguish etched his features and tortured his voice. "He was thrashing her, and she was screaming. Ma tried to pull him off Sally, but he shook her loose and shoved her to the floor."

He lowered his head and leveled his gaze on Jessy. "Something in me snapped. I grabbed him and jerked Sally free. I was big, near as big as I am now. I punched him hard, right in the jaw, and he went down. When he fell, his head hit the corner of the bench. It must have hit wrong, because by the time he struck the floor, he was dead."

The echoing shock rang through his matter-of-fact words. She reached for him, slid her arms around his waist, and laid her head against his chest. He allowed her to hold him but made no move to return the embrace.

"I'll remember his eyes as long as I live."

"You didn't mean to kill him. It was an accident." His jacket muffled her voice.

He raised his hands to her shoulders and stepped back. "You don't understand. At that moment I hated him. I wanted him dead."

"But you didn't intend to kill him when you pushed him to the ground."

"No, but I felt a thrill when I did it." He dropped his hands. "I've lived in fear of that feeling ever since."

"Is that when you found out he wasn't your real father?"

He nodded. "When we realized he was dead, Ma told me. Maybe she was trying to make it easier on me. She was young when they married, real young. She'd been in love with someone else, but he died before they could marry. Caleb knew I wasn't his son, of course, right from the beginning, and he never forgave me or her."

"Did she ever tell you who your father was?"

Morgan nodded again. "He was David McTaggart, the younger brother of Old Man McTaggart, who owns the land next to ours."

"Is that the reason for the feud?"

He shrugged. "As long as I can remember, Caleb hated the McTaggarts. My birth must have had something to do with it."

Her mind worked to digest what he'd told her. She was beginning to understand why he pushed her away whenever she tried to get close, why he insisted he wasn't good enough for her. It was much more than a simple matter of money. The burden of guilt and self-loathing had twisted and crushed his sense of his own worth. But his revelations only strengthened her feelings for him.

"Is that when you left home?" Her voice caught in her throat.

"Yes. Caleb and his brother, Thomas, the man you saw at Boone's store, were involved in moonshining and counterfeiting with some fellows who wouldn't think twice about ambush and murder. Ma was afraid for me, so she made me leave."

"But you were only seventeen. Where did you go? What did you do?"

"I wandered from place to place, doing my best to prove Caleb had been right about me—I'd never be worth spit."

A suspicion stirred in Jessy's brain. "Is that why you joined up with Jesse and Frank James?"

"Sure." His lips tilted up in a self-deprecating smile. "By that time, I hadn't done anything to be proud of in years. I figured if I was going to go wrong, I might as well do it in a big way."

His expression sobered. "Now you know the truth, and you know why you never should have followed me, why you'll stay away from me if you have any sense. I'm no good, and I never have been."

"How can you say that?" She threw her arms around him again and peered into his tight, drawn face. "Back in Weston, you risked your life to save me. Now, you've come home to help your family. You must leave what happened with Caleb in the past. You're the bravest, strongest man I know, and I love you very much."

She blinked back unshed tears and tried to read the expression in Morgan's eyes in the dim moonlight. With all her strength, she willed him to believe her. He hesitated, staring at her in searing agony, before his arms reached out and pulled her hard against him.

"Oh, God, Jessy..." The words ripped from his throat, and his mouth descended on hers.

One hand clutched her back, pressing her against his unyielding body. The other plunged into her unbound hair and held her head in place while his lips plied hers with growing hunger. Without hesitation, she opened to him and rejoiced as their tongues met, thrust, and parried, struggling for dominance in the sensual battle.

"Oh, Jessy," he moaned between kisses. "I can't get enough. I'll never get enough." His mouth caressed her cheekbone and the delicate line of her jaw.

"I love you," she repeated breathlessly.

In response, his lips captured hers again, this time with even greater force. Of all the emotions pouring into her through his kiss, raw need was paramount. The need to touch, to hold, to possess. The need to be absorbed, surrounded, and protected. He needed her physically, emotionally, and spiritually—every way a man could need a woman.

And she responded with joy. No plea had ever been as strong as the need of this man. She opened herself and gave. his need could never deplete her—he was the source of her renewal.

Soon mouths were not enough. Hands sought feverishly but were thwarted by layers of clothing.

"Jessy, I...I've got to..." His breath warmed her ear. His hand slid inside her jacket.

"Let me."

She peeled off her jacket and shivered from a combination of cold and desire. Her trembling fingers reached for the fastenings on her bodice but stilled at the first hook. She stood on the verge of a momentous threshold. She couldn't claim later, even to herself, that Morgan had pushed her across. This had to be her decision. She was about to bare herself, body and soul, to the man she loved. There could be no going back.

She raised her gaze to his, seeking reassurance. The fiery tenderness stole her breath and banished every doubt. Her fingers moved, slipping the metal hooks from their eyes until her bodice gaped open.

She flinched when his cold hands touched her heated flesh. He gathered her sleeves and the straps of her camisole and pushed them down over her shoulders, trapping her arms against her sides.

Her breath caught in her throat at his look of awed reverence as he stared at her breasts illuminated in the soft moonlight.

"You're the most perfect thing I've ever seen." His voice was low and raspy and unbearably exciting.

She moaned and leaned against the support of his arm.

"Morgan, please..."

"Do you want more?"

"Mmmmm," she murmured in assent, beyond coherent speech.

He trailed a string of hot kisses down her neck. When he reached her breast, the strength left Jessy's knees, and tiny bolts of lightning shot through her. She grasped his arms for support.

"That's right," he murmured against her skin. "Hold on to me."

Eyes closed, she tightened her grip. While his mouth worshipped her breast, one hand slowly crept downward until it pressed against her most tender parts and began to draw slow, maddening circles. she moaned aloud.

Without warning, he jerked back, and her eyes flew open. He faced her, chest heaving in the cold night air. Why had he stopped? Surely something so wonderful shouldn't end in quaking frustration.

"What...?"

He tugged the sides of her bodice together. "Make yourself decent."

"W-what?" she repeated, too stunned to put her question into words.

One minute he was taking her to the brink of discovery, and the next he was growling at her like an angry bear. Her body ached while her mind fumbled to understand. "What's the matter?"

"I said, get dressed. And try to remember you're supposed to be a lady, not some two-bit saloon girl begging for more."

Without stopping to think, she slapped him hard across the face.

Morgan smiled with grim satisfaction. "You better watch out. All that fire's going to get you in trouble someday."

Her palm stung, and her cheeks burned. She wasn't sure if he was referring to the slap or her passionate response to his lovemaking, but it didn't matter. "I didn't think I had to watch out. I thought I was with the man I love, the man I trust."

His gaze fell to his boots. "That was your first mistake. Now get back to the house."

She turned away in humiliation. She wasn't the least bit sorry she'd slapped him. Under her breath, she called him every nasty name she could think of, stoking her anger into a towering blaze in a valiant, but futile, attempt to ward off the desperate, crushing blow he'd dealt her heart.

****

Morgan watched Jessy disappear into the trees. Hellfire, that was close. His body shook with the effort it had cost to pull back. He didn't know where he'd found the strength. He'd hurt her, but he had to find a way to push her away, to force her to keep her distance. If he ever got that close again, he'd never be able to stop. And that would be a disaster. One slip of his self-control could leave Jessy pregnant with his child.

Jessy pregnant with his child.

The thought conjured an image so seductive in its forbidden sweetness he could almost reach out and grab it. He dashed the vision from his mind. Such blessings were for other men, men who deserved them. Never for a man like him.

He thought of his ruthless words. He reminded himself he'd had to do it—it was for her own good. Better for her to think him capable of deliberate cruelty than to start rebuilding her fantasies about a life together. They could never have a life together. He knew it as sure as he knew he'd never want another woman for the rest of his sorry, misbegotten life.

He hated hurting her. Sweet mercy, it had nearly killed him to see the pain in those brave green eyes. And she was brave—thoughtless and foolish sometimes, but never a coward. He needled her about her privileged upbringing, but he had to admit, if only to himself, that most girls of Jessy's background would never have had the gumption to follow him into unknown country. And they certainly wouldn't insist on staying once they saw the primitive accommodations.

Yes, Jessy was unique. But that didn't make him the man for her. What was it the Good Book said about casting pearls before swine?

****

Sleep eluded Jessy as she lay in her narrow bed under the rafters. Morgan's words had left her battered and bruised, but her initial rage had burned out, taking with it some of the sting. Now her mind struggled to make sense of what had happened.

She allowed herself to review each word, each touch, each sensation. What made him stop? Thinking back to her own urgent arousal, she wondered where he had found the strength. She couldn't have stopped him. What had happened to turn him from ardent lover to cold, insulting stranger in a heartbeat?

The last time he had stopped their lovemaking so abruptly, he'd said he didn't want to make her pregnant.

Her mother always warned that men would take whatever they could from a girl, and it was up to her to protect herself. What made Morgan different? He didn't find her unattractive. His desire had been obvious.

Perhaps his miserable childhood made him reluctant to take the risk of becoming a father. But he could never be a brutal, uncaring father like Caleb Bingham, whatever the circumstances. In spite of his rigid exterior, he was a man of strong emotions, capable of tenderness and compassion. She couldn't allow his fears to keep him isolated in the solitary prison he'd built for himself. She had to help him find the door.

The next day, Morgan began work on the main house. He split and nailed shingles, mixed fresh mud with icy water from the springhouse to repair the chinking between the logs, and rehung the front door. He worked like a man possessed by demons, barely speaking and pausing just long enough to eat the food Sally brought.

Jessy spent the day indoors sewing with Sally, adding to her meager wardrobe. Her most pressing need was a warm nightdress. She didn't want to spend another night huddled beneath the quilt wearing only her underwear. Since the nightdress was to be a simple affair, she was able to do most of it alone while

Sally cut the more complicated garments from the calicos.

At one point, Jessy glanced up from her stitching. "Sally, there's much more here than I can use. Wouldn't you like to make a dress for yourself after we finish mine? I'd be happy to help you."

Sally hesitated. Her hands smoothed the bright new cloth lovingly, almost covetously, and her eyes glowed with excitement. Then her face fell like a child in a candy store being told there would be no treat that day.

"Not right now. Maybe later, after we've finished your things. Maybe in the spring."

Jessy puckered her brow. Sally wanted a new dress. Why wait? "Are you sure? Winter is a perfect time to sew. It helps pass the time when the weather's bad."

Sally forced a little smile. "There's always plenty of work around here. Besides, Corrine's baby will come in January, and that'll keep us busy."

Jessy nodded, focusing on the tiny stitches on the ruffled hem of a sleeve. "I was an only child, so I haven't been around many babies."

"I love babies." Sally kept her eyes on her sewing, but a tiny smile tilted the corners of her mouth.

"What do you do around here for fun in the winter?" Jessy asked. With no close neighbors except the hostile McTaggarts, it seemed unlikely the young people got together on Saturday nights for dances or socials.

"Fun?" Sally sounded surprised. "I'm not sure what you mean."

"You know, like parties or sleigh rides, things like that."

"Oh. We don't much see anyone else, winter or any other time."

"Don't you go into town?" Jessy had driven to Camdenton. It wasn't close, but it wasn't too far to make the trip once a week.

"I haven't been to town since I was a little girl. Pa or Morgan used to take me...before. Ethan went before he went off to war. Nobody's been since, until Morgan came back."

"What about church?"

Sally shook her head. "Ma hasn't set foot in church since before I was born. I'm not sure why. She keeps the Bible by her bed, though, and she knows some of what it says."

Jessy tilted her head. The kernel of an idea sprouted. This might be the opportunity she'd been waiting for. "I wonder if she would mind if I borrowed it. I've always enjoyed reading in the evening before bed."

Sally glanced up from her work, her blue eyes wide with wonder. "You can read?"

Jessy nodded. "I was a teacher in Weston before a bunch of rabble burned down the school."

"Why would anyone burn a school?"

"It was a school for the children of former slaves."

"Oh." Sally pursed her lips. "I saw a slave once, in town when I was little. He had chains around his wrists and ankles, and he was bleeding. Pa said he was a runaway who was being taken back to his master in Mississippi. He looked so sad."

Jessy straightened in her chair and let her sewing fall idle in her lap. "Well, Mr. Lincoln may have freed the slaves, but I don't believe anyone can be truly free unless he can read, so I taught their children to read."

Sally looked puzzled. "But I can't read. I don't know anyone who can."

"Morgan can read. I taught him. Do you think you or anyone else in the family would like to learn?"

"I don't know. I'm not sure how Ma would feel about that."

"Maybe at first everyone could just listen while I read, if she agrees."

"You can ask her."

Satisfaction rushed through Jessy. It was a small victory, but it was a start.

That evening after supper she washed the dishes and Sally dried. As usual, Ethan returned to his cabin as soon as he finished eating, but tonight his wife and son lingered with the rest of the family. Morgan stretched out in a chair near the fire. His eyelids drooped, and his head nodded.

It was the perfect time to set her plan in motion.

"Mrs. Bingham, I wonder if I might borrow your Bible as soon as I finish these dishes."

Rachel regarded her with suspicion. "What for?"

"I'd like to read aloud, if you don't mind. I think it's a good way to rest after the labors of the day."

"Labors. Huh!" Rachel snorted under her breath. "I guess I have no objection."

After handing the last plate to Sally, Jessy untied her apron. She was surprised to find that Morgan's mother had placed the Bible on the table behind her. She picked up the heavy book and carried it to the chair opposite Morgan. It was a venerable book, large and beautifully bound in dark brown leather.

She opened the cover and found the entire history of the Bingham clan painstakingly recorded—each birth, marriage, and death, generation after generation, next to the date. Someone in the family had been able read and write well enough to record the names. Scanning the list, she was struck by the continuity and cohesiveness represented there. This was a family, a line of people who derived their identity and security from the knowledge of who they were and where they came from.

She glanced at Samuel, who stood glued to his mother's side with her arm wrapped around his thin shoulders. His huge blue eyes focused on Jessy. She smiled and opened the Bible to the book of Exodus, where she read the story of Moses, from his discovery in the bulrushes by pharaoh's daughter to his triumphant escape with the people of Israel across the Red Sea.

As the beautiful, ancient words rolled from her tongue, Samuel detached himself from his mother, drawn by the power and drama of the story. Soon he stood next to Jessy staring in amazement at the open book.

"Would you like to sit on my lap?"

He shook his head.

She smiled. "That's all right. Maybe next time."

The corners of the boy's mouth twitched, as though he would smile if he dared, and she had to restrain a sudden urge to hug him. Her first convert in the Bingham family!

She glanced around the room. Morgan was fast asleep in his chair, and Rachel appeared to be concentrating on her knitting. But Sally and Corrine both wore the look of awe and excitement that Jessy never tired of seeing on the faces of her students. Samuel might be too young, but with a little encouragement his mother and aunt might be willing to learn to read to him.

She closed the book. "That's all for tonight. Shall we read some more tomorrow?" Samuel gave a shy nod.

"Good. Now I'm sure it's past your bedtime. You go home and sleep tight."

Samuel trotted back to his mother, who had risen to her feet and was massaging her lower back.

"That was beautiful, Jessy," Corrine said. "It's good for Samuel to be around someone with book learning."

Jessy beamed. Two converts!

Rachel set her knitting aside. "I have to admit it's good to hear the Good Book again."

Three! She'd show Morgan yet.

As if on cue, he stirred and straightened in his chair. Feet on the floor, he unfolded to his full height. "Time for me to head to the barn." He glanced at Jessy. "Walk with me outside for a minute."

She wasn't sure if it was an order or a request, but she followed him to the door, taking her jacket from a peg before stepping outside. They walked in silence across the dark yard, past the lights in Ethan and Corrine's cabin, toward the barn. It was so dark she could barely discern his shape next to her. After their disastrous encounter the night before, she wondered why he'd brought her out here. Maybe he wanted to lecture her again about minding her own business.

"I heard you read."

Uh-oh. Here it comes.

He stopped, and she nearly bumped into him. He caught her arms to steady her. Jessy wished she could see his face clearly enough to read his mood.

"It was nice," he said. "Maybe you were right."

What? Was he admitting he might have been wrong? That she might have something worthwhile to offer his family? Her heart leapt. This admission might be the closest thing to an apology she would ever get from him.

Before she had a chance to adjust to the idea, Morgan jerked her toward him, branded her lips with a swift, hard kiss, and set her back. While she stared after him in numb shock, he stalked off toward the barn.

And men complained women were unpredictable. Hah!

Chapter Seven

The next evening, Rachel set the Bible out without being asked. Jessy picked up the book with a small smile of triumph and carried it to the chair by the fireplace. Samuel's watchful eyes followed her. Settling herself, she beckoned to him. "Samuel, why don't you bring that little stool over here? You can sit next to me while I read."

"It's time to go home," Ethan interrupted. "The boy don't need to hear any more of that. Come on, Corrine."

Samuel shrank against his mother, and her arm slipped around his shoulders. "But Ethan..." Corrine protested.

Ethan's handsome face darkened to a deep shade of red. "I said we're going. I'm still head of my own family."

"But—"

"Shut up, woman! You'll do as I say."

He lashed out toward her. Corrine ducked and covered her son with her body, even though her husband was too far away for the blow to reach her. He growled and leaned down to pick up his crutches.

Jessy leapt to her feet, but before she could intervene Morgan stepped between his brother and Corrine.

"There'll be none of that in this house ever again."

Ethan shook in impotent fury and glared at his brother, standing straight and tall in front of him, ready to back his edict with force if need be. "They're mine!"

"They're yours to protect and provide for, not bully and abuse. Be a man."

"Damn you, you bastard! Don't you see? I can't...I can't." Ethan's voice caught in his throat, and he crumbled. Struggling against the ultimate humiliation of tears, he whispered, "I can't," once more. Without raising his head, he thumped across the room, banged open the door, and disappeared.

Morgan turned to Corrine and squatted down next to where she sat clutching her son. "Corrine," he said in a gentle voice, "I want you to tell me the truth. Does Ethan beat you or Samuel?"

"N-no. He's never hit us. He just has this temper. It's the drink...that and his leg."

"You don't have to stay in the house with him if you're afraid. We can always make room for you and Samuel here."

Corrine shook her head and straightened her back. "No, though I thank you for offering. My place is with Ethan. He's my husband, and I love him. He's just hurting so bad inside, so bad. I'm more afraid for him than for Samuel and me. God knows what he might do to himself."

"You'll promise to come to me if you need help of any kind?"

She nodded and stood. "I think it's time to go home. Ethan'll be feeling poorly, and I don't want to leave him alone."

"All right, but remember your promise." Morgan stood and ruffled Samuel's dark hair. The boy stared at him, his face offering no clues to his thoughts.

After they left, Jessy closed the Bible. "Maybe tonight's not the best night to read."

Over in the corner, Rachel glanced up from her mending. "I think it might do the rest of us good to hear it."

"If you really think so..."

"Read," Morgan said. "Please. His voice softened as he met her gaze.

The pain in his eyes gnawed at her soul. "Yes, of course."

She opened the book and read the story of the stoning of the adulteress. She tried to concentrate on the message of empathy and forgiveness, but her immediate response to Ethan was to throw stones, even if only in her heart.

The next day was unusually pleasant for early November. A brisk wind rattled the leaves in the trees and brought many sailing to the ground like a golden snowstorm. In spite of the breeze, the sun shone, and thin, wispy clouds raced across the sky. After breakfast, Sally asked Morgan to haul the big black laundry cauldron out behind the house.

"We probably won't have another day this good for washing and drying for several months," she explained to Jessy.

In Weston, the Randalls had a maid to do the laundry, but Jessy was determined to pull her weight. "I'd be happy to help. I don't have much experience, but I'm sure I can learn."

Sally laughed. "Oh, it's not complicated. All you have to do is stir the pot and hang the wet clothes on the line."

Three hours later, Jessy cursed that blithe description. Her arms ached from stirring the heavy, wet garments in the boiling pot, and the front of her dress was soaked from wringing them out before hanging them on the lines Morgan had strung between the trees. The steam had curled her hair into an unruly mass of ringlets, and she was sure her face was a matching shade of scarlet.

The women decided to take advantage of the fine weather to wash the linens as well, and big white sheets flapped on the lines like sails on a schooner. Samuel raced between the rows of sheets laughing like any ordinary four-year-old. His laughter brought a smile to Jessy's face despite her discomfort. It was the first sound she'd ever heard him make. He was such a silent child, she had begun to wonder if something was wrong with him.

After tucking the last sheet into the last open spot on the last line, she surveyed the fruits of the morning's labor. She'd had no idea such backbreaking effort went into maintaining clean clothes and bedding for a family. At home, her dresser was always full of clean garments, and her linens were always fresh. It pained her to realize the trouble the maid had taken to keep them that way.

Strong hands grasped her shoulders from behind, and she started, letting out a little shriek.

"It's only me."

She relaxed into Morgan's grip. "What do you mean, sneaking up on a person that way?"

"I didn't mean to scare you." His fingers set to work massaging the kinks out of the aching muscles in her shoulders. "I never thought I'd see the elegant Jessamine Randall bent over a washing cauldron. What would your mother say?"

Jessy laughed. "She'd probably faint dead away." She paused and stretched like a satisfied cat, closing her eyes in pleasure. "Mmmm. You're awfully good at that."

"Thank you, ma'am." He moved his hands down from her shoulders to the small of her back.

She sighed, grateful no one else was around to see them. His family already thought the worst of her. It wouldn't help if someone saw them together like this.

The action of his thumbs soon pushed all thoughts of his family aside. After the other night, she had been afraid she'd never feel the magic of his touch again. His hands were less intimate this time, but still personal even without the passion. He offered comfort and unselfish pleasure. She knew she should stop him, but she was so sore and tired.

Several blissful moments later, she feared she was in danger of melting like a lump of butter left in the sun. Just as her knees started to waver, she heard voices. She stiffened under Morgan's hands, and they both stilled.

The voices belonged to Sally and Corrine, who were hidden somewhere in the forest of sheets and clothes. The women spoke softly, but Jessy heard every word. From his rigid attention, she knew Morgan heard them, too.

"Corrine, can I ask you something kind of personal?"

"I guess so."

"How did you know when you were first expecting Samuel, and now this new baby?"

"Well, my monthly stopped. And I didn't feel like eating much, but I swelled up anyway and felt kind of tender-like."

"Hmm."

"Sally, what's this about?"

"Nothing. I was just curious."

"You can tell me anything, you know. Sometimes it helps to talk to another woman. Is anything wrong?"

A long silence followed.

"Oh, Corrine, I've just got to tell someone, or I'll bust. I don't know what to do!" Sally wailed before breaking into noisy sobs.

"Hush, hush now. It's going to be all right," Corrine crooned softly with the sound of a mother well experienced at soothing tears.

"Oh, n-no, it's n-not."

Morgan's fingers dug into Jessy's shoulders.

"Bringing a new life into the world is cause for joy, not sorrow."

Sally's sobbing halted. "W-what?"

"I'm a woman, a mother. I've noticed the changes."

"You know?"

"I didn't know. I suspected. How long has it been since you bled?"

"Almost four months. Oh, Corrine, what am I going to do?"

Morgan dropped his hands from Jessy's shoulders. She turned, and their gazes locked. Fury blazed in his eyes.

"I think you should tell your Ma, and Morgan and Ethan," Corrine said. "They're your family. They love you, and they'll help you."

"I can't do that. They'd never understand. They'll think I'm a fallen woman and put me out of the house. It would be better if I just went away."

Jessy's heart turned over at the pain in Sally's voice. "You've got to do something," she whispered.

"You're damn right I do." Morgan's voice shook.

He shoved his way through the laundry with Jessy following in his wake, thrusting wet sheets, dresses, shirts, and undergarments out of his way. He burst through the last barrier, and the startled women gasped.

Corrine clutched her belly. "Morgan, you like to scared me to death!"

He ignored her and grabbed his sister by the arms. "Sally, who did this to you? What low-down, son of a polecat... Tell me his name, and I'll skin him alive. I swear it."

Sally jerked out of his hands. "No, no!"

Jessy tugged his elbow. "Morgan, stop. You're frightening her."

He released his sister but frowned like Zeus with a fistful of thunderbolts.

Jessy approached Sally. "It's all right. No one's going to hurt anyone. But you should tell Morgan the name of the father of your child. I'm sure he'll see the man does right by you."

"I'd rather see him dead," Morgan muttered.

Jessy shot him a quelling look. "That's enough. You're not helping the situation. If you frighten her, she'll never tell you anything."

He took a deep breath and let it out slowly. "All right, Sally. If you swear the man didn't force you or take advantage of you, I won't kill him. But I sure as hell want to talk to him."

"No."

He narrowed his eyes to dangerous slits, like a mountain lion eyeing its prey. "No what?"

"No, he didn't force me, and no, I won't tell you his name."

He reached for her again. "Sally, by God —"

"No, no! Stay away from me. I won't tell you anything, and you can't make me." She gathered her skirts and dashed into the woods.

Jessy turned to Morgan. "Maybe I should go after her."

"You'd get lost in a second. I'll go." He stared into the trees, worry carving deep furrows in his brow. "Sally's lived here all her life. She knows these woods like a mother knows her own child. She can probably keep away from me if she really wants to." He glanced at the sky. "I've got about four hours of daylight left. With luck, I'll have her back by suppertime."

Jessy watched his back disappear into the woods in the direction Sally had taken and prayed he would be all right.

All afternoon, she and Corrine watched and waited, but Morgan didn't return. It was nearly suppertime when they carried the folded laundry back to the cabin. Rachel glanced up from a kettle hanging over the fire from a big iron hook.

"Isn't Sally with you? Where's that girl gone to?"

Jessy didn't know what to say. "I'm not certain, but I'm sure she'll be back any time now."

Rachel muttered something about irresponsible children and went on with her preparations for supper. When the food was ready, Corrine called Ethan. She settled Samuel into his place, but Ethan shrugged off her helping hand.

Rachel glanced around the table, and her lips tightened. "Jessy, I suppose you'd better see about Morgan. He's late. I don't know what's come over those two today."

Before she could formulate a response, the front door opened, and Morgan stepped into the room, alone. Her heart sank.

"Son, do you know where your sister is?" Rachel asked. "No one seems to have seen her."

He hesitated, and Ethan answered in his stead. "Sally's run off."

His mother whipped her head around. "Why would she do a thing like that?"

"Corrine says Sally's got herself in the family way and won't say who did it." His matter-of-fact tone did little to lessen the impact of the words.

The spoon in Rachel's hand clattered to the floor. Her face paled, and she turned to Morgan. "Is it true?" Her voice was barely audible.

"I'm afraid so, Ma."

"Oh, no." Rachel sank to the bench. "Not my baby. It can't happen to her, too." She drew a shallow, shuddering breath. "I was afraid...I saw the signs, but I didn't want to admit it, even to myself."

Hoping to offer comfort, Jessy reached out and touched Rachel's shoulder. "Don't' worry, Mrs. Bingham. I'm sure everything will work out. Sally said she wasn't forced, so she must love the man. If she'll tell us his name, they can get married."

Rachel raised watery brown eyes. "It ain't always that easy."

"I'm worried about her," Corrine said. "She's nearly four months gone. She shouldn't be out in the woods all night."

Morgan shrugged off his coat and draped it over a peg. "I lost her trail in the dark. If she doesn't come home tonight, I'll go out again at first light."

He crossed the room to his mother and dropped to one knee. "I don't want you to worry, Ma." He took her hands. "Sally knows how to take care of herself. She'll be all right. I'll bring her back tomorrow, I promise."

His mother nodded, but a tear slipped from the corner of her eye and trickled down her lined cheek until it fell, making a small dark spot on the bodice of her brown dress.

Rachel left the kerosene lamp burning all night as a beacon for her daughter, but Sally never returned. The only sounds Jessy heard from her bed in the loft were the snap and hiss of the fire and the older woman's fitful tossing in her bed below.

Unable to sleep, she pondered Sally and her problem. She also considered Morgan's response to his sister's pregnancy. Supportive wasn't the word she would choose to describe his reaction. It was easier to picture him as an armed angel of vengeance than a peacemaker who would place the feelings of others first. What would he do to Sally when he found her? What would he say? What if he found her with the man responsible for her condition? Jessy could envision several scenarios, none of them pretty.

There was only one way to make sure he didn't allow his fraternal protectiveness to make a bad situation worse.

Her fretful imaginings kept her awake the rest of the night. She finally gave up and rose to dress and wait for daybreak. The darkness lightened from black to gray, and Rachel began the daily ritual of preparing food for her family. When the first pink streaks lit the eastern sky, heavy footsteps sounded on the front porch. Jessy peeked down over the edge of the loft.

Morgan stepped into the room, and her breath caught in her throat. Dressed in buckskins with a rifle slung over his shoulder, he looked like a man hunting big game, not his own sister.

"I'll take a cup of coffee and some of those grits, Ma, then I'll be gone."

Rachel glanced up from the loaf of yesterday's bread she was slicing. "Take half this loaf with you, son. I've got another, and Sally won't have had anything to eat since yesterday."

He slipped the bread into the small pack he carried. "Thanks, Ma. And don't you worry. I'll be back with her before nightfall."

"You won't be too hard on her now, will you, son?" Rachel's voice trembled.

"I'll do the best I can."

She nodded and sighed. "That's all a body can ask."

Morgan wolfed his grits and downed his coffee in minutes. He rose from the table, kissed his mother on the forehead, and disappeared out the door.

Jessy wondered how long she should wait. A hollow gurgling reminded her if she wanted any breakfast, she'd better hurry. Nimble in her pants and boots, she scurried down the ladder.

"Where are you going dressed like that?" Rachel's harsh question caught her before her feet hit the floor.

She stepped down and turned. She drew herself up to her full height, which, although petite, was still greater than Rachel's. "I'm going after Morgan, Mrs. Bingham. I think Sally could use my help when he finds her."

Rachel didn't respond immediately. She looked Jessy up and down. Her expression softened, and she nodded several times. "That might be for the best. Here, take this bread with you." She handed Jessy three slices of the soft, brown bread. "You'd better hurry, or Morgan will get too far ahead. Then there'll be two of you to find."

Jessy smiled. She felt a tiny thrill of victory. The bread was almost like a peace offering. Perhaps Morgan's mother was beginning to accept her after all.

"Thank you. Don't worry. I'll take care of Sally." Bread in hand, she dashed out the door.

She assumed Morgan had started his search at the point where Sally had bolted into the woods, so she started there. From the clearing, the line of trees and underbrush appeared impenetrable. However, when she reached the edge, she spied a path of sorts winding into the trees. Reasoning that both Morgan and Sally had followed this path, she set off in pursuit.

The early morning light played eerily through the trees in the dense woods. The wind had blown in a mass of clouds and brought with it colder weather. Her breath steamed in front of her face, and her boots crunched and rustled in the fresh layer of walnut, oak, and maple leaves. Only an occasional birdcall from high in the branches overhead reminded her she was not alone.

She walked and walked without seeing any sign of Morgan. After a while, worry began to gnaw at her. He was an experienced woodsman. He might have seen signs indicating Sally had gone another way, signs Jessy would have missed. If Morgan were still on this path, he couldn't be very far ahead. If he'd left the path, she might never find him. She decided to continue. At least she could always find her way back to the Bingham farm as long as she stuck to the trail.

She focused on the track. The trees appeared to thin out some distance ahead. Walking closer, she saw a small natural clearing.

She stepped into the clearing and stopped short.

There, on the trunk of a strangely bent tree, sat Morgan. He stared at her, arms crossed, waiting.

"Morgan, what are you doing?"

"Waiting for you to catch up." He slid off the tree trunk, which defied nature by growing horizontally for several feet, forming a natural bench, before rising skyward again.

"How did you know I was coming?"

He gave a short laugh. "You're about as quiet as a buffalo."

"I wasn't trying to be quiet," she retorted.

"You're lucky there weren't any poachers out this morning. Someone might have taken you for a deer and filled you full of lead."

Poachers? The suggestion there might be others in the woods with guns led her to a worrisome thought. "Whose land are we on now?"

"Ours, but not for long. Come over here and sit for a minute. I don't suppose you brought any water."

She hated the knowing look in his eyes. She'd come unprepared again. She might as well face it—she'd never make a woodsman.

After she joined him on the tree trunk, he handed her his canteen. "You can have some of mine."

Jessy hadn't realized how thirsty she was until she tasted the cool, pure water. After a long, satisfying drink, she returned the canteen.

Morgan closed his eyes, took a long swallow, then wiped his mouth on the back of his hand and screwed the lid back on. "I guess I shouldn't be surprised you decided to come along."

She pointed a warning finger at him. "Now don't you start in on me about meddling. I came to offer my support to Sally. She's going to need it, dealing with you."

"She's my sister, and I can take care of her myself."

"That's what I'm afraid of. It might interest you to know your mother approved my coming."

"My mother knows you're here?" There was no mistaking his genuine surprise.

She bobbed her chin. "Your mother and I have reached an understanding."

"When pigs grow wings," he muttered. "At any rate, I don't have time to take you back now. I don't suppose I could trust you to return by yourself."

She shook her head.

"I didn't think so. I guess you'll just have to come along."

Victory lifted her spirits, and she smiled. He didn't smile back.

"This is the strangest tree I've ever seen," she commented, changing the subject. She ran her hand along the bark. "What is it?"

"It's a thong tree. The Osage Indians used to bend saplings to mark the locations of important landmarks, like trails, or springs, or caves. After a few years the trees just continued to grow in the bent shape."

"Indians were right here?" She glanced around.

"Years ago. You're safe enough now. The white men pushed most of the Indians out before I was born, and the ones who are left don't cause any trouble."

"What does this tree mark?"

"That trail you were following was an old Osage trail. It turns here and heads down to the river. There are some caves below we need to check. I hope to God we find Sally in one of them."

"Why?"

"Because this tree marks something else, too. It marks the dividing line between Bingham land and McTaggart land."

Jessy's eyes rounded in horror. She had visions of sweet, pretty Sally lying somewhere, shot by the murderous McTaggarts. "You don't think Sally could have been so upset she accidentally ran onto their land, do you?"

Morgan's expression was grim. "Not accidentally, no."

Chapter Eight

"Morgan, after what you told me about the McTaggarts, you don't think Sally would run to them on purpose, do you?"

He glanced at the trees on the rising slope of the hill. "I don't know. I guess we'll find out, if we can get close enough without getting shot. But first, let's check the caves."

He lifted Jessy from the tree branch, and she followed him to a spot at the opposite side of the clearing where the thread of a path cut into the underbrush.

He reached back. "Take my hand. I'll go first. The trail gets steep up ahead, with lots of loose rock underfoot."

She entrusted her small hand to his and followed him.

He was right. A few yards into the woods, the trail began a steep descent toward the rushing cataracts of the river. The trees barely muffled the splashing sounds of water racing over rocks, fallen tree trunks, and any other impediments nature had the nerve to throw in its path. Several times her feet slipped on loose pebbles, but Morgan's strong grip held her upright.

"Where are the caves?" She tried to subdue her panic. The incline was so steep it seemed they were sliding down the face of a tree-covered cliff.

"The caves are above the river on this side." He squeezed her hand. "We're almost there."

They skittered down another short section of trail before coming to rest on a ledge of solid rock. The sounds of the water were very close now. Hesitantly, she stepped toward the edge of the rock ledge and peered over. About twenty feet below, the river coursed through the wide gorge it had carved in the rock. An unfamiliar fear of heights assailed her at the sight of the sheer drop, and she jumped back.

He clasped her hand, drawing her toward him. "Don't worry. I won't let you fall."

"That's very reassuring." She tried to sound unconcerned as she regained her footing.

He tugged her hand. "The caves are over here."

She turned to follow but stopped short when she spotted the gaping black maw in the side of the hill. A prickly chill raced up her arms. The dusky mouth of the cave was ominous enough, but the striped limestone walls soon disappeared into an inky blackness that appeared to descend straight to the center of the earth.

She held back at the entrance and tried to mask her anxiety with logic. "How can you search in there? It's too dark to see anything. There might be animals in there, a bear or something."

"What's the matter? Lost your nerve?"

His teasing voice raised her hackles. She jerked her hand from his grasp. "It just seems like a waste of time if we can't see."

He slid the small pack off his shoulder. "Unlike you, I came prepared. I brought a candle." He struck a match.

She crossed her arms. "I'll wait for you here."

He reached out a long arm, snagging her elbow and pulling her with him toward the cave. "You'll be safer with me. You're more likely to be eaten by a bear out here, anyway. It's too early for the bears to hibernate. They're out hunting for food, fattening up for the winter."

At his mention of bears, she grudgingly ceased her resistance. She had managed to avoid meeting a bear for twenty-one years, and she didn't want to spoil her record this morning. At least Morgan was armed if they should encounter any hungry wildlife.

The entrance of the cave was tall enough to stand in. She glanced at the rock walls lit by the candle's yellow glow. Strange markings and drawings covered the walls, and the ceiling near the entrance had been blackened by smoke.

She shivered. "Someone's been here, but I don't think it's Sally."

"These caves have been used as long as there have been people in these hills. Those drawings were made by the Indians long before white men moved into this part of the country, maybe even before they came to America. Since the Indians left, the caves have been used to hide all sorts of things. Caleb and his friends used to hide whiskey and counterfeit money here."

"Well, Sally's not here, so I think we should go back outside."

"I want to check a couple of smaller chambers in the back. I might be able to tell if she spent the night here." He held the candle closer to the back wall, and Jessy saw a smaller opening, just big enough to crawl through.

Her heart began to pound, and she couldn't seem to draw a full breath. "If you think I'm going through that hole, you can think again."

He crouched near the entrance to the smaller chamber. "You want to stay out here by yourself?"

"I'm not moving from this spot. If a bear comes, I'll scream. I promise."

He cocked a brow. "Suit yourself. I won't need my rifle, so I'll leave it with you. Try not to shoot yourself." With that ringing vote of confidence, he laid the weapon on the floor of the cave and disappeared through the hole, taking the candle with him.

Although her eyes had partially adjusted to the dim light, she inched back toward the entrance. If she stayed just inside the mouth of the cave, she would be keeping her promise, but she would also be able to see out and breathe fresh air. Maybe that would help fight the feeling that the walls and ceiling were closing in on her.

Suddenly, the light dimmed, and a dark outline filled the entrance, the outline of a man with a gun. Jessy gasped. With a speed belying his size, the man reached in, grabbed her, and clamped a filthy hand over her mouth, stifling her cry. She struggled in his grasp, but he was huge-huge and unkempt and as malodorous as fetid swamp water.

"Stop wiggling," he growled low in her ear. He pinched his meaty fingers together for emphasis, grinding her soft inner cheeks into her teeth.

The metallic taste of blood filled her mouth, and she fought harder. She struggled to form sounds in her throat. She had to make some kind of noise. She had to warn Morgan.

"Shut up and hold still, or I'll have to knock your head against the wall." The giant lifted her off her feet and made a motion to follow through on his words.

She stopped struggling. She couldn't do Morgan any good if she were unconscious or dead.

"We're going to wait here quiet-like 'til he comes out." His hand pinched tighter, and her eyes watered from the pain. "You understand?"

She nodded the best she could.

Who was this monster, and what did he want? He must have watched them enter the cave, because he obviously knew Morgan was with her and intended to capture him, too.

"There's no sign of her here, but I did find a sizeable stash of corn liquor." Morgan's voice echoed from the smaller chamber.

Jessy struggled and tried to cry out, but the hand across her mouth tightened brutally.

"I wonder if it's part of Ethan's supply," Morgan continued. His head reappeared through the opening.

At that moment, she gave a sudden, sharp kick backward into the shin of the man who held her, catching him by surprise.

He howled, but his grip remained as tight as ever.

Morgan's hand shot forward toward the rifle he'd left on the floor of the cave.

"Drop it, Bingham, and come on out of there," the monster growled. "I got your lady friend here, if that's what you call this hellcat in pants. If you want to make sure she don't get hurt no worse, you'll come out real careful-like."

"What the—"

"Now, Bingham." The big man squeezed Jessy's cheeks again, and she let out an involuntary whimper.

At the sound of her pain, Morgan shot through the opening. He stared at the attacker's face in the darkened cave. "Zeke McTaggart, is that you under all those whiskers and dirt? What the hell do you think you're doing? Let go of her now!"

Zeke released Jessy but kept his gun trained on his captives. She rushed to Morgan's side, and he slid his arm around her, drawing her to him.

"Are you hurt?" he asked.

She rubbed her jaw. The insides of her cheeks ached. His body was taut with coiled tension. He might not have his gun, but she knew he carried a knife in his boot and wouldn't hesitate to use it if necessary.

"Not too much."

He tightened his grip on her and returned his attention to the hulking man with the gun. "I ought to slit your hide and skin you from top to bottom like the no-account varmint you are."

"Not today, you ain't," the hairy giant replied with a gap-toothed grin. "Pap said you'd be a'comin', and he sent me to fetch you. I didn't want to take no chances." He nodded to Jessy. "Sorry if I hurt you, ma'am, but Bingham here is a known killer, killed his own pa. Did he tell you that?

"But—"

"Shut up, Jessy," Morgan interrupted. "Zeke isn't interested in anything we have to say. Are you, Zeke?"

"Nope. Just march on out of this cave, and we'll go see Pap." He motioned with the gun.

Morgan took Jessy's elbow and steered her out of the dank cave into the fresh morning air. Even though a thin layer of gray clouds obscured the sun, her eyes took a moment to adjust to the glare. As Zeke stepped out behind them, Morgan gave her a hard shove. She cried out and stumbled to the side.

Morgan took advantage of the temporary blinding effect and knocked the rifle from Zeke's hands then leapt at him. They fell to the ground in front of the cave, locked in combat. Zeke was taller and had at least fifty pounds on his adversary, but Morgan's speed and flexibility gave him the advantage. In a matter of seconds, he knelt atop his would-be captor with his knife poking the flesh beneath Zeke's ear.

Morgan hauled the big man to his feet. "All right, Zeke. Now we'll go see your pap." He tossed the man's gun to Jessy and picked up his own in his left hand, keeping a firm grip on his knife with his right.

All the fight seemed to drain out of Zeke. "But what will Pap do when he sees what you done to me?"

"That's your problem," Morgan replied without sympathy. "Now get going." He prodded the lumbering giant in the back with his knife, and they set off single file back up the path toward the top of the hill.

When they reached the clearing with the thong tree, Zeke headed for another trail that led further up the hill. Jessy followed, her breath coming faster with each step. She was more accustomed to leisurely strolls in town than vigorous hikes up the sides of mountains.

Morgan ordered Zeke to stop, and Jessy collapsed onto the trunk of a fallen tree, certain she couldn't take another step. In spite of the cool mountain air, she was sticky with perspiration beneath her jacket, and her feet ached. "Do you have any more water in your canteen?"

Morgan glanced at her, keeping his knife to his captive's back. "We didn't stop so you could rest. We stopped so Zeke's danged fool brothers won't blow our heads off when we get close to the cabin."

"Oh." They might have captured one McTaggart, but apparently that didn't guarantee safe passage.

"If you can reach my canteen, you can have a drink."

She unclipped the canteen from its strap across his shoulder, removed the lid, and took a long drink. The cold water chilled her throat all the way to her stomach.

Morgan returned his attention to Zeke. "All right, now I want you to call out and let Jonah and Will know we're coming, and we don't want any surprises." He nudged Zeke in the back a little harder as a not-so-gentle reminder of his position.

Zeke raised his hands to cup his mouth and let out a perfect imitation of the cry of a hawk. From off in the distance came two echoing cries. "Hallooo," he shouted. "I'm coming in with 'em. Don't shoot."

Morgan listened for a moment. Apparently satisfied, he said, "Let's go. Jessy, you stick close to me. When we get there, just keep quiet. I'll do the talking."

"But what do they want? Do you think they have Sally?" She hurried to walk next to him.

His face was set in grim lines. "We'll soon find out."

A few minutes later, they stepped into a clearing much like the one surrounding the Bingham homestead. Several log buildings were scattered about, but they were larger and sturdier and appeared to be in much better repair than those at Morgan's home. As they walked toward the house, two young men materialized from the edge of the forest with rifles in their hands.

"Tell them to put those down," Morgan ordered in a low voice.

Zeke glanced around with nervous eyes. "It's all right, boys. Put down your guns. He won't hurt nobody."

Morgan showed his teeth in a wolfish grin. "That's right—not as long as everyone cooperates." The young men lowered their weapons, and Jessy stared. The older one looked like Zeke, with a bushy beard and a wild mop of sandy hair. But the younger one was a teenage version of Morgan. The boy was slimmer and not yet as hardened, but he had the same rugged bone structure and piercing hazel eyes. She glanced at Morgan, then back at the young man. The resemblance was unnerving. If Morgan's father had been a McTaggart, this boy must be his cousin.

She thought for a moment. That would also make Zeke and the other man cousins and the man waiting for them in the house Morgan's uncle. Since they were all family, why were they acting like this, pointing guns at each other? Surely the circumstances of Morgan's birth no longer mattered after so many years.

Morgan stared at the boy, too. "You must be Will."

"That's right." The young man regarded him with suspicion.

Morgan simply nodded. He nudged Zeke's back again. "Let's go inside and see what your pap wants."

Jessy walked as close to him as she could. These men might be relatives, but there was clearly no love lost between them.

Zeke opened the cabin door and stepped inside with Morgan and Jessy right behind. In front of the fire sat a mountain of a man with a craggy face and sharp eyes beneath ridged brows. She guessed he might be in his fifties, but he had a timeless quality, like the limestone hills outside the cabin door.

"You're here," the old man said.

"Hello, Uncle Dermott."

Dermott McTaggart quivered. Rage mottled his face, and he rose to his feet. "Never call me that! You're no kin of mine."

"Oh, but I am. You can see it for yourself."

The old man didn't answer, and Morgan continued. "I saw Will outside. A blind man could see the resemblance. There's no denying I'm your brother's son."

"You might have McTaggart blood in your veins because of a whore's trick, but I'll never claim you as kin."

Morgan crossed the room in three long strides and grabbed the old man by the front of his tobacco-stained shirt. "Say one more word about my mother, and I'll cut your tongue out." He pressed his knife against his uncle's throat.

"She killed my brother David, she and that black-hearted scum she married. She's nothing but a—"

Morgan tightened his grip until the old man's breath gurgled in his throat. "I said, shut up!"

Jessy shuddered in horror. Listening to their hate-filled words, she wracked her brain for a way to stop them before one or the other drew blood and the family rift became an all-out war. From the corner of her eye, she spotted Zeke advancing on Morgan with an axe handle raised above his head like a club. "Morgan!"

He whipped his head around and tightened his grip, pressing the knife until it made an indentation in Dermott's throat. "Drop it, Zeke."

"You let go of Pap, or I'll bash your head in." Zeke brandished the axe in the air.

Jessy couldn't stand another second of this madness. Without stopping to think, she ran to Zeke and grabbed his upraised arm. "Stop it, all of you! This minute!"

Her ringing plea cut through the violence hanging in the air as effectively as Zeke's big axe through a pine log and brought the men to their senses. Zeke lowered the axe, and Morgan released his hold on his uncle's shirt. He stepped back but kept a firm grip on his knife.

"All right," he said. "I didn't come here for that. You know why I'm here." He looked hard into Dermott's face. "She's here, isn't she?"

The old man nodded.

"I want to know why."

"Ask them." Dermott McTaggart pointed toward the doorway with his chin.

Morgan, Jessy, Jonah, and Zeke all turned to see Will McTaggart standing with his arm around Sally Bingham, a fiercely protective scowl on his young face.

"What do you want here?" he demanded.

"I've come for Sally."

Sally clutched Will, and tears formed in her blue eyes. Fear warred with determination in her gaze "I'm not coming home." She wiped her eyes with the back of her hand. "I love Will, and I'm staying with him."

Dermott scowled at the young couple. "Take her away. I'll not have that jezebel in my house."

Sally's face crumpled at the cruel words, and her defiance melted. Pooled tears brimmed and spilled down her cheeks before she buried her face in Will's shirt.

"I can't send her away, Pap." Will's hands stroked Sally's dark hair. "I love her, and she's carrying my baby."

His father beetled his bushy brows. "How do you know that? If she's truly breeding, the brat could be any man's. Send her back to her own people. She's no good, just like her mother."

Sally gasped, and Jessy flinched at the insult. First Rachel and now Sally. The old man overflowed with hatred. She had only known Morgan's sister a short time, but she knew Sally was a decent, honest girl, regardless of her current predicament. If Sally said she was carrying Will McTaggart's child, then she was. Seeing the young couple together, it was obvious the child had been conceived in love and deserved to be welcomed the same way.

Jessy faced the old man. "Mr. McTaggart, you're talking about your own grandchild."

Dermott slowly turned his head. "Who the hell are you?" He stared at her. "Better yet, what are you?"

"She's Morgan's woman, Pap," Zeke volunteered.

"I might have known," the old man replied with disgust. "No natural woman would have a whore's spawn like him."

"That's enough!" Morgan stepped forward and jerked Sally away from Will with one hand and grabbed Jessy with the other. "We're going home. If we stay here one more minute, I'll kill him. I swear it."

"No, no!" Sally struggled to free herself from the manacle of her brother's grasp. "I want to stay with Will. We're going to be married."

"Never." Dermott spat. "No son of mine will ever marry a Bingham. He's only seventeen, and I refuse to give my permission."

"We'll run away." Will's young face was red, and his hands balled into fists.

His father snapped his shaggy head around, eyes blazing at his son's defiance. "And live on what? You don't know how to do anything except hunt and trap and brew a little 'shine, and you haven't got a dime to buy land of your own."

"I'll find a way."

"None of this makes a shred of difference," Morgan interrupted. "I'm taking Sally home now. She's my responsibility, and I won't allow her to spend another minute listening to your poison, old man."

"I won't let you take her!" Will reached for Sally.

"Zeke, stop him," Dermott commanded sharply, bobbing his head at his youngest son.

Zeke wrapped his arms around Will, restraining him in a bear-like embrace. "I got him, Pap."

"Now get out," Dermott ordered Morgan.

"Gladly."

The McTaggart men stood aside and watched with expressions ranging from satisfaction to burning resentment as Morgan dragged his weeping sister from the cabin. Jessy needed no encouragement to follow. She couldn't remember when she'd ever been so glad to get away from anyone. Dermott McTaggart and his two eldest sons were physically revolting and morally despicable.

She couldn't bring herself to include Will in her sweeping condemnation of the McTaggart men. His startling resemblance to Morgan and the stricken look on his face as he watched Sally being led away touched a chord deep in her heart. It would be a tragedy if Will and Sally's young lives were ruined by their families' hatreds.

Unspoken thoughts hung thick in the air on the long walk back. When they reached the Bingham homestead, Sally broke away and rushed into the house in tears, her face buried in her hands. Morgan swore under his breath.

"You did the right thing." Jessy rested her hand on his arm. "You couldn't leave her there. Will has no way to take care of her."

He shrugged off her hand. "I've got work to do." He shot one last look at the house before stalking off toward the barn.

She clenched her teeth in frustration. Why did he always refuse comfort? Perhaps he'd kept his guard up so long he'd forgotten how to let it down. Or maybe there was so much dammed up behind that wall he didn't dare open the gates for fear the resulting flood of emotions would overwhelm him.

Inside the house, she found Sally in the consoling arms of her sister-in-law. Corrine patted her back and murmured soothing words.

"I-I just w-want to die!" Sally wailed.

"No, you don't. You've got your baby to think of now."

"But I n-need Will. I love him."

"Ssh. Maybe something will work out."

"No, never." Sally shook her head vehemently. "His father hates me. He said the awfullest things. It had something to do with Ma, but I didn't understand."

Jessy glanced at Rachel, who stood by the cupboard with a ladle dangling forgotten in her hand. The haunted look on the woman's face renewed Jessy's desire to halt the destructive hatreds spreading their poison to a new generation.

Sally drew back and snuffled. "What am I going to do?" She dashed the tears from her thick black lashes with the back of her hand.

Corrine smoothed the girl's tousled hair away from her temples. "You're going to do what women have always done. You're going to do your best to take care of your child, whether your man is there to help or not."

"How do you do it? How do you manage to be so strong? I know Ethan's no help to you."

Corrine smiled a small, sad smile and patted Sally's hand. "Ethan does what he can. And I do what I have to. Pretty soon you'll find out what that means. You'll find you can do just about anything when you have to." Her tired face brightened. "Besides, I have the rest of the family to help me, and we'll be here to help you, too. Don't you worry, honey. Everything's going to be fine."

Sally sniffed and managed a watery smile. Corrine eased her bulk up from the bench. "Now let's see what we can do about supper, shall we?"

At supper, Morgan and Ethan looked as dark and threatening as a pair of thunderclouds, but they swallowed any words of condemnation along with their food. Jessy ate mechanically, barely noticing the ham and biscuits on her plate as her mind concocted schemes and plans to end the feud between the McTaggarts and the Binghams.

The two families were tied by bonds too strong to sever, no matter how they might pretend otherwise. There had to be a way to force them to recognize and accept that truth. The coming baby should bind them together and heal the old wounds, not force them further apart.

When everyone finished eating and the dishes were cleared, she brought out the Bible. Ethan got up to leave, and she held her breath, wondering if he was going to force Corrine and Samuel to leave. But tonight, if he had any complaints, he kept them to himself. Morgan stayed, but he ignored them all and sat staring at the fire.

She settled into her chair, opened the book, and began to read. Samuel leaned close and listened in silence with eyes wide. Nearby, his mother rubbed the worn calico stretched across her belly, caressing her unborn child. Even Sally looked calmer by the time Jessy finished.

At the soft thump of the book closing, Morgan rose from his chair and stretched like a cat in front of the fire. "Night, ladies." He walked to the door and lifted his coat and hat from their peg.

"Just a minute." Jessy laid the book down and hurried across the room. "If you don't mind, I'd like to take a walk before turning in."

His eyes mocked her. "Haven't you had enough walking for one day?" He settled his hat firmly on his head.

She reached for her jacket. "No, I'm fine, and I think a breath of fresh air would do me good, unless you're too tired, of course."

He shrugged. "Let's go." He held the door open for her with one hand.

They stepped out from under the overhang of the porch roof, and tiny cold droplets stung her cheeks. "Oh, it's beginning to rain!"

"Yeah, nice night for a walk," he drawled.

She wrapped her arms around herself and shivered as the rain intensified. "Can we go somewhere, to the barn perhaps?"

"Sure." Morgan grabbed her hand, and they ran across the rain-slicked mud toward the barn. He rolled the heavy door aside wide enough for them to slip in then slid it shut.

The barn was pitch black and redolent with the smells of old hay and warm horseflesh. "Do you think we could have some light?" Jessy whispered.

"You don't have to whisper. The horses aren't going to tell anybody your secrets. I'll go up and get the lamp."

She sensed rather than saw him leave her side. His boots scraped the rungs of the ladder then echoed across the floorboards above her head. He was so sure-footed in the dark. Must be those mountain lion instincts. Moments later the barn glowed with light from the kerosene lamp. He appeared at the top of the ladder, but she stopped him. "If you've got any place to sit up there, I'll come up."

He shook his head. "There's only the bed, and that's not a good idea."

But she was already on the second rung. "Don't be silly. I promise I won't attack you." She climbed onto the loft platform and found Morgan lounging on a narrow wooden cot. She sat beside him.

He leaned back on one elbow and regarded her through lazy eyes. "Since you've promised my virtue is safe, what do you want?"

"Stop teasing. This is serious."

"What's serious?"

"Everything."

"I agree, but I'm sure you had something more specific in mind when you lured me out here." The shadow of a smile hovered around his lips.

"I did not lure you anywhere. I just want to talk to you."

He straightened in one swift movement, all traces of humor erased from his hard features. "You've got five minutes. Then you're going back to the house."

"Why?"

He leaned closer until they were nose-to-nose. "Because I'm no saint, far from it. I've done things that would make every beautiful hair on your head stand on end." His voice was low and husky, with a rough edge.

"But you'd never hurt me."

He stared at her long and hard, then closed his eyes. "I don't want to. God knows I don't want to."

When his eyes opened again, the torment in them burned her.

"I'm a man, not a statue carved in stone. Don't you understand?" He clutched her upper arms, his fingers digging into her soft flesh. "Dammit, Jessy, we're alone and you're sitting on my bed. We're not on the sofa in your mother's parlor drinking tea."

"I just want to talk to you."

He surged to his feet, dragging her with him. Giving her a little shake, he glared into her startled face. "But that's not all I want from you, and I'll be damned if you'll end up like Sally on my account. Do I make myself clear?"

Chapter Nine

Jessy gazed into Morgan's blazing eyes. "If you're trying to frighten me, you won't succeed."

"If I don't scare you, you're not as smart as you think, because sometimes I scare the hell out of myself."

Keeping her eyes trained on his face, she allowed her fingers to caress the rigid muscles of his arm. "Nothing about you scares me, no matter how hard you try. In spite of your past, I know you're a strong, decent man, and you love me."

He swore and thrust her away. In the golden lamplight, his body shook. She reached out to touch him, but he stepped back beyond her reach.

"Did you come out here just to torture me?" His voice shook with anger, but his eyes gave witness to a deep underlying pain.

She dropped her hand. "Of course not. I wanted to talk about Sally. What do you intend to do about her situation?"

Some of the stiffness left his body. "I don't know." He ran one hand through his thick, sandy hair. "Part of me wants to skin Will alive, cut his heart out, and nail it to a tree."

She shivered at the hideous image and the violent intensity of his words.

"Shocks you, doesn't it? That's good. I told you what I am. Only a fool would want any part of me."

She lifted her chin and faced him. "But you wouldn't do it." Her voice was steady with confidence and conviction.

He released a pent-up breath. "No. You're right." His bleak hazel gaze met hers. "I think she really loves him."

"I think so, too. And I think he loves her back."

Morgan sat on the bed and buried his face in his hands. When he finally raised his head, pain ravaged his rugged features. "I haven't seen Will since he was a little boy. God, Jessy, it's like looking in a mirror that can turn back time."

"He's your cousin, Morgan, your kin. You could no more hurt that boy than you could hurt Sally or Ethan."

He turned away to stare at the lamp. "You have no idea what I can do."

She sat beside him, resisting the temptation to throw her arms around him. He needed support, but his pain and self-condemnation were too great to accept the full force of her love. "I know that once, years ago, you did what you had to do to protect your mother and sister. That doesn't make you a killer."

"There's more. Things you don't know about, things I've never told anyone."

"During the war?"

"And after."

"Lots of people do things they aren't proud of during wartime." She took a risk and placed a hand on his arm. "Look at me."

He dragged his head around to face her.

"As for the time you spent with the James boys, that's in the past." She tightened her grip, praying for the words to convince him he deserved forgiveness, especially from himself. "I don't know what you did, and I don't care. All I care about is us, here and now, and what we make of the rest of our lives."

He didn't acknowledge her hand. "Try to understand. I can't just forget everything, or pretend it never happened. It's a part of me now, part of who I am. Anything good in me died years ago. All that's left of my soul is an ugly, scarred shell."

"If that were true, you wouldn't be here helping your family."

He shrugged and glanced away, staring into the glowing flame of the lamp, withdrawing into his own dark world before her eyes.

She wanted to scream. To lash out. Anything to bring him back. "I have an idea about what we might do for Sally and Will." When he remained silent, she continued. "I brought quite a bit of money with me, and since there isn't much to spend it on here, I thought I might give some to Sally and Will. They could take it and make a new start somewhere, away from both families."

Morgan's eyes blazed. "Keep your damned money. I told you before—we're not one of your charities. I've got plenty of money to take care of my family."

Even though she understood the wounded pride behind his angry outburst, she couldn't protect herself from the stab of pain. "I was only trying to help."

Her injured tone seemed to soften him. "You've seen Sally and Will—they're just kids. Neither of them has ever been out of these hills. Even if I gave them enough to get started, do you think they'd be happy and safe away from everything they know, with no way to make a living and a baby on the way?"

"They'd have each other."

"Sometimes that's not enough."

"But their families are the root of their problem."

He pushed to his feet, dragging her with him. The shadows made his face appear as hard and craggy as the weathered rocks of the Ozark bluffs. "Drop it, Jessy. This isn't your problem. If I think something needs to be done, I'll do it, without any meddling from you. Now go on back to the house and get some sleep. It's been a long day."

She was about to argue that she had every right to be interested in the welfare of the family when her brain registered the crushing fatigue, of both body and spirit, shadowing his eyes. Even in the golden light, his skin carried the gray tinge of exhaustion. Dark hollows under his eyes defined the bony ridges of his cheekbones.

She felt a flash of contrition. Although she had no intention of abandoning her efforts to help the family, she also had no wish to add to his burdens. He hadn't conceded yet, but tonight he appeared to have lost the upper hand in his relentless battle against the obstacles life threw in his path.

She stood on tiptoe, clasped his shoulders, pulling him down, and leaned forward until her breath caressed his lips. "Kiss me goodnight, then I'll go." She closed her eyes.

He groaned, but his arms closed around her. He hesitated for a fraction of a second, resisting the pressure of her hands before giving in and molding his lips to hers. Their breaths mingled in a joining of sighs—triumph in hers, surrender in his.

The kiss was like no other they had shared. It was gentle and sweet, almost devoid of the passion she had come to expect from him. His lips did not demand. Instead, he approached her as a supplicant. He asked. He begged. He needed. And she gave, over and over, gladly and with her whole heart.

Her heart ached at the exquisite tenderness of the kiss. It swelled as the force ebbed from Morgan and flowed into her. He relinquished control. She gained it. Along with the power, she gained an awesome responsibility, for she sensed he was unconsciously entrusting her with the burdens of his heart, burdens she rejoiced to share.

Slowly, he released her lips, but they remained joined, forehead to forehead. "Go, now," he pleaded in a hoarse whisper.

She pressed one last, light kiss against his mouth. Then she slipped away and was gone.

The next morning, prickles of anticipation raced through Jessy's body. After a night of stirring dreams, she had arisen early, anxious to see Morgan, to see what traces of the night's shattering exchange would linger in the light of day.

She had taken extra pains with her appearance, brushing her unruly hair until it crackled before taming the fiery curls into a respectable braided coronet. She wore her new green calico dress and dainty slippers. When Rachel looked her over and nodded in taciturn approval, she knew she had passed muster with her harshest critic. Now she could hardly wait for Morgan to walk through the door.

Would his eyes glow hot and hungry like they used to every time he saw her? The memories spurred her heartbeat. From the moment they met, he had intrigued her. His behavior and demeanor were painfully respectful, but he'd never been able to keep the raw hunger from his eyes.

She wondered if his tenderness and capitulation last night meant he was ready to acknowledge his need for her, or even his love. Her pulse picked up speed. Perhaps they could be married soon and turn the lie she'd written her parents into truth.

The door clattered open, and a smile lit her face. Morgan stepped into the room. Their gazes met, and she froze. Instead of the warmth she hoped for, she encountered the flat expression of a disinterested stranger.

"Better sit down and eat while it's hot." Rachel didn't glance up from the griddle. Her words interrupted the charge of tension.

Morgan sat at the table, and his mother delivered a heaping plate of bacon and eggs along with several slices of yesterday's bread. From a speckled blue and white enameled pot, she poured a steaming stream of rich, black coffee into a matching cup.

"It's mighty good to have real coffee again," she remarked as she poured cups for herself and Jessy. There was no sign yet of Ethan and his family, and Sally was still in bed.

"I'm going over to Newt Martin's this morning to see if I can buy a cow. Samuel and Corrine need milk."

His mother nodded. "The butter would be nice, too. We've been making do with lard and bacon drippings, but I miss the taste of real butter now and again."

A muscle contracted in his cheek. "You'll never have to do without again, Ma. I swear."

"You mustn't take so much on yourself. Our situation is not your fault. Lots of families suffered worse during the war."

"Everything would have been different if I'd been here."

Rachel clucked. "I daresay you like to think so, but the truth is, there wasn't much you could have done. If you'd stayed, the soldiers would have come for you, just like they came for Ethan."

He stood, scraping the bench against the wooden floor. "Well, I'm here now, and things are going to be different."

He left the cabin without so much as a glance in Jessy's direction. Disappointment choked her. He'd done it again, spurned her love and walked away. She hoped one day he'd learn the world wouldn't end if he exhibited a normal human frailty or two.

A few minutes later, Ethan, Corrine, and Samuel arrived for breakfast. In the big bed against the wall, Sally still didn't stir.

Corrine cast a worried glance at the quilt-covered lump. "Is Sally feeling poorly this morning?" She dished up plates of food for her husband and son.

"She's feeling just the way you'd think," Rachel replied. "Cried most of the night."

Corrine sighed. "I 'spect we ought to leave her alone 'til she's had a chance to think this all out."

"A day or two, anyway. After that, work is what she'll need. Idle hands are an invitation to the devil." Rachel's tone bespoke hard-gained experience. "Morgan went over to Martin's to buy a cow."

Corrine brightened. "That would be a blessing."

Ethan lifted his head from his breakfast. "Big brother sure is throwing his money around. Life must have been good to him the past ten years."

The women ignored his comment and continued eating, but in her heart, Jessy disagreed. The past ten years hadn't been easy for Morgan. They'd been hell on earth. He might not have suffered the same disabling injury as his brother, but he was deeply scarred, inside and out. Nothing short of a miracle could heal him. The problem was getting him to accept the miracle she offered.

After breakfast Ethan returned to his cabin, leaving his wife behind to help clean up. Jessy cleared the table with Samuel's help while Corrine washed the dishes and Rachel dried.

Corrine handed the last plate to her mother-in-law. "It's so cold and damp this morning, I thought I'd bring some mending over as soon as we finish. If you have anything, I'd be glad to do it along with my own."

Rachel nodded. "That's right kind of you, Corrine. As it happens, Morgan gave me two shirts yesterday that need mending."

"I'll do them," Jessy volunteered before Corrine could reply.

Rachel nodded. "They're over there on the chair by the bed."

A few minutes later, Corrine left and returned with an armful of clothes balanced in front of her protruding belly. Jessy hurried over. "Here, let me take those. You'll bump into something."

Corrine surrendered her load then patted her belly with a rueful smile. "I can't always see what's in front of me these days."

"How soon is your baby due?"

"In a couple of months, sometime in January."

"Why don't you sit here?" Jessy steered Corrine to the chair she used for reading in the evenings. "It'll ease your back, and the light from the lamp is better."

Corrine's grateful smile reminded Jessy how no one made much of a fuss about Corrine's delicate condition. They seemed to ignore it or accept it as a matter of course. She couldn't understand such a casual attitude. She was used to women who treated their confinements like nine-month-long, life-threatening emergencies. They seldom appeared in public, and when they did they were coddled and petted as if they were made of spun glass. Corrine went about her daily tasks, more slowly and awkwardly than usual perhaps, but without expecting or receiving special help from anyone. Jessy decided she deserved a medal for the simple heroism of getting out of bed every morning to tend to the needs of her family.

She and Corrine worked on their mending, murmuring occasional words of encouragement to Samuel, who sat at their feet drawing pictures on a flat rock with the charred end of a small stick. Jessy finished securing the carved horn buttons to the soft blue fabric of Morgan's shirt and spread the garment across her lap. Smoothing it with her hands, she closed her eyes. It was easy to imagine the shirt stretched across his back and her hands caressing the width of his shoulders and chest.

"You love him, don't you?" Corrine's gentle voice intruded.

Jessy opened her eyes, startled at being caught. "How could you tell?"

Corrine smiled a soft, tired smile. "I know the look. After my pa died, Ma used to hold one of his old shirts up to her face, late at night when she thought we wouldn't see. She had the same look as you, sad but full of love."

Heat rose in Jessy's cheeks. "You must think I'm shameless to love Morgan when he refuses to marry me."

"No. You're not like any woman I've ever met. You're bolder and you speak your mind. But I don't think you're shameless. Shame has no place in love, and I can see you love him."

"I know he loves me, too." Jessy sighed. "But I'm not sure he'll ever admit it."

Corrine nodded. "Men can be stubborn."

Jessy had a sudden thought. "What was Ethan like when you first married him? You know...before."

"Well, he was stubborn, too, even then." Corrine smiled, remembering. "I met him in town at the mercantile when I was just fifteen. I thought he was the handsomest man in the world—I still do. We married that spring, and Samuel was started before my sixteenth birthday. Times were tight, but we were happy until the soldiers came to take him away. When he came back, I hardly knew him, he was so bitter and angry. And then the drinking started."

She paused, staring at the patch she was applying to the knee of a pair of Samuel's pants. When she glanced up, tears sparkled in her sapphire eyes. "But I know my Ethan is still inside there, and he's hurting. He's hurting so bad."

The raw pain in her voice seared Jessy. She reached out and clasped the young woman's arm. "I know, and I want to help him. We all do."

Corrine sniffed. "I don't know what to do for him."

"Have you tried to keep the liquor away, destroying his bottles?"

"I've thought of it, but I'm afraid." A delicate shudder passed through her thin, but swollen, frame. "It would make him so mad. Besides, he would just get more. I don't know where he gets it, but he's able to get around pretty well on his crutches, and I can't lock him in the house."

"I suppose not."

"I think he could give it up if he wanted to bad enough, but he doesn't feel like he has anything to live for."

Jessy frowned. "But he has you and Samuel and the new baby."

"Yes, but he doesn't feel like he's any use to us. He can't take care of us the way he thinks a man should."

"But you said he can get around pretty well on crutches. There must be lots of things he could do."

Corrine smiled as if Jessy were simple. "He can't hunt, he can't chop wood, he can't walk behind a plow, and he can't ride a horse. That pretty much takes care of the ways for a man to support his family around here."

"There must be something else."

"If you think of anything, you let me know."

Jessy's mind whirred as she finished stitching up a torn cuff. In Weston, she knew lots of men who didn't do any of those things, yet they managed to make a comfortable living. Unfortunately, every occupation she could think of required a basic level of education, or living in a town, or both.

"Would you consider moving to town?"

Corrine's eyes rounded. "Leave the hills? No. Ethan would never leave the hills again."

Jessy considered arguing that continuing to live here might bring about his premature death from alcohol and melancholia, but the tight line of Corrine's lips and the firm set of her jaw caused her to keep still. She could always bring up the idea again later.

Morgan didn't return for the noon meal, and by two o'clock Jessy felt stifled in the house. Sally had remained in bed, refusing even the light meal her mother offered. Ethan was in his usual foul humor and returned to his cabin as soon as he finished eating. Faced with the harsh reality of her children's suffering, Rachel was more sour-faced than ever.

Jessy walked to the door and took a heavy shawl from one of the pegs. If she didn't get outside and away from the grim mood, at least for a little while, she might scream. "I'm going for a walk."

Corrine glanced up from the string game she was playing with her son and frowned. "But it's so cold and damp out today. You'll take a chill."

"I need some fresh air." Jessy opened the door. "I won't be gone long." She slipped out and closed the door.

Once outside, she pulled the shawl up to cover her head and wrapped it tighter around her shoulders. Her breath hung in the heavy, misty air. It was like standing in the middle of a cloud. She drew in a deep breath then let it out. A slight freshening breeze seemed to carry with it the scent of snow, but that was impossible. It wasn't even the middle of November. Surely it didn't snow so early this far south, even in the mountains.

She dismissed the thought and stepped off the porch into the yard. Despite the chill, she was glad to be out of the smoky little cabin. She had told Corrine the truth—both her mind and body needed a breath of fresh air.

She walked aimlessly at first, toward the cornfield, along the path that led down the mountain. The ground was soft and muddy, not yet frozen, and the moisture seeped through the seams of her slippers.

She wound her way down the mountainside toward the rushing waters of the river and gradually became aware of a sound. At first it sounded like wind whistling through the bare branches of the oak trees, but the air was still. Then she thought it might be water tinkling down some small tributary to the river. She walked closer to the river, and the sound separated itself from the natural sounds around it.

It wasn't wind or water. It wasn't a sound of nature. It was a sound of man. It was music.

She stopped in her tracks and listened closely. The tune was high and thin, mournful and pleading. The intricate melody was ancient, reminiscent of older, higher hills far across the sea. It reminded her of bagpipes she had once heard in a parade in Philadelphia during the war, but it was purer and less reedy.

She walked down the path a little farther, and the sound grew clearer. It seemed to be coming from behind a feathery clump of cedar trees near the water. She approached with caution. Who could be playing such a sweet, sorrowful tune? This was still Bingham land. She was sure of it. Had some trespassing wayfarer stopped to rest his weary feet and lighten his load with a song?

Taking care not to brush against the bushes or snap any twigs underfoot, she crept closer. She reached the trees, and tried to peek between the branches, but the cedars were too dense. She leaned over and peered around the edge of the last tree.

"Ethan!" Her exclamation came out more as a squeak than a shout.

He struggled to swing around on the fallen log he was using for a chair without losing his balance. "Who the hell—"

She stepped out from behind the tree. "It's me. Jessy."

He scowled and swore an ugly oath, but she ignored his words and stared at his hands. Dangling from his left hand was a beautiful old violin. The bow still hung from his right.

Ethan had made that wondrous sound, that haunting cry from the soul. She could hardly believe her eyes.

"I heard you play. It was beautiful." Inadequate praise, but she felt compelled to offer it anyway.

He scowled deeper. "No."

She rushed forward. "Yes, yes, it was. I had no idea you played the violin."

"No one knows, and if you know what's good for you, you'll keep it to yourself."

She gave him a puzzled frown. "No one knows? Not even your family?"

"No one," he growled. "And it's going to stay that way."

"But you mustn't keep such talent to yourself. It's a rare gift. Your family would be so pleased."

His blue eyes narrowed. "Don't you tell me what to do, Miss Fancy Pants. You don't belong here. You're not family, and you never will be."

Jessy winced but refused to back down. This was too important. She had found something Ethan was good at, something he felt passionate about. His love of music might prove the key to his salvation. "I'm sure if I told Morgan—"

"Dammit, woman!" Ethan shook with anger. "You won't say a word to Morgan or anyone else. My fiddling is mine, my own and no one else's. Do you understand?"

She persisted. "But you could use it to make a living. You could play for dances and such in town."

"No!" He raised his fists, still clutching the violin, high in the air and brought it crashing down to the fallen log.

She cried out at the splintering sound then stared in horror at the jagged slivers of the smashed instrument. Ethan stared, too, at the ruin in his hands. He raised his head, and she took an involuntary step back. Hatred blazed in his eyes.

"Get away." His voice was no more than a ragged whisper. "Get away from me before I do the same to you."

She ran all the way back to the house, not because he was chasing her, but because she was sick with horror at what she'd caused. Ethan had destroyed the one source of solace in his miserable life, all because she had tried to help.

She burst through the door, out of breath, with tears streaming down her face. Rachel and Corrine glanced up from their sewing. Sally was out of bed now and sat huddled on a stool next to the fire with a quilt wrapped around her, staring at the floor.

Rachel was the first to speak. "What happened to you, girl?"

Jessy dragged the shawl off her shoulders and draped it across one of the pegs. It slid to the floor, but she ignored it. "It's Ethan."

"Ethan?" Corrine struggled to rise from her chair. "What's the matter? What's happened to him?"

"I found him, down by the river." Jessy dashed the tears from her cheeks and tried to catch her breath.

Corrine clutched her belly, and the color drained from her thin face. "Oh, no," she whispered, sinking back down.

Jessy realized what she must be thinking. "No, no. It's nothing like that. He's not hurt."

Corrine's expression turned to puzzlement. "Then what did you see?"

"It's not so much what I saw as what I heard. Ethan was playing the most beautiful music, on a violin."

"Fiddlin'?" Rachel stared in amazement. "My Ethan was fiddlin'?"

"Yes. He said you didn't know."

The older woman was quiet for a moment. "No, can't say I did."

Jessy turned to Corrine. "Did you know Ethan played the violin?"

Corrine shook her head. "No. I can't imagine where he ever got one. Lord knows there hasn't been enough money to buy such a thing, and even if there was, Ethan can't ride into town. He hasn't left the farm since he came home from the war."

"It's his grandpa's." Rachel's voice was wistful. "My pa's."

"Then he's had it a long time?" Jessy asked.

"Ever since he was a little boy. Ethan was always Pa's favorite, and he left him the fiddle when he died. I haven't seen it in years. I'd forgotten it. Pa used to play beautifully." Rachel stared at the sock she'd been darning, lost in a long-ago time.

"Well, your son must have inherited his talent along with the instrument."

"I wish he'd play it in the house some time," Corrine said.

Jessy sank onto the other chair by the fireplace, unable to face them, remembering the destruction she'd caused. "I'm afraid he won't be playing it anywhere ever again."

"Why not?" Corrine cocked her head and knit her brows.

"It's my fault." Jessy kept her gaze on her hands balled into fists in her lap, but the waver in her voice betrayed her emotion. "The music was so lovely, and I got so excited. I suggested he might use it to earn a living by playing for gatherings around the area. Ethan was infuriated by my suggestion, and he...he smashed the violin to pieces."

Corrine paled.

"Pa's fiddle." Rachel's voice was soft and sad.

Jessy shook her head. "And I was so hopeful music might be the key to getting him to take an interest in life again."

"I guess we'll never know." Corrine sighed.

A moment later the front door banged open, and Morgan stepped into the cabin. "What the hell's going on around here?"

Jessy was the first to recover. "What do you mean?"

"I just got back with the cow I bought from Newt Martin and found Ethan outside swinging an axe and smashing up everything in sight."

Jessy gasped. "Oh, no!"

"He knocked down most of the fence and put a sizeable hole in the side of the barn. Now I've got to fix it before nightfall, or we can kiss that new cow good-bye."

"Is he still out there?" Corrine's gaze darted toward the door.

"Of course not. Do you think I'd leave him to bust the place up? I took the axe away and got him into the house."

"Is he alright?

"I had a hell of a time getting him calmed down, but once he got the anger out, he kind of collapsed. He's resting now." Morgan shifted his gaze from one woman to the next. "What I want to know is what started it. He was screaming something about a fiddle, but it didn't make any sense."

Rachel and Corrine glanced at Jessy.

Morgan's lips thinned. "You know something about this, don't you?"

She shifted in her seat. "I'm afraid so."

"Out with it."

In halting words, she relayed what happened down by the river. "I was only thinking of his welfare. Don't you see? I was only trying to help."

"What I saw was my little brother turned into a raging animal."

She flinched. "I never meant—"

"You never do, but because of your interference, Ethan has lost the one pleasure he had in life."

"Don't you think I know that?" Fresh tears welled in her eyes, and her voice broke.

Corrine appealed to him to soften his harsh accusations. "She didn't mean any harm."

"She never does, but you can see what happens."

He turned to his mother. "I checked the smoke house, and there's not enough meat to last the winter. I'll mend the fences and the hole in the barn today while it's still light. First thing in the morning, I'm heading to that old hunting shack up on the ridge for a few days. I'll bring back enough game to last a couple of months. There's snow in the air, and a light snow always makes tracking easier."

Rachel nodded, but Jessy sensed her mind was on her younger son, alone and suffering in his cabin.

Corrine rose from her chair and took Samuel's hand. "I'd better go see to Ethan."

"Would you like to leave Samuel here for a while?" Jessy offered, unsure what condition they might find Ethan in. "I'd be glad to watch him until supper time."

Corrine gave her a grateful smile. "Thank you. It might be best." She slid one hand under her belly for support and waddled toward the door.

For the rest of the afternoon, Jessy read to Samuel and told him stories she remembered from her childhood. He sat on her lap and was a receptive, if silent, audience, but she was concerned that he still refused to speak. From the expression on his small, serious face, it was obvious he had sufficient intelligence. And she'd heard him laugh, so it was unlikely he was mute. Perhaps it was a reaction to his father's violent temper and vicious words.

The more she thought about it, the more the idea made sense, and the more determined she became to do something to help the whole family. Ethan's love of music might still be the key. She might have caused the loss of his grandfather's instrument, but there had to be a way to make it up to him.

At suppertime, Corrine returned to fetch Samuel. Tears streaked her cheeks, and she declined Rachel's suggestion to stay for the meal. "If you could put some stew in a small pot and wrap up a couple of those biscuits, I'd be obliged."

Her mother-in law complied without comment. But when she handed the food to Corrine, Rachel reached out a gnarled old hand and squeezed her daughter-in-law's thin, young hand. Corrine squeezed back and slipped out the door.

While she ate, Jessy's mind worked on the problem of Ethan and his family. Soon the glimmer of an idea appeared. She molded and tested it until it was solid and perfect.

"Morgan, how soon can you take me to town?"

He glanced up from his food. "What for?"

"For Ethan."

"Don't you think you've done enough for Ethan?"

A sharp pang of guilt stabbed her, but she refused to back down. "No, I don't. And if you'd just listen—"

He stood, almost knocking over the bench. "I don't want to hear another word. You keep your half-baked ideas to yourself."

She followed him to the door. "You will listen to me, Morgan Bingham, this is important. If I have to hound your every footstep for the next week, I will."

"You won't have the chance, thank God." He stepped onto the porch. "I'm leaving at first light."

"I'll follow you," she called as he crossed the yard to the barn.

He stopped and turned. "You won't." It was an order, one he clearly expected her to obey.

Oh, yes, I will. We've got a lot to work out, and you're going to listen to me if I have to hog-tie and gag you.

The hunting shack on the ridge might be the perfect place.

Chapter Ten

Morgan had been right about the weather. The soles of his boots melted patchy brown prints through a thin layer of fresh snow when he set out through the woods to the hunting shack early the next morning. Snow still drifted through the leafless branches of the trees, but he paid scant attention. The wide brim of his hat protected his head and face, and the thick sheepskin of his coat prevented the cold from penetrating through to his body. After ten years, he could still climb the ridge to the tiny cabin almost by instinct. And that was fortunate—getting lost was the last thing he needed to worry about now.

He shifted his rifle and reached to grasp a sapling to pull himself onto a rocky outcropping. He stood looking down. From here he could see across the treetops all the way to the rushing white water of the Osage River and beyond. Muted and austere without the softening effect of leaves, the land still called to him. It was right for him to come back, not pleasant or easy, but right.

The hunting shack was very close now. It would be good to be alone for a few days, away from his family and Jessy, especially Jessy. As much as he needed to work on the farm, he needed time to think even more. And he needed to be away from her to think.

Jessy was a real problem. She had set her mind on making a place for herself in his family, and she seemed to be succeeding. She refused to keep her distance, and every day it grew harder to push her away.

But he had to keep trying. His reaction the other night in the barn had scared him spitless. He hadn't come that close to breaking down in ten years. If he didn't guard himself, she would expose every ugly, sordid secret he'd managed to hide.

In spite of his efforts to hold back, she drew him like a seductive flame. She promised light where he languished in darkness. She offered warmth where he dwelt in numbing cold. But she was too bright, too warm, and he was too black, too hollow. If he ever truly attached himself to her, he would drain all the fire from her, leaving a lifeless shell. He could never let that happen. Never.

The small hunting cabin was only a short distance away, but most of the distance was straight up. By the time he finished the climb, his shirt clung damply to his skin beneath the heavy coat. Just enough trees had been cleared from the thick woods on top of the ridge to accommodate the tiny structure. It blended so well into its surroundings that unless smoke escaped from the stacked-stone chimney, it was nearly invisible to the human eye. The rocky hill was impossible to farm, so no permanent structure had ever been built, but game abounded in the woods, making it a perfect hunting base.

He approached the cabin with care, checking for signs of recent use. It wouldn't surprise him to find the isolated building being used by moonshiners, fugitives on the run, or anyone else who didn't want their activities scrutinized. The war had created such chaos throughout the state that hundreds of displaced men roamed the countryside scavenging for food, shelter, or anything they could carry away and sell.

From the outside, the cabin looked undisturbed. He nudged the door with the muzzle of his rifle, and the hinges complained from lack of use. Inside, the tiny room appeared untouched. In fact, it looked exactly as it had ten years earlier, when he'd fled to its sanctuary in the terrifying aftermath of Caleb's death. Dust formed a smooth, hazy coating on the rough plank floor and small stone hearth. The mattress and blanket on the sagging, rope-bottomed cot opposite the fireplace bore a few water stains, but he'd brought his bedroll to spread on top. If the snow didn't turn to rain, he'd be comfortable enough.

He carried his rifle back outside. His first job after checking the rain barrel would be to gather firewood, but he never left his rifle out of reach. In this country, a man never knew when he might encounter a predator, four-footed or two. It paid to be prepared.

He tipped up the wooden lid of the rain barrel that sat under one corner of the roof. Beneath the skim of ice, it was almost full. That was a piece of luck. There were no springs at this elevation, and the closest stream was a narrow trickle several hundred yards away. It would have been a mighty dry two or three days if he had to rely on the water in his canteen and what he could carry from the stream.

With the question of water answered, he set about gathering wood. There was no axe at the cabin, but he'd brought a small hatchet as well as his big skinning knife. He ought to be able to find enough fallen logs and limbs close to the cabin to last the short time he'd be here.

Sometime later, he dragged a long oak branch into the clearing. After stripping off the smallest branches where clusters of rustling brown leaves still clung, he picked up his hatchet and reduced the remaining limb to a neat pile of small logs and sticks just the right length for the fireplace.

Stepping through the cabin door, he dropped his load to the floor in a sudden clatter. "Hellfire! How the devil did you get here?"

Jessy sat on the bed facing him, dressed in her boy's clothes and sturdy boots, with legs crossed at the ankles and hands folded in her lap. "It's about time you got back. It's freezing in here."

"You didn't answer my question."

"It's simple. I followed your tracks in the snow." She rose and began to gather the fallen sticks as if the situation were perfectly normal.

"Why?"

She continued her task without looking up. "Because I wanted to talk, and you refused to listen. I figure with just the two of us here, you won't be able to ignore me."

Morgan swore again. "You're out of your mind, but I'll be damned if I'll take you home down now. There's not enough daylight left to get back here before dark."

She glanced at him with a patient smile. "Of course not. That's the whole idea."

"Jessy, sometimes you don't have the sense God gave a June bug. We can't stay up here alone for several days."

"I borrowed a loaf of bread, and this time I remembered water." Arms full, she pointed her chin toward a battered old canteen sitting on the floor.

"That's not what I meant. What's everyone going to think when they find out what you've done?"

She flashed him an impish smile. "That we're young and in love and desperate for a chance to be alone?"

"This isn't funny." He glared at her. "I won't be trapped into marrying you."

The unfairness of his accusation stung. She'd had no such intention when she hatched her plan to follow him. To be honest, she hadn't stopped to consider the long-range consequences. She just wanted to be alone with him, to have his undivided attention.

"I wouldn't have you under those circumstances anyway." She hoped he wouldn't see how much his words hurt. "I would never marry a man who didn't want to marry me."

His brows shot up. "That's exactly what you've been trying to do for the past two months."

"I have not. I've been trying to help you recognize how much you do want to marry me."

"Well, whatever you call it, it won't work. I can't marry you, and we both know it." He reached to take the wood from her arms. "Now give me those damned logs."

She glared at him. "Gladly!"

She swiftly withdrew her arms, and the pile clattered to the floor. Glaring at Morgan once more for good measure, she stomped from the cabin.

****

Outside, the snow had picked up, but she paid little notice. She had no intention of trying to make her way back down the mountain to the homestead. She just needed to walk off some of her anger.

He had always been stubborn and hardheaded, but why was he so determined to avoid happiness? She could make him happy, if he'd let her. She appreciated his resistance to feeling pushed into something—she never liked being pushed either. But she wasn't really pushing him—well, maybe just a little. But it was for his own good.

Caught up in a spirited mental debate, she ignored her surroundings. After a while, she noticed the snow was getting deeper underfoot. She stopped to brush the accumulating flakes off her jacket and hat and glanced around. The trees stood as stark sentinels crowding in around her. The gathering gloom told her it was getting late. She'd better get back or Morgan would be even madder than when she'd left.

Thanks to the snow, she had no trouble retracing her steps part of the way. However, the light faded and the wind picked up, blowing snow across her tracks until she could no longer see her path.

She glanced up, and a dark shape loomed ahead. She squinted, but the blowing snow obscured her view. It had to be a bear. Nothing else could be that big or lumber along on its hind legs that way. Her mind raced. Should she run away, or climb a tree? Her frozen muscles refused to obey the garbled commands of her brain. Instead, she did the only thing that came into her paralyzed mind.

She screamed.

The thing broke into a run and loped straight toward her. She screamed again, rooted to the spot where she stood in horror, awaiting her grisly demise.

The thing halted directly in front of her, and the scream died in her throat. Her mouth open, she stared into the furious face of her pursuer.

"Dammit, Jessy!" Morgan's shout echoed through the silent woods. "One of these days you're going to get one of us shot."

Relief flooded through her. She was not going to be eaten by a bear after all. Then her mouth snapped shut and her brow furrowed. "What do you mean scaring me that way?"

"Scaring you? Scaring you?" He grabbed her wrist. "How the hell do you think I felt when the storm picked up and you still hadn't come back?"

Her face relaxed. He'd been worried about her. He did love her.

"Don't give me that look, you little baggage. I'd turn you over my knee right here and warm your backside, but it's too damned cold to take my gloves off." He jerked her toward him. "We're going back to the cabin, and you're going to stay put until I take you back to the house tomorrow morning. Do you understand?"

She nodded. He might be angry, but his anger never frightened her. In fact, she enjoyed stirring him up. A rousing battle was always more satisfying than his cold, controlled rejections. Whenever she managed to break through his defenses, she gloried in the resulting sparks, no matter how dangerous.

Morgan half dragged her through the snow back to the cabin, never hesitating or pausing to get his bearings. Those mountain lion senses again, she mused, stumbling along beside him. That must be why her fears vanished the minute she recognized him. Even a bear would think twice before tangling with an enraged mountain lion.

They reached the cabin door, and he opened it, shoving her inside. She closed her eyes and smiled. The heat was glorious. She hadn't realized how cold she was until she stepped into the cabin. A cheery fire crackled in the stone fireplace, filling the small space with warmth. She pulled off her gloves and removed her hat, shaking loose the cascade of curls.

Turning to face him, she smiled. "What's for supper?"

His look skewered her. "You said you brought bread and water, so I guess that's what you'll be eating."

"I thought you came here to hunt."

"I did, but you arrived before I got started, and even I can't hit much in the dark. Tomorrow will be a loss, too, by the time I take you home and hike back through the snow."

"Then the obvious answer is to let me stay." She continued to smile, proud of her logic. "Besides, whether I stay one night or three, the damage will be done as far as your family is concerned."

"You don't care a fig about what they think, do you?"

She sobered. "Of course, I do. You have no idea how hard I've tried to make your family like and accept me. But as you pointed out, it's too late to go back today, so we might as well make the best of the situation."

He studied her through narrowed eyes. "And what's your idea of making the best of the situation?"

She raised a tentative hand to the padded solidity of his chest. "I want to talk, really talk. I have an idea about how to help Ethan, and I want you to listen."

She didn't add that she also wanted to come to an understanding about their relationship. There would be time for that later. When they did, the matter of his family would become irrelevant. Either Morgan would admit he loved her and agree to marry her as soon as possible, or she would leave and it wouldn't matter what his family thought.

"I told you to leave Ethan alone."

She rummaged through her small pack of provisions and produced a half loaf of bread. "We'll discuss it after supper." She perched on the edge of the cot, tore off a bite of the soft, fresh bread with her teeth, and washed it down with water from her canteen.

Morgan removed his hat and gloves and reached for his own pack. "There's nothing to discuss."

She swallowed and took another swig. "There certainly is, and I'm sure you'll feel more like talking after you've had something to eat. Now why don't you join me?"

She patted the thin, worn mattress, and a cloud of dust rose into the air. "Goodness!" She choked. "This place is filthy. I'll have to give it a good cleaning tomorrow."

"You won't be here tomorrow."

She dismissed his statement. "We'll talk about that later, too. Now sit and eat."

He half surprised her by doing just that. He had two pieces of chicken from dinner the day before and what appeared to be the other half of her loaf of bread. She watched his strong, white teeth bite into the tender meat, and her mouth began to water. She defiantly took another bite of bread and watched him while she chewed.

She couldn't be certain, but she thought she saw the hint of a dimple in his cheek. The big oaf! He probably thought it was funny, sitting there eating chicken while she had only bread and water. She ripped another bite from her bread and munched with exaggerated gusto.

He raised one brow. "Bread good?"

"Delicious."

"Good." He nodded and went back to work on his own supper.

After they finished eating, she made a big show of unrolling the bedroll she'd made from the blanket and quilt from her bed. She hated to spread them on the dusty floor, but it couldn't be helped. She would have to shake everything out in the morning and find some way to clean the floor.

"You planning on sleeping down there?" Morgan drawled from his vantage point on the cot.

She glanced over her shoulder. "Of course. I wouldn't dream of putting you out of your bed. Besides, I wasn't sure what the accommodations would be, so I came prepared."

She was proud of herself for remembering to bring food, water, and bedding. Perhaps she was adjusting to life in the wilderness after all.

His face remained impassive. "Fine." He walked to the door and opened it a crack. "If you want to step outside before turning in, I'd suggest you stick close to the cabin. The snow's coming down even heavier now. Looks like we've got six or seven inches already."

Step outside? Why would she want to step outside in a snowstorm? Then realization struck her. The tiny building had no facilities, not even a chamber pot. Of course, even if it had, they would have to take turns stepping outside. As if on cue, her bladder felt uncomfortably full.

She snatched her hat and gloves. "Uh, yes, I believe I will."

Stepping through the door into the snow, she saw he was right. The snow had already piled up to the top of her boots and showed no signs of stopping. She wished she could ignore the pressing ache in her abdomen and go back inside where it was warm and dry, if not clean. Unfortunately, the result would be even worse than the discomfort of relieving herself outside.

"Stay close to the cabin," Morgan reminded her from inside.

She didn't deign to answer. She made her way around the side of the shack, holding onto the wall for support against the driving wind. Fortunately, the little building had no windows, because she didn't dare go out of sight of the cabin. In the storm, she might never find her way back.

A freezing eternity later, firmly convinced she had just accomplished the most difficult and miserable task of her life, she reached the cabin door. He met her with his hat on his head and a scowl on his face.

"I was about to come looking for you."

She was in no mood for his disapproval. "As you can see, I'm fine." She pushed past him into the room. "I can do a few things for myself, you know."

He frowned. "I'll be back in a minute." He stepped outside and disappeared.

By the time he returned, Jessy was sitting in front of the fire wrapped in her quilt. "I'm ready," she announced, staring into the flames.

"Ready for what?"

"To talk."

"And if I don't feel like talking?"

"Then you'll listen. In fact, that might be better.

He made a small choking sound, but she ignored him while she gathered her thoughts before announcing, "I've decided."

"Decided what?" He pulled off his gloves, hat, and coat.

She glanced at him in irritation. "What to do about Ethan. That's what I followed you up here to discuss."

Morgan sat on the bed behind her and crossed his arms. "All right, let's hear it. I can see I won't get any peace until you get it off your chest."

She scooted around to face him. "First, we must agree I caused the destruction of Ethan's violin, albeit inadvertently."

"You won't get any argument here."

She frowned at his ready agreement. She was willing to accept the blame for her part in the incident, but the least he could do was try to make her feel better about it. "Yes. Well...therefore, I must be the one to replace the instrument. I'm convinced Ethan's love of music is the key to his recovery."

Morgan looked dubious. "Maybe, but how do you plan to replace a violin?"

"As soon as we get back, you will take me to town, and I'll order him a new one."

He released a snort of laughter. "You can't do that."

Her lips thinned. "Now you listen to me. You wouldn't let me help Sally and Will, but I insist on buying Ethan a new violin."

He raised his brows and shook his head. "Where do you think you are? This isn't New York, or Philadelphia, or even Kansas City. The closest town is miles away and doesn't even have a working telegraph."

She refused to be deterred. "Mr. Boone must have some way to order merchandise for his store. I'll place my order with him."

"Hiram would laugh you right out the door."

"Well, then, Mr. Know-it-all, how am I going to get Ethan a new violin if there's no way to buy one?"

He shrugged. "Damned if I know."

Ignoring his attitude for the moment, Jessy pursed her lips and considered the problem. "Perhaps I could hire someone to make one for him. Do you know anyone who could do that?"

"The only fiddle-maker I ever knew was my grandfather, and he's been dead for fifteen years."

"Your mother's father? The same man who gave Ethan his fiddle?"

"Uh-huh."

She considered the possibilities. "Do you think he might have taught Ethan how to make one himself?"

Morgan leaned down and jerked his left boot off by the heel, dropping it to the ground. "I doubt it. Ethan was just a little boy when Grandpa died."

"But it is possible, isn't it? After all, no one knew Ethan could play, either, but he can. And he's handled that instrument for years. Maybe with the right materials, he could make a new one."

He let out a sigh. "Jessy, you've had some farfetched ideas before, but this one rates up there with the best."

She knit her brows. "Don't you patronize me. It's a very good idea."

"It's completely impractical." He yanked the right boot off and dropped it to the floor with a resounding thud.

She tried to be patient, but he could be so unimaginative sometimes. "If we limit ourselves to the practical, we never accomplish anything."

"Is that one of your school teacher sayings?"

She was losing patience with his recalcitrance. "Yes, and it's one you'd do well to take to heart."

He yawned rudely. "This conversation is making me tired. Lie down and go to sleep. We need to get an early start in the morning." He stretched out on the cot, pulled his blanket over his shoulders, and turned his back to her.

She stuck her tongue out at his arrogant back, not caring about the childishness of the gesture. He could be so closed-minded. She uncoiled and tried to get comfortable, but the floor was cold and hard, and she was too wound up about her plans for Ethan's violin to relax. She tossed and turned, grinding her protesting shoulders and hips into the unforgiving floor until she finally drifted off to sleep.

Hours later—she had no clear idea when—she stirred and tried to roll over. A warm, solid body blocked her movements. She opened her eyes but couldn't see much. The fire had burned down to glowing coals, and the tiny windowless cabin was as dark as pitch. Feeling around, she determined she was no longer on the floor but had somehow ended up on the cot. The big, warm body could only belong to one person.

She shoved hard against his chest. "Morgan, wake up."

"Hmm? What's the matter?" His voice was gruff and his words slurred by sleep.

"What am I doing in this bed with you?"

"You were sleeping." He sounded irritated at being awakened.

"No. I mean, how did I get here?"

"I picked you up and put you here. You were huddled in a tight little ball on the floor, moaning in your sleep. Should I have left you there?"

"Hmph."

"We slept together like this on the trail." He pulled her against his chest and settled his arm around her. "It didn't bother you then."

Then, she reminded herself, she had thought they were about to be married. Now, with each passing day, she felt progressively less certain.

"Oh, go back to sleep," she muttered. He snorted and gathered her close.

She spent the rest of the night in the loneliest place in the world, wrapped in the arms of the man she loved, who refused to love her in return.

He was a puzzling collection of contradictions. Most of the time he held his emotions in such tight check one might question whether he had any. But she knew better. When she managed to breach the stronghold of his iron will, his body quaked with anger, his voice shook with passion, and his eyes danced with humor.

He expected little of others but everything of himself. He never complained about the cruel blows life dealt him, but neither was he willing to take the risks necessary to change that life.

She wondered if he would ever bend enough to make a place for her in his life. One thing she did know—in the time they'd spent together, his need for her had not diminished. If anything, it had grown stronger as he faced the harsh realities of returning home. Of all his qualities, it was need that drew and held her in the face of his rejection, and she would never let him push her away as long as his need remained.

By the time he finally stirred, the fire had petered out, and the air inside the cabin was as cold as the air outside. She shivered and felt a pang of regret when his body shifted and stretched. Wrapped in his arms, she could pretend she was cherished and protected. As long as he slept, she could pretend they were the only two people in the world, perfectly alone and perfectly in love. With Morgan awake, her fantasy was doomed.

He stretched again and groaned.

Time to face the music.

Chapter Eleven

"Time to get your cute little backside out of bed. It's a long walk down the mountain."

Jessy grimaced. It was a far cry from "Good morning, sweetheart," or any other reasonably civil greeting. She lifted one corner of the pile of blankets. Icy air rushed in to chill her sleep-warmed body. She snatched the blankets back around her.

"It's too cold." Her voice was muffled by the blanket half covering her face.

Morgan lay between her and the frigid boards of the cabin wall, insulating her from the worst of the cold. Without warning, he reached around and ripped the covers off them both. She gasped and tried to cover herself again.

"I said it's time to get up."

"I will, I promise. After you get the fire going again."

He propped up on one elbow. "There isn't going to be a fire this morning. We're leaving as soon as we're ready."

She refused to budge. She remained on her side with her head pillowed on her hands and her back to him. With the blanket gone, she drew her knees up even further in an attempt to conserve body heat. "I can't go out in the snow without at least having something hot to drink." She craned her neck and peered at him over her shoulder. "Did you bring any coffee?"

"Get up. Now."

Smack! He brought his hand down on her unsuspecting backside.

She yelped. "What do you think you're doing?" She rubbed her posterior.

"Just trying to warm you. Now get out of this bed before I roll you onto the floor and climb over you."

Grudgingly, she sat up and slid her legs around to the side of the bed. He clambered over to sit beside her and reached for his boots. She scowled but followed suit. She slid one foot part-way in then sucked in a swift breath. The rigid leather was as stiff and cold as if it were carved out of ice. She didn't know how she'd be able to walk several hours through the snow.

"There's no need to go back this morning." She wriggled her toes to keep them from freezing.

He pulled on his second boot, and she noted his slight wince with satisfaction. It was encouraging to see he wasn't completely superhuman.

He stood. "We're not going to discuss it. Pack your things and be ready to go in ten minutes."

Her rebellious gaze followed him while he shrugged into his coat, stuck his hat on his head, picked up his rifle, and stepped outside. Two minutes later he was back, knocking a huge clump of snow off his hat and swearing a blue streak.

"What's the matter?"

"A big load of snow slid off the roof onto my head, and it's melting down the back of my neck. There's no way I can take you back today. The damned snow's knee-high. You'd never make it."

She smiled to herself.

He threw his hat on the cot in disgust. "I wouldn't look so pleased if I were you. I don't have enough provisions for two, and you sure didn't bring much."

She turned a level gaze to him. "Will you please calm down? I'm sure everything will be fine. Is it still snowing?"

"No," he admitted grudgingly. "In fact, the sun's out."

"So, if the snow melts some, we can probably get back tomorrow or the next day."

"Probably."

"Then there's nothing to get so excited about."

He muttered something that sounded like, "That's what you think," and leaned down to retrieve his soggy hat.

"What was that?"

"Nothing. I'm going hunting."

"Now? Without breakfast?"

"I'll take my pack with me."

She crossed her arms in front of her chest. "Fine. Then maybe we'll have something more substantial than bread and water for dinner."

He ignored her jibe about his refusal to share his food the night before.

"What should I do while you're gone?" she asked.

"That's your problem. If you remember, I didn't invite you here."

She glanced around the tiny room. "I guess I'll try to clean this place the best I can. Is there any water?"

"There's a rain barrel outside. You can use that pot to carry it in." He pointed to a black iron pot in the fireplace.

"When will you be back?"

"When I catch something, or when I don't. You'll be all right as long as you stay in sight of the cabin."

He closed the door without a word of farewell, leaving her alone.

Jessy ate some more of her bread but was careful to save enough for another meal or two in case Morgan had no luck hunting. After breakfast, she ventured outside with the pot in search of water. She didn't have any soap, but hot water would go a long way toward making both the cabin and herself more presentable.

Outside, the air sparkled clean and bright. The storm had passed during the night, leaving behind more than a foot of fresh snow and a brilliant blue sky. She drew a deep breath. She smelled...nothing. No smoke, no animals, no people. Just the faint hint of spicy cedar in the fresh morning air.

She stepped down from the doorway and sank into snow past the tops of her boots. Morgan was right. She'd never be able to climb down the mountain in such deep snow. Even forging a path to the bushes to relieve herself and then to the rain barrel for water was a challenge. But the sun shone warm on her face, and drips from the tree branches drilled tiny holes in the pristine surface of the snow. If the melting continued at this pace, by tomorrow they should be able to make the trip.

Back inside, she built the fire up to heat the pot of water. By the time it was steaming, the tiny room had warmed enough to take her coat off and wash her face and hands. She hadn't brought a towel, so she had to make do with the end of her blanket. After she brushed and re-braided her hair, she was ready to tackle the cabin. There was no mop or broom, but she found an old shirt wadded under the cot which served her purpose well enough.

She washed every surface until she was steaming along with the wash water. She opened the door to empty the pot, and a bright beam of sunlight flooded the room. The brisk air cooled her flushed cheeks and helped dry the damp floor and walls. She dragged the thin mattress to the door and beat as much dust out of it as she could before making the bed with clean blankets.

Wiping her hands on her pants, she surveyed the room and decided she'd done all she could. All that was left was to wait for Morgan to return, so she sat on the bed.

She waited, and waited, and waited. When she could no longer ignore the growling of her stomach, she ate a little more of her bread. The light coming through the half-opened door began to fade, and the room grew colder in spite of the logs she added to the fire.

She hated waiting. She'd never been patient, and waiting encouraged her overactive imagination to conjure all sorts of horrible possibilities. She pictured him falling and breaking a leg, being mauled by a bear, or shot by one of his dreadful cousins. What if he never returned? She doubted she could find her way back to the homestead alone.

In the midst of her morbid thoughts, she was distracted by a faint noise. It sounded again, and she listened closely. Someone was calling. She pulled on her coat and stepped outside.

"Jessy!" Only one person could be calling her name.

"Morgan!" she shouted, stumbling through the snow toward the sound of his voice.

"Over here."

She struggled through the trees, following his voice, imagining him injured or dying. When she reached him, she stopped short.

"Take this turkey, will you?" He held out the plump, feathered carcass of a wild turkey dangling by its scrawny feet. "I've got all I can handle here."

He was dragging a huge buck by the antlers. She wrinkled her nose and reached out gingerly to take the turkey. She'd never held a dead animal in her life.

"For Pete's sake, it's not going to bite you."

She snatched the bird from his hand.

He turned his attention to his main kill, trying to get the best grip to drag it to the cabin. "You can pluck it while I butcher this buck."

She dangled the turkey in front of her. She couldn't believe he expected her to pluck the feathers off a dead bird with her bare hands.

Morgan kept his attention on the buck. "We can have some of this venison tonight, and the rest will freeze by morning. I want to take the turkey home. It used to be one of Sally's favorites when she was a little girl."

Jessy thought of Sally, pregnant, frightened, and withdrawn. If a turkey dinner would help Morgan's sister feel better, then she would get the feathers off the bird, one way or another.

They reached the cabin, and he dragged the buck around back. Withdrawing a wicked-looking skinning knife, he glanced at the sky. "I hope there's enough light left to get this done." He motioned to a stump. "You might as well sit to pluck that turkey."

She swallowed hard, uncertain she could do it. There was only one way to find out. She sat, facing away from him and began to pluck at the feathers.

"It's a lot faster if you scald the bird first, but we don't have a big enough pot. You'll just have to do the best you can."

Metal scraped bone behind her back. She didn't turn, and she didn't answer. She concentrated on her task and tried to disregard the hot smell of blood and death coming from behind her. If she could do this, and do it without being sick, she would have proved something to both of them.

Her determination battled the natural inclinations of her stomach but eventually won out. By the time she finished, she was quite proud of herself and not the least bit squeamish. "All done." She held up the turkey.

Morgan glanced over. "I guess that will have to do until we get it home."

She almost flung the bird at his head. Instead, she plopped it down on the stump and marched back inside. Fuming, she washed her hands and set a fresh pot of water over the fire.

Why was he always so negative? Life was infinitely more rewarding if one approached it with a positive outlook. Of course, to be fair, he hadn't had much proof up until now that life could be good, but she was willing to prove it to him if he gave her a chance.

A short time later, he opened the door holding a bloody hunk of meat. "You'll probably want to boil this. It might be a little tough." He thrust it toward her, and she accepted it without thinking. "I've got to go back out," he continued, "and rig up some sort of sled so we can pull the rest with us in the morning."

After he left, she viewed the quivering red mass with distaste. It didn't look very appetizing, even though she'd had nothing to eat all day except a little bread. If Morgan thought it should be boiled, she would boil it. But that didn't mean she had to eat it. She plopped the venison into the pot of simmering water and sat down to wait.

When he returned carrying his pack, he dropped it on the floor and peered into the pot. "Is the meat done? I'm starved."

"How should I know?" She didn't care if she sounded sullen. Of all the hours in the day, the short time she hadn't spent waiting for him she'd been pulling the feathers off a dead bird. On top of that, she was hungry, and the gray mass bobbing in the pot looked about as appealing as a boiled boot. Her tension level had been building for days. Her emotions teetered on the brink. And now here was Morgan, who hadn't said a pleasant word to her all day, demanding his dinner.

"Stick it with a fork or something," he suggested.

"I don't have a fork."

"There's one in my pack."

She glanced from his face to the pack lying on the floor and back. Tears of anger and frustration welled in her eyes, and she leapt to her feet. "Why don't you stick it yourself? If I weren't a lady I'd tell you exactly what you can do with that fork!"

"What's the matter with you?"

She balled her hands into tight fists against her thighs. "If you weren't such an insensitive dolt, you'd know what's wrong with me!"

He threw his hat on top of his pack and unbuttoned his coat with rough, jerky motions. "Now look, I didn't ask you to come here. Hell, I didn't ask you to follow me from Weston."

"No, you didn't, did you?" She was yelling and crying at the same time. "You couldn't wait to get away from me. All I offered you was a lifetime of love and comfort. Who in his right mind wouldn't run away from that?" Tears streamed down her face.

He grabbed her shoulders and gave her a little shake. "Jessy, pull yourself together. You're hysterical."

"Of course, I'm hysterical! The man I love has done everything possible to reject and humiliate me."

"I'm just trying to do what's right for you."

"Ha!" She waved one hand in the air. "Was it right for me to stand in church, in front of my family and friends, waiting for hours for a man who never showed up?"

His expression hardened. "We've been through this before. I can't marry you."

"Horseapples! Can't or won't, it doesn't matter. Just stop trying to pretend you don't love me, you don't want me." She glared in defiance.

His eyes darkened, and his grip tightened on her shoulders. "I've done a lot of things, but I've never tried to pretend I don't want you. Never."

"Then prove it. Right here and now."

"Dammit, Jessy—"

"Right here, right now," she whispered. "And I'll prove to you just how much you care."

****

He stared into her eyes, and the unselfish love glimmering there brought him to his knees as no blow ever had. He had wanted her so desperately for so long. He no longer had the strength to fight it.

His hands shook as he raised them to frame her face. "I can't—"

"You can." She slid her arms around his waist. "Let me give you this happiness, this pleasure. You deserve it."

He shook his head and squeezed his eyes shut. "I don't deserve you. I never have, and I never will."

"Yes, you do. And I deserve you." She pulled him closer and rose on tiptoe until only a breath separated their lips.

"Oh, Jessy..." He closed the gap.

His fingers gripped her head as if she might vanish at any moment, and his thumbs brushed her delicate cheekbones before his lips claimed hers. There was no room for tenderness in his kiss, no room for leisurely exploration or sensuous indulgence. He was driven by a furious need to act before his inner voices became loud enough to stop him one more time.

And she needed no seduction, no gentle persuasion. She accepted his passion with a love as fiery as her temper and met it with equal strength. Her lips parted at the first sign of pressure. Her tongue twined with his in joyous frenzy. Her soft moan joined his. And her hands sought his body as eagerly as his sought her.

His hungry mouth slid away to explore the contours of her face. Her soft gasp warmed his ear, fueling his fire. He pressed frantic kisses across her cheekbones, eyelids, and brows before being drawn again to the honeyed lure of her mouth. His lips and tongue moved to trace the curve of her ear. His hands fumbled with the buttons of her shirt.

"Jessy, I've got to have you...I can't stop this time...I'm sorry."

She responded by reaching for his buttons. "Don't stop. I'll die if you do."

Her confession of desire jolted him. "I'll die, too." He drew back and gazed deep into her eyes, searching for fear or reluctance. "I don't want you to be afraid."

"I'm not." Her loving smile assured him of the truth of her words.

Together they made short work of the rest of the fastenings. Removing her clothing piece by piece, he stroked and caressed, learned and enjoyed in sweetest torture.

When she was completely naked and he wore only pants and boots, he stepped back and held her at arm's length. He let his eyes feast on the wonder of her. Slender and pale, her body gleamed in the golden firelight.

She was beautiful. She was perfect. She was a breathtaking gift. He didn't deserve her, but she was here, offering herself, and he could deny her no longer.

"I can't wait." His voice rasped with desire, and he reached again.

She flashed a small, teasing smile. "Can you wait long enough to take off your pants?"

"Huh...what? Oh, sure." If he could, he would have blushed. He was the one with the experience, the one who was supposed to soothe her fears, but he shook with anticipation like a green boy.

He jerked his boots off, and his pants and long johns quickly followed, leaving him to face her with a stab of uncertainty. He reached for her again, but she raised a hand to hold him back.

"Not so fast. I want to look, too."

This time, heat rose to his cheeks. He'd never in his life stood stripped naked in front of a woman who stared at him the way Jessy stared. Her eyes gleamed. Slowly, she examined him from head to foot.

Hellfire! He hadn't felt like this since he was fifteen.

Slipping one arm beneath her knees, he lifted her and carried her to the bed without breaking contact. He laid her on the quilt and followed her down. After kissing her thoroughly one more time, he lifted his head and stared into her green eyes. Reading the passion and joyous consent shimmering there, he slowly joined their bodies.

She gasped and squirmed. Closing her eyes, she clasped his head with both hands and moaned. He raised his head and drank in the sight of her—eyes closed, cheeks flushed with passion, rosy lips parted. She was magnificent.

She moaned softly. "Morgan, I need..."

He nuzzled her neck. "What do you need?"

She tossed her head. "I don't know."

"Lucky for both of us, I do."

At her small sounds of pleasure, he knew he was lost. Even as he felt himself falling, he was determined to take her with him. A shower of sparks consumed them both.

Hours, or seconds, later, he groaned and rolled off to lie beside her. He lay still, drained of all energy, while his breathing and heartbeat returned to normal and the sweat dried on his body. He was too stunned to move. Nothing like that had ever happened to him. Jessy was incredible. She was so open and loving. Despite her lack of experience, she gave as much as she took, and more.

He glanced at her, and sudden fear choked him. What had he done? How could things ever go back to the way they were? How could he go back to holding her at arm's length?

He had to make himself do it, of course. Nothing fundamental had changed. He was still the same man, and he still had nothing to offer a woman like her. He would have to hope he hadn't gotten her pregnant and pray for the strength to resist her. Loving Jessy was the closest to heaven he could ever hope to come, and he had to force himself to accept their lovemaking for what it was, a fleeting reprieve from his life sentence of loneliness and pain.

****

Jessy lay on her back with her eyes closed, concentrating on the rhythmic throbbing between her legs that kept pace with her heartbeat. The tiny aftershocks were small-scale reminders of the glorious and overwhelming feeling she had just experienced. She had understood the mechanics of lovemaking before, but nothing could have prepared her for the overpowering sensations that swept through her body like a tidal wave. She could easily envision becoming addicted to this sort of pleasure.

She opened her eyes and found Morgan staring at her with a hooded and unreadable expression.

"How do you feel?" he asked.

She purred like a satisfied cat. "Wonderful." She sighed and stretched. "How about you?"

He ignored her question. "I'm sorry, Jessy."

She smiled again. "Whatever for? I'm not."

"I never meant this to happen. It doesn't change anything."

It changes everything, you foolish man.

But she was feeling indulgent, so she yawned and said, "Don't worry. I won't force you to marry me at gunpoint in the morning."

He frowned. "This is serious. What we just did could have made you pregnant."

She sighed and rolled to her side to face him. "I doubt this one time will make me pregnant, but if it does, I'll take care of it." She wasn't worried. Morgan would never abandon her to raise their child alone.

His frown deepened. "What does that mean?"

"It means stop worrying. It isn't your problem right now."

"Don't be simple. Of course, it's my problem."

"Why are we arguing? We don't even know if I'm pregnant, and I'm probably not."

"It's important to be prepared."

"We'll deal with it if, and when, the problem arises. Now will you stop trying to ruin what has been the loveliest night of my life?

"I'm not trying to ruin anything. I'm trying to keep from ruining anything."

This time, her sigh was filled with exasperation. "Just shut up and pull those blankets over us, will you? I'm freezing. Now put your arms around me and go to sleep."

He surprised her by following her instructions to the letter. Lulled by the warmth and lingering physical satiety, she was soon fast asleep.

She awoke several hours later to a dull gnawing in her stomach, reminding her they'd never gotten around to eating the night before. The fire had gone out, but the hunk of meat still floated in the greasy, cold water in the pot. The thought of overboiled venison revolted her, but maybe Morgan had some food left in his pack.

She rolled over to nudge him awake and realized he was gone. Clutching the blankets around her bare shoulders, she sat up and glanced around the room. Her racing pulse slowed when she saw his pack on the floor next to hers. At least he wasn't so upset by his lapse last night that he'd gone off and left her. He must already be up and preparing for the trip down the mountain.

She was climbing into her pants when the door opened and he stepped into the cabin. The clear gray light that entered with him told her it was morning, and his closed expression told her he was ready to leave. She glanced at him, unsure of what to say. How did one greet one's lover the morning after a night of earth-shattering passion, especially when that lover claimed to regret the entire affair?

She settled for something basic. "Good morning."

"Are you almost ready to go? I've got the meat packed on the sled."

So much for tender expressions of emotion.

She began to button her pants. "I'll be dressed in a few minutes, but I'm starved. Do you have anything to eat?"

"There are a couple of biscuits and one more piece of chicken in my pack. I wasn't hungry."

She offered a teasing smile, hoping to lighten the mood. "After last night, I'd think you'd be famished."

He scowled at her effort. "I don't know how you can make light of this."

She walked over and slid her arms around his waist, ignoring his stiff stance. "Because it's not the end of the world. In fact, it was wonderful. Can you look me in the eye and tell me you don't want to hop back in that bed and do it again?"

His stern expression faltered in the face of her cheerful decadence. "You're completely shameless. Did you know that?"

"I am where you're concerned."

Pain flashed through his eyes before he jerked her into his arms, crushing her against his chest. His lips descended and branded hers with a searing fire.

A loud gurgle from her stomach interrupted their passion. He set her back. "You'd better get something to eat."

She nodded. "I guess so. Do you think it will take long to get back?"

"The snow has melted some, but it's still at least six inches deep. It'll be rough going in places."

He was right. It was much harder climbing down slippery, snow-covered rocks than it had been climbing up, especially dragging the makeshift sled loaded with venison and turkey. The sun was warm and bright, melting the snow in the trees so it seemed to be raining, making the footing all the more treacherous. By the time they reached the clearing around the Bingham homestead, Jessy's legs wobbled from exhaustion.

"I'll take this meat to the smokehouse first," Morgan said.

"I'll come with you." Her stomach tightened at the thought of facing his family. When she'd sneaked off two days earlier, she hadn't given much thought to what would happen when they returned. She'd been concentrating on settling things with Morgan. Now, instead of being settled, things between them were more complicated than ever. She hadn't even persuaded him to go along with her plan to help Ethan.

Morgan hung the meat in the smokehouse. He left the hide and antlers there, too, for the time being. She was surprised when he turned and offered his hand. Sliding her small hand into his, she returned his reassuring squeeze, and together they walked toward the house.

Inside, the family sat gathered around the table. Every head turned, and all eyes were riveted on the couple in the doorway.

Finally, Rachel spoke. "I see you're back. I reckon it's time to send for the preacher."

Chapter Twelve

Jessy tightened her grip on Morgan's hand. His family had assumed she'd left to join him. They'd been gone for nearly three days, and now everyone expected him to do the honorable thing and marry her.

But she didn't want him to marry her because it was the honorable thing. She wanted him to marry her because he was ready to admit he loved her and couldn't live without her. And if the last two days had taught her anything, it was that he wasn't ready.

He squeezed her hand again and released it. "No preacher, Ma."

"Son, you've been gone two nights."

"This is between Jessy and me. We'll handle it ourselves."

Rachel frowned. "I don't see how. There's only one way to take care of this, and you need a preacher for a wedding."

Morgan stiffened but remained steadfast in the face of his mother's mounting disapproval. "There isn't going to be a wedding."

"Just because the girl's father isn't here pointing a gun at your head doesn't mean you don't have to do right by her."

"You didn't insist that Sally marry Will McTaggart," he pointed out.

"That's different." Rachel spared Jessy a quick glance. "Whatever this girl is, at least she's not a McTaggart."

Jessy glanced at the rapt expressions on the faces of Corrine, Ethan, Sally, and even little Samuel. If Morgan and his mother didn't end this humiliating discussion soon, she was likely to explode.

"Please, Mrs. Bingham, this is a very personal matter. Morgan and I have some things to work out between us first."

Rachel stared at Jessy's waistline, then raised her gaze to her face. "Well, you'd best be quick about it."

Her ears burned. The woman certainly didn't believe in beating around the bush. Her own mother would have swooned before speaking so frankly in mixed company.

Rachel faced her son. "I can't force you to marry the girl, but I feel responsible for her while she's living in my house, even if she is a brazen, city-bred hussy who wears britches and traipses off all over the countryside after a man who isn't her husband."

The words stung like an open palm against Jessy's cheek.

Rachel continued, "As long as you're under my roof, I won't have no carrying on."

"There won't be any carrying on." Morgan delivered his assurance with uncompromising hardness.

On the surface, his words might appear to be directed at his mother, but Jessy didn't miss their true intent. His message to Rachel was secondary. His main purpose was to remind her that he considered their lovemaking a mistake he did not intend to repeat.

Well, she wasn't ashamed and she wasn't sorry, but he'd have to get down on his knees and beg before she offered herself to him again.

Rachel studied him. "I'll accept your word on that. You've never lied to me."

He nodded in acknowledgment of their bargain. Propping his rifle against the wall near the door, he turned to hang up his hat and coat. "I brought a turkey and a buck. They're in the smokehouse."

"Fine." His mother moved toward the fireplace. "I'll see to the meat in the morning. Now I expect you could both use some hot food. Sit down, and I'll see what's left in the pot."

Jessy pulled off her hat and fumbled with the peg, as the gravity of her situation struck her for the first time. When only she and Morgan had been affected, she'd felt no shame. But now the whole family was involved. Would she be shunned, tolerated, or accepted?

Rachel's matter-of-fact offer of dinner seemed to indicate she was willing to put the issue of marriage aside for the time being, but there was no mistaking her silent censure. Trying to view the matter objectively, Jessy couldn't blame her. Rachel had actually remained quite calm. Annabelle Randall would have had a conniption and taken to her bed for a month.

Jessy slumped in her seat at the table. Because of her impulsive action, she had lost every inch of ground she'd gained with Morgan's family over the past weeks, and then some. On top of that, she hadn't even persuaded him to help with her plan to replace Ethan's violin.

A gentle touch on her shoulder brought her head up. "I know what you need." Corrine set a steaming bowl in front of her. "After you eat, we'll fix you a nice hot bath."

A bath. She sighed at the thought. Heaven. She pictured her bathtub at home and could almost feel the sensual luxury of sinking all the way up to her chin in the hot, sweet-scented water.

Corrine smiled. "After supper, come to my house with me, and you can use the tub there."

Despite her hunger, Jessy barely tasted her beans and bacon. She couldn't wait to get out of the cabin. She blessed Morgan's sister-in-law for her offer of escape.

Corrine patted her son's dark head. "Samuel, honey, you stay with Grandma Rachel until I come for you." He nodded, staring at Jessy with huge eyes.

Jessy scurried up the ladder to the loft and returned with a bundle containing fresh clothing, a hairbrush, and her precious bar of lavender soap. Avoiding the gazes of the rest of the family, she followed Corrine through the connecting door to the dogtrot leading to the small cabin she shared with her husband and son.

Once inside, Corrine waddled over to a tin tub propped against one wall. "Here's the tub. You set it by the fire, and I'll heat some water."

Jessy dragged the tub to the center of the small room and eyed it skeptically. It was round and only about a foot deep and bore no resemblance to her bathtub at home. In fact, it looked more like something a horse might drink from than a bathtub. If she sat in it, her knees would bump her chin. Nevertheless, it offered her first chance for a full bath since she'd left Independence. The tub might not be the height of luxury, but if it didn't leak, it should serve its purpose.

"I can't thank you enough."

Corrine checked the kettle for steam. "Don't be silly. It's just a simple kindness."

Jessy grimaced. "I don't think the rest of the family is feeling too kindly toward me at the moment."

"I expect you knew what you were doing."

She let out a short laugh. "Hardly. When I left, I told myself I just wanted the chance to talk to Morgan alone." She dropped her gaze to the floor. "It turned into something much more complicated."

Corrine hefted the heavy kettle from its hook over the fire and poured the steaming contents into the tub. "I expect everything will work out."

Jessy rushed to take the kettle from her hands. "Let me do that. I can't have you waiting on me."

Corrine brushed her away. "I'm used to it, and besides, we all need to be waited on every now and again."

"Who waits on you?"

It was Corrine's turn to glance away. "In his better moments, Ethan tries to ease my way."

"I followed Morgan to the cabin to talk about Ethan." Jessy knelt to unlace her boots.

"Why?"

"I had the idea I might be able to replace his broken violin, but Morgan doesn't seem to think that's possible."

Corrine sighed and pressed a hand to the small of her back. "That surely would be a blessing. He needs to have something to occupy his hands and mind."

At the wistful sadness in her voice, Jessy determined not to give up on her idea. There had to be a way, and she would find it.

Corrine picked up her shawl and wrapped it around her shoulders. "I'll go back to the house and leave you to your bath. Take all the time you want. I'll help you empty the tub when you're through."

"I think we'll let Morgan empty the tub. It's the least he can do."

Corrine smiled. "I'm glad to see you haven't let this dampen your mettle."

The implicit approval in her words acted as a balm to Jessy's bruised spirit. It seemed like ages since anyone had approved of her. Impulsively, she reached out to hug Corrine. "If Morgan and I do end up married, one of the best things about it will be having you for a sister."

Corrine's thin face flushed, and she slipped out of Jessy's embrace. "I just want you to know you have a friend here—no matter what happens."

Jessy watched her go with mixed emotions. Her spontaneous display of affection might have embarrassed Corrine, but not enough to cause Morgan's sister-in-law to withdraw her friendship.

She shook her head and reached up to unbutton her shirt. She doubted she would ever fully understand these hill people. They had feelings, strong feelings, but they suppressed any outward display of emotion. She couldn't imagine living like that. She would burst if she tried to keep her feelings bottled up that way.

Yet she knew the Binghams, with the exception of Ethan, well enough to know they were honest, honorable, and sincere people. They were strong enough not to give up in the face of discouragement and deprivation. They simply refused to ease the reins on their self-control. And none of them knew how to have any fun.

Well, Christmas was coming soon, and she'd have to see what she could do to remedy that.

In spite of how appealing the bath had sounded, she soon found that crouching naked in a small, round tub of water in a chilly cabin bore no relation to her previous concept of bathing. She gritted her teeth to still their chattering and scrubbed her body and hair in record time. With her hair damp and curling and her skin glowing from the rough towel, she returned to the main cabin.

There was no sign of Morgan.

"Morgan decided to use the tub after you finished," Corrine said.

She nodded but noted the irony of their back-to-back baths. In the isolation of the hunting cabin, she and Morgan had been as close as two people could get. Yet as soon as they returned to the company of others, each hurried to wash the smell and feel of the other from their bodies. She only wished he could wash away his guilt and self-hatred as easily.

****

Christmas was less than a month away. It had always been Jessy's favorite holiday. As a child, she thrived on the bustle that began several weeks before the actual day.

Her mother relished her role as the wife of a prominent judge, but never more than at Christmas. The entire month of December was given over to endless rounds of teas, soirées, and caroling parties. Jessy was allowed to help the cook in the kitchen, and as she grew older, Mama let her help decorate the house as well. As an only child, she was often permitted to attend social gatherings, scrubbed, curled, and impeccably dressed.

Thoughts of Christmas brought memories of the sweet, spicy scents of fresh cedar and baking gingerbread, the crisp rustle of taffeta, and a constant flurry of activity. And then there were the presents. Although most of her friends were lucky to receive a single toy or a treat of candy or fresh fruit, Jessy had amassed a beautiful collection of porcelain dolls all the way from France, attired in miniature copies of the latest Paris fashions.

Without warning, the image of Morgan's family filled her mind, along with an uncomfortable twinge. In comparison to their Spartan lives, her family's holiday excesses seemed almost obscene. Yet, there had been much more than mere overindulgence. She remembered the excitement and anticipation, the feeling something wonderful was coming. She doubted anyone in the Bingham household had ever known that feeling. And most important, she remembered basking in the glow of being cherished. For, although her parents might have spoiled her, they loved her and weren't reluctant to show it.

She couldn't duplicate the kind of Christmas she'd enjoyed as a girl, but she could still give the Binghams a festive celebration. There would be no problem with food since Morgan had stocked up on staples at Mr. Boone's store. They might not have the candied fruits or some of the other delicacies she was used to, but she could produce a respectable plum pudding from the jars of wild plums lining the kitchen shelves, and Morgan could provide a fresh turkey or goose.

That left the problem of gifts. The family was no longer destitute, but they had lived in oppressive poverty for so long she wasn't sure they would think of presents, even for Samuel. She had plenty of money to buy something for everyone—the problem was how and where. She was no longer in Philadelphia, or even Weston. She was in a log cabin in the Ozark Mountains, miles from the nearest town, with no way to get there, even if the single store had anything to buy. That left only one option. She would have to use her imagination and whatever materials she could find.

That night she snuggled under the quilts in her narrow bed beneath the rafters, plotting and planning. By the next morning, she was ready to begin. The remaining snow had nearly melted, leaving slippery, oozing mud everywhere. With a sigh of regret, she dressed in her pants and boots. After Rachel's comments about her attire and behavior the night before, she would have preferred to appear at breakfast looking as feminine as possible, but she would never be able to do what she wanted to do today in a dress and slippers.

She might as well accept that she was doomed to make a bad impression on the woman and quit worrying. If things with Morgan didn't improve, she would be leaving in a few weeks anyway and would never see any of them again. The thought brought an empty ache.

After breakfast, when the others set about their chores, Jessy slipped away unnoticed. She followed the muddy path through the trees and across the cornfield before beginning her descent to the river. The slick stones and slimy mud were treacherous underfoot. Several times she had to grab the branches lining the trail to keep her balance.

The roaring sounds of rushing water grew louder and louder. She couldn't remember how far she'd come the day she heard the sounds of Ethan's violin. She stopped and glanced around. Then she remembered. The cedars. He had been sitting behind three big cedars. She continued, scanning the right side of the path for the landmark trees. As soon as she saw them, she hurried to the clearing behind.

She couldn't believe her luck. It was still there. She bent and picked up the splintered pieces of the instrument. The neck was broken but still dangled from the smashed body by the strings. She turned the pieces over in her hands. It had been a beautiful thing, fragile and delicately carved. The varnished wood still glowed with the markings of the grain.

The instrument itself was a total loss, but the strings appeared to be undamaged, and the strings were what Jessy sought. Given the right materials, Ethan might be able to make another violin, but without strings it would never sing as this one had, and she could imagine what Hiram Boone would say if she walked into his store and tried to order a set of violin strings.

She surveyed the debris to see if any other parts might be salvaged. The tuning pegs appeared to be whole, so she removed them and wound the strings loosely before placing them in the pocket of her jacket. As an afterthought, she retrieved a couple of fragments of the body of the instrument and tucked them into the other pocket.

As she was leaving, she spied an odd stick dangling from the top of one of the cedars. She took a closer look and recognized the bow. Ethan must have flung it away in his anger, and it had caught in the tree. With a long branch, she reached up and knocked the bow loose. She ran her fingers over the satin-smooth wood. The snow might have warped it—she couldn't be sure—and it would have to be restrung, but she tucked it under her jacket and headed back to the house.

She found Morgan in the barn mending tack and rushed to show him her treasures. "Look what I found."

He turned the smoothly carved pegs with their thumb-sized keys over in his hand and examined the coiled strings.

"They're from Ethan's violin," she added.

"I guessed that." He handed them back to her. "What were you planning to do? Give them to him as a memento?"

She snatched the strings and pegs. "Of course not. Must you always be so difficult?"

"Yes."

Was he teasing her? Her delight bubbled up into a grin. The answering flash in his eyes might have been humor, or something else. "These are for Ethan to use when he rebuilds his violin."

Morgan leaned back against the side of a stall and crossed his arms. "And how is he going to do that?"

"With the wood you're going to find for me to give him for Christmas." She fished in her other pocket and brought out the pieces she had saved from the body of the instrument. "Look at these. All you have to do is find some more wood like this."

He took the samples. He studied them closely, turning them over and rubbing his thumbs across the smooth finish. "Maple."

"Well, there are lots of maple trees around here, aren't there? Go out and chop one down."

He glanced at her and sighed. "Jessy, you can't make anything out of green wood. Only good, seasoned wood with a tight grain will work for something like this."

Her eyes narrowed, and she perched her hands on her hips. "Are you trying to tell me that in this entire forest there is no wood suitable for making a violin?"

"No. There's probably a fallen tree somewhere that would work."

"Then all we have to do is find it."

He shifted his weight and stood. "In case you haven't noticed, I have more important work to do than wander around the woods looking for some damned log."

She refused to be cowed. "More important than helping your brother?"

"Dammit, Jessy. How many times do I have to tell you to stop interfering?"

She gave him a sweet smile. "It doesn't matter how many times you tell me. I'm going to do what I know is right, and you're going to help me."

He stared at her long and hard before his features relaxed. "Okay."

Her smile widened, and she flung herself at him. "You'll do it? That's wonderful! I knew I could count on you. When can we go?"

"Just a minute." He peeled her arms from around his waist. "I've got work."

"How about tomorrow?"

"We'll see. Depends on the weather."

She pointed her index finger at his nose. "All right, but I have your promise, so don't you go trying to weasel out on me."

She squeaked when Morgan jerked her into his arms. "As if I could ever hope to get away with it," he muttered before planting a swift kiss on her lips.

She giggled and leaned forward for another kiss, but he set her aside.

"Now get out of here and let me work."

Whistling under her breath, she marched out of the barn and back to the house.

They did not go hunting for Ethan's wood the next day, or the next, or even the next. A hard, cold rain began to fall that afternoon, and it rained for three days, soaking everything and shortening tempers in the cabin. Ethan began drinking shortly after the noon meal each day and was surly and argumentative by suppertime. Jessy didn't see Morgan at all, except for mealtimes, and assumed he was working in the barn.

It was just as well, because the second day her monthly bleeding commenced, and the dragging pain that always accompanied it left her weak and as sociable as a snapping turtle. The knowledge she wasn't pregnant should have lifted her spirits — Rachel and Corrine certainly seemed relieved by her discomfort. Instead, she felt disappointed, no matter how hard she tried to persuade herself she had escaped potential disaster.

Since she couldn't go outside and wasn't up to strenuous chores, she spent the three days working on her Christmas gifts for the family. The women were the easiest. She could sew for them. She was a good seamstress, and since they all spent time each evening sewing and mending, no one paid much attention to what she was working on.

She had taken inventory of her remaining fabric and decided to make a dress of the red calico in a high-waisted, loose-fitting style for Sally. The bright color would complement her dark hair and fair skin, and a new dress might help lift her sagging spirits. For Corrine, she would make some gowns for the new baby from scraps of the soft flannel she had used for her nightdress. Rachel was more difficult, but after watching her handling hot pots over the fire, Jessy decided to quilt together several pieces of the two calicos into colorful potholders.

The men were another matter. Until the rain stopped, she couldn't do anything about the wood for Ethan's violin. She knew exactly what she wanted to give Samuel—a book. She could write down one of the stories she remembered from her childhood, maybe even draw a few pictures to illustrate it, if only she had paper, pen, and ink. But she had only tucked a single sheet of paper and one envelope into her bag to be used in case of emergency. She couldn't fashion a whole book from a single sheet of paper, and the Bingham household didn't have any. She would have to ponder that problem further. A solution was bound to come to her. One always did.

That left Morgan. She had already offered him her most precious gifts, and he had rejected them. What was left? There must be something, something he could hold and treasure, whether they were together or apart. But what? That, too, she would have to ponder.

The passing days confirmed her suspicions about the coming holiday. No one paid it any mind. There was no special baking, no boughs or ribbons, no preparations of any kind. No whispered secrets or furtive glances passed between the members of the family to suggest anything out of the ordinary. Even Samuel showed no signs of excitement or anticipation.

One evening, she brought up the subject of Christmas. Rachel answered with a disapproving frown. "We don't hold with useless frippery."

"Of course not. I just thought I might start reading the Christmas story in the evenings."

"I guess there's no harm in that."

So, she did. She loved watching Samuel's round blue eyes widen as he listened to the story of the baby born in the stable and laid in the straw and heard about the mysteries of the angels and shepherds and wise men.

"Our baby will come close to Christmas," he whispered.

Jessy's heart leapt to her throat. He could talk. Clearly and sensibly. She slid an arm around his narrow shoulders and hugged him. "Yes, and won't it be lucky to have a warm cradle in a house and a big brother to help watch over it?"

Samuel's thin chest swelled, and he looked at her with a new glimmer of pride in his eyes. "I'll be a big brother."

She glanced over his head at Corrine. Watery joy radiated from her thin face, and Jessy's eyes stung in response. She returned her attention to Samuel and smiled. "Yes, sweetheart, you will." She could barely speak around the lump in her throat.

When the story was finished, Samuel walked back over to his mother. "It's a wonder, Ma, ain't it?" he whispered.

A tear trickled down Corrine's cheek before she brushed it aside. "Yes, honey. It's a wonder."

Watching them, Jessy knew exactly what she wanted to give Samuel for Christmas. She would to make him a book of the Christmas story, and she had an idea of how to do it.

She glanced at his mother. "Corrine, I need some dark brown dye. I need to…to…patch my jacket. I'd like to dye it to match."

Corrine considered. "Well, walnut hulls make a good dark brown that ought to match pretty close. In fact, I've got some in a jar left over from last year if you don't need too much."

"Oh, no. Just a small amount. That would be wonderful."

"I'll fetch it for you before I go to bed."

"Thank you."

Tomorrow she would start Samuel's book. She might not have the proper supplies, but she could fashion a makeshift pen from a turkey feather and use the walnut dye to write and draw on squares of the white flannel. She could stitch the cloth pages together when she finished. It wouldn't be a real book, but if she worked slowly and carefully she should be able to print large, simple words the little boy could learn to read for himself.

The next morning, she gathered her flannel scraps, old jacket, and the jar of dye and escaped to the barn after breakfast. She wanted to keep the book a secret from Samuel and his mother, and she needed a place to work where she had a flat surface and plenty of light. She found Morgan sharpening the teeth of a rusty old saw with a file that looked even worse. "Good morning."

He glanced up from his work. "Is it?" With disgust, he tossed the file on the bench where he sat. "There's not a single thing around here that's worth a damn. Sometimes I'd like to knock the whole place down and start over."

She reached out with her free hand and rubbed his tense shoulders. "You've already done so much. You'll be amazed at how much better the place will look by spring."

"We'll see." But his muscles relaxed beneath her fingers.

"I came to ask if I could work on the little table in your loft."

He flexed his shoulders with a sigh. "Why?"

"It's something I want to do for Samuel."

"I guess so, but you'll get pretty cold up there without a fire."

At the mention of cold, she shivered. He was right. It was chilly in the unheated barn, yet he spent most of his days, and all his nights, out here. "Are you planning to sleep in the loft all winter?"

"There isn't any place else. The house is already crowded. Maybe in a month or two I'll start building a cabin of my own."

A cabin of his own. Where Morgan could be alone. Maybe where they could be alone together. She shied away from the turn of her thoughts. "Um...by the way, when can we go looking for Ethan's wood?"

"Do you still want to do that?"

"Of course. You didn't think I'd give up on the idea, did you?"

His lips twisted into a wry smile. "No. You never give up on anything."

She didn't return his smile. "Not when it's something I believe in."

He rose and dusted off the seat of his buckskin pants. "I'll take you this afternoon, but you'd better change your clothes first."

She glanced at her pretty green dress and grimaced. She couldn't win. No matter what she wore, it always seemed to be wrong. Who would have expected such a dilemma from the best customer of Mrs. Twitty's Fine Fashions for Ladies?

That afternoon she was dressed and waiting when Morgan came to fetch her.

"You ready? Let's go."

Rachel stepped forward waving a big wooden spoon. "Just a minute, you two. I don't know where you're going, and I don't want to know, but you be sure to be back by suppertime, you hear?"

Jessy flinched, but Morgan nodded and replied, "Yes, Ma."

Several minutes later, she struggled behind him on the path, trying to match his long-legged strides. "Do you have any idea where we should look for the wood?"

He didn't miss a step or turn his head. "There's a stand of maples about a mile from here, on the way up to the hunting cabin. I expect we can find a good-sized fallen tree there."

She didn't answer. She needed all her breath to keep pace with him. They were almost running. Obviously, Morgan intended to make certain they didn't have to spend another night in the woods.

By the time they reached the grove, she was grateful for the chance to stop and catch her breath. She plopped down and leaned her back against a tree trunk. Morgan dropped his canteen in her lap and started scouting for a fallen tree. She unscrewed the lid and took a long, satisfying drink.

They were beginning to get used to each other, to anticipate the other's needs. Of course, she sought to fill Morgan's emotional needs, while he sensed only her physical ones. When the day came that he looked beyond the physical, her hopes for the future would have a fighting chance.

He finally found a suitable trunk and used the hatchet hanging from his belt to remove a section about two feet long. "Do you think this will be enough?" he asked.

She studied the log. "I suppose so. Ethan will need enough for a front, a back, sides, and a neck, but all the pieces except the neck are very thin."

"That's true, but from looking at the pieces you gave me, the front and back were made by cutting away the back side of the wood until only a thin shell was left. The sides seemed to be a single thin strip that was bent into the right shape."

"How will he do that?"

He shrugged. "That's up to him. It's probably soaked or steamed—the way a cooper forms barrel staves."

She had never seen anyone make barrel staves, but his suggestion made sense. She examined the rough wood. It was hard to believe it could be transformed into a beautiful musical instrument, but it was worth a try. "I don't know if this will work, but at least it will give him something to do."

He turned the wood over in his hands, examining the fine, tight grain. "I don't know what he's going to use to cut this. It's not as hard as oak, but nearly."

"We'll think of something. Don't worry."

His hands stilled, and he raised his head. "You know the one thing I've always envied you for?" His voice was utterly serious.

"What?"

"Your complete faith in the future. You always seem so certain everything will work out just the way you want."

It might have been an accusation, but it wasn't. A sharp pain jabbed her heart. What would it be like to live without confidence and hope for the future? Morgan had done it for years, and obviously expected nothing more. She longed to turn his thinking around and make him see that good things could happen, that he had it in his power to change the course of his life.

She smiled. "Maybe I'm a foolish optimist, or simple-minded, or maybe I just live a charmed life."

He shook his head. "Whatever it is, I don't want to be the one to break the spell." He slid his hatchet into the leather sheath on his belt and hefted the log onto one shoulder. "Let's go."

Chapter Thirteen

For the next few weeks, Jessy sought out every opportunity to inject the joy of the season into the dreary routine on the farm. She continued reading the Christmas story. She asked Rachel and Corrine about favorite family foods. She told Samuel stories of childhood Christmas memories, stories that involved simple family activities rather than elaborate parties or presents and made sure the others heard as well.

But it was an uphill battle. Rachel showed no interest in holiday baking. Corrine was so near her confinement that she concentrated most of her energy on getting around. Sally remained withdrawn, speaking only when necessary. And Morgan and Ethan were oblivious.

Jessy found them all enormously frustrating.

However, she had never been one to knuckle under to frustration. Sheer persistence could overcome most obstacles, so she redoubled her efforts.

She brought feathery branches clipped from a cedar tree into the cabin and arranged them on the rough log mantel above the stone fireplace. When questioned, she replied that she liked their fresh scent. Rachel muttered something about a fire hazard but allowed the greenery to remain.

A few days later, Jessy cut strips from the scraps of red calico and tied bows to the branches. Corrine made the only comment, remarking that it made a cheery display, but soon Jessy noticed a subtle change in the mood inside the cabin. People spoke to each other with more kindness. Brief smiles appeared from time to time. Even Sally showed signs of emerging from her self-imposed emotional exile. These ironbound hill-folk were softening under her relentless barrage of Christmas spirit.

The next day, when Jessy requested permission to bake cookies, Rachel not only granted it, she offered to help. Soon the mouth-watering smells of oatmeal and molasses cookies filled the house. The aroma must have made its way outside, because as soon as she removed the cookies from the baking oven in the fireplace, Morgan appeared. He said he needed a pair of scissors, but lingered, scissors in hand, sniffing the air.

She waved a warm, spicy molasses cookie, glistening with sprinkles of sugar, in front of his nose. "I thought you had work to do."

He snatched the cookie and consumed it in two bites.

She rapped his knuckles with a wooden spoon. "Remember your manners."

"It serves you right. You should know better than to tease a starving man."

The pretense of severity melted from her face. "I never tease."

He met her gaze, and his lips parted as if to form words…or a kiss.

"Morgan Bingham, are you eating sweets before supper?" Rachel's scolding broke the mood.

He glanced at her. "I—"

Jessy grabbed an oatmeal cookie and took a bite. "Mmm. They taste better now than they will later." She smiled at Rachel. "We might as well each have one. It's nearly Christmas. Besides, if everyone ruins their appetite, we won't have to cook supper."

Rachel hemmed and hawed, but eventually Jessy's good spirits snared her. Soon the whole family sat munching fresh cookies and drinking cold milk from the springhouse.

Jessy glanced at the faces around her, and a warm glow filled her heart. A few short weeks ago, such a scene would have been unimaginable. None of the problems had disappeared, but at least Morgan's family was willing to take a respite from their troubles. The only dark spot was Ethan, who had refused his wife's invitation to join them. Jessy could only pray her hunch about the violin would prove correct.

****

Day by day, fighting years of tradition, or lack thereof, Jessy dragged Morgan and the rest of the Binghams toward her goal of a happy family Christmas. By Christmas Eve, she was exhausted, but satisfied. Her presents were finished, and nearly everyone had contributed something to Christmas dinner. She sent Morgan hunting, and he returned with a fat goose. Rachel agreed to make the corn pudding that had been her sons' favorite food since childhood. Sally and Corrine baked soft potato rolls and churned fresh butter.

Jessy hoped her plum pudding would be the pièce de résistance. Even without a proper mold, it had steamed perfectly and sat on a shelf in the springhouse, waiting to make its entrance. At home, her mother had always soaked the pudding in brandy and flamed it before serving, but she didn't think corn liquor would be an appropriate substitute. And besides, she wasn't sure she could convince Morgan's family to eat something they'd just seen on fire.

On Christmas morning, she was the first to wake. In her two months at the farm, she had grown casual about some details of grooming, such as wearing stays and elaborate hairstyles, but today of all days, she wanted to look her best. She had burned herself twice ironing her green dress and two petticoats the day before, but the result was worth it, even if her skirt wasn't as full as it would have been with a proper crinoline. No one would know. Morgan was probably the only other person in the house who had ever seen a woman in a crinoline. Fully dressed and with her wild curls subdued in a smooth, twisted coronet, she gathered her gifts in one arm and picked her way down the rickety ladder.

Rachel bent over the fire, stirring the remaining coals with a poker and adding fresh wood. She straightened at the soft sound of Jessy's slippers on the plank floor. "You look fine today."

Even though she had taken great pains to make a good impression, Jessy flushed at the unexpected compliment. "Thank you, Mrs. Bingham. Merry Christmas."

"Hmph."

Well, maybe two pleasant comments in a row were too much to ask.

She laid her pile of gifts in a chair and gathered the utensils to set the table for breakfast. Soon, the rest of the family straggled in. On the surface, it might have been any ordinary day, but she detected underlying signs of anticipation. Hair was damp and carefully combed. Clothing, though plain and worn, was better than everyday work clothes. Eyes shone brighter than usual in the early morning darkness.

Morgan was the last to arrive after he'd milked the cow and fed the animals in the barn. He was freshly shaven and wore wool trousers and a clean blue shirt instead of the buckskins he had affected since returning home.

Jessy waited while they took their places at the table. Before Rachel served the porridge and bacon, she spoke. "Just a moment. Before we eat, I have something to say." She glanced around the table. "I think we all know today is a very special day."

Samuel piped up, "We're going to have a party, ain't we, Aunt Jessy?"

She caught Morgan's frown at his nephew's form of address but ignored him and smiled at the bright-eyed little boy. "Yes, sweetheart, we are. And I have something for you to help make the day even more special."

Samuel's eyes widened.

"Do you remember the story of the wise men bringing presents to baby Jesus?"

Samuel nodded.

"Well, I have a present to help you remember this special day." She took his gift from the top of the stack. "This is a book just for you. I'll read it to you, and later you can learn to read it for yourself." The little boy stared at the offering.

"Take it," she urged. "I made it for you."

He glanced at his mother, and Corrine nodded with tears in her eyes. He accepted the gift as if the floppy flannel pages were leaves of gold.

"Go ahead. Look at the pictures. I have some things for the rest of the family, too."

Jessy proceeded to give Sally her new red dress, Rachel her pot holders, and Corrine the gowns for the new baby. All three were stunned speechless. Sally stared at the bright cloth in her lap. Corrine began to cry. And Rachel turned the quilted squares over and over in her hands.

Jessy turned to Morgan and caught him regarding her with an unfathomable look in his hazel eyes. "Would you please go out to the barn and get Ethan's gift?"

He rose from the table. "It's on the front porch. I had a feeling you might be up to something this morning." He returned carrying the large maple log, which he set on the table in front of his baffled younger brother.

"What the—"

"These are to go with it." Jessy triumphantly handed Ethan the coil of strings, the tuning pegs, and the bow she had rescued from the clearing.

Ethan stared at the array. Then he turned on her with a snarling scowl. "What is this? Some kind of sick joke?"

The furious hostility in his voice pushed her back a step. "N-no. It's for you...to make a new violin...to replace the one that was broken."

Ethan roared an obscenity that made a mockery of the holiness of the day, struggled to stand with his crutches, and stormed out of the cabin.

She stared at his back, heedless of the shaking that had overtaken her limbs and the tears streaming down her face. She thought she had prepared herself for the possibility of rejection, but the reality was much worse than her imagination. "I just wanted to help."

Corrine hefted herself from her seat and came around the table to hug Jessy's trembling body against the hard bulk of her belly. "I know you did, and he'll come around. You'll see."

Jessy swiped at her cheeks. "I'm not so sure."

"Don't pay him no mind," Rachel said gruffly. "Now everybody eat before the food gets cold."

They ate in silence, with solemn faces reflecting the lost magic, the broken promise of the day.

"Aunt Jessy." A small voice broke the stillness. "Thank you for the book."

She glanced at Samuel, who sat beside her. His eyes were huge, and his voice wavered a little, as if he had summoned all his courage to speak in the gathering of silent adults.

She smiled. "You're welcome. Would you like me to read it to you after breakfast?"

He nodded.

"Good. We'll do that." She smoothed his shiny hair. "This afternoon, I thought we might have a taffy pull. I always used to like that when I was a little girl."

"What's taffy, and why do you pull it?"

She smiled at his puzzlement. "It's wonderful candy, made of sugar and butter. You'll love it, but it's mighty sticky. You have to make sure all your teeth are in tight. Are they?"

Samuel's dark brows drew together. He poked a tiny thumb and forefinger into his mouth to check his teeth. After testing each one, he nodded again.

"Good." She hugged him, and unable to resist the temptation, dropped a quick kiss on his silky black hair. The little boy jerked back then offered her a shy smile.

She glanced up to find Morgan staring at her with an intensity that would have frightened her, had it been anger. But it wasn't anger burning in his mountain lion eyes. It was something more powerful, a yearning so fiery she feared she might incinerate where she sat.

He wanted her. Not merely her body, but her. She blinked. When she opened her eyes, the fire had been banked—but not extinguished. It continued to smolder until she could no longer meet his gaze.

After breakfast, she kept her promise and read Samuel's new book. He even allowed her to hold him on her lap. They snuggled together in the big chair, and she delighted in the weight of his slight body resting against hers and the feel of his slender fingers helping her turn the pages. She'd always had a special love for young children, and this one, with his too-solemn eyes, tore at her heart.

The finished book bore little resemblance to any book she'd ever seen, but Samuel treated it with touching reverence. The walnut dye had bled into the soft fibers of the flannel, and the words were not as clear as she would have liked, but the resulting fuzzy effect gave the pictures a charming, magical quality that fit the story perfectly.

They finished the story, and Samuel hopped off her lap. She glanced up and saw that Sally had changed into her new red dress. The color suited her beautifully, contrasting with her porcelain-fair skin and black hair. It even seemed to bring some color to her pale cheeks.

"Thank you for the dress." Her voice was quiet, and she kept her gaze trained on the floor.

"You look beautiful in it."

"I wish Will could see it."

Jessy reached for her hand and squeezed. "I'm sure he will, one day soon. Everyone will settle down, and we'll try again. I'm sure we can persuade Morgan to be reasonable."

"Maybe." Sally looked skeptical. "But I don't know about Will's pa. I'm not sure anything could make him reasonable."

"Don't worry. We'll think of something."

Sally sighed and raised wistful blue eyes to meet Jessy's. "I wish I could be like you. You're always so sure."

Inwardly, Jessy winced. She was always sure where other people were concerned. It was her own life that gave her trouble.

Christmas dinner was an unqualified success. The goose was perfectly roasted, and the corn pudding light and flavorful. Rachel used her new potholders and complimented Jessy on her plum pudding. The accompanying hard sauce didn't taste quite right without the bourbon her mother always added, but she doubted anyone noticed the lack. At his wife's request, Ethan joined the family for dinner. He wasn't jovial, but he wasn't surly either, and the meal proceeded in peace.

After the dishes had been washed and put away, Jessy got out the sack of sugar and sent Samuel to the springhouse for the rest of yesterday's butter. She poured sugar into the large black kettle and swung it over the fire to melt.

"Sugar don't grow on trees, you know." Rachel's voice stopped her.

Her hands froze. Had she pushed the frivolity too far? Rachel had gone along with her plans so far without balking. "I'd be glad to pay for it, Mrs. Bingham. I just wanted to make something special for Samuel."

"Seems to me you've done enough." Rachel's tone wasn't unkind, just a statement of fact.

"I'll buy more sugar, Ma," Morgan said from across the room. "I need to go to town for supplies again soon, anyway. I plan to start work on my cabin next week if the weather holds."

His cabin. A leaden lump formed in Jessy's chest. It was one more sign he had no plans to return to Weston with her. She sensed he would be happy spending the rest of his days in these hills.

When the melted sugar and butter had cooled into a semi-firm mass, she told everyone to grease their hands with the remaining butter. She divided them into groups of two and handed each pair a big lump of the warm mixture.

"Pull it between you, like this." She handed Morgan the other end of her piece and stretched it out like a ribbon. "Then double it back and do the same thing again. As you stretch it over and over, the taffy gets softer. When you can't pull it one more time, it's ready."

Everyone pulled, and the mood grew lighter, until it was almost silly. Corrine and Sally giggled when Morgan threatened to tie Jessy up in the soft, sticky rope and dangle her above the floor. Even Ethan cracked a smile as he engaged in a tug-of-war with his wife and son.

When no one could pull another pull, Jessy pronounced the taffy done, and Morgan cut it into small pieces with a sharp knife. Everyone collapsed onto benches and chairs to sample the results of their hard work.

"I remember doing this once, when I was a girl." Rachel bit into a piece of the sweet candy. "It was so long ago I'd forgotten."

Everyone was quiet for a moment, enjoying both their exhaustion and its reward.

Rachel finished her taffy and wiped her hands on her apron. "In all my life, I can't remember another day quite like this."

"Neither can I," Morgan echoed.

The look in his eyes melted Jessy like the sugar in the hot kettle. "I hope you enjoyed it. That's all I wanted."

Morgan rose. "Come outside with me."

"But there's the pan to wash, and—"

"Go on." Rachel shooed Jessy toward the door. "Sally and I will wash up. You've done enough."

"All right, if you're sure. I'll get my jacket."

She removed her apron and draped it over the back of the chair, making sure no one saw the roll of fabric she picked up from the seat and concealed in the folds of her skirt. She slid her arms into her jacket, slipping the roll into her pocket.

Morgan held the door then followed her out, closing it firmly behind them. He clasped her elbow and guided her down the steps. His determination was evident in the strength of his grip and the purposeful measure of his stride. He was obviously a man with a mission. Well, she had a mission, too.

"Morgan, I—"

"I don't know—"

They spoke at once, stopped, then Jessy smiled. "You first."

"No, you."

She wrapped her arms around her body to ward off the chill. "You're the one who invited me out here, so you must have something important to say. You go first."

He looked flustered. "You know I've never been very good with words. I guess all I really wanted to say was thank you."

That was all. And it was enough.

She searched his tawny hazel eyes. They said much more than his lips. "You're welcome." She placed a hand on his arm, leaned forward on tiptoe, and pressed a light kiss to his lips. "Now I have something for you. Could we go somewhere more private?"

"Private?"

"Yes. And preferably out of the wind."

He glanced around. "The barn?"

"That would be fine. I have something to give you, and I'd rather not be interrupted."

He didn't ask questions until they were inside the barn and the heavy doors shut out the rest of the world. "Now, what's this about having something for me? You shouldn't—"

"Will you please be gracious, just this once?" She reached into her pocket and withdrew the roll of fabric. "This is your Christmas present. I didn't want to give it to you in front of everyone else because...well...I just didn't."

He took the cloth and unrolled it.

She watched his face. What did he think? Did he like it? It was impossible to tell from his expression. She thought she might go crazy if one of them didn't speak to fill the gaping silence.

"I had the worst time trying to think of something to give you," she began, "and I didn't have any of the supplies I needed, so I'm afraid it's not very good—"

"Shut up, Jessy," he said softly.

"I beg your pardon."

He faced her with the fabric clutched in his fist. "Shut up, Jessy. It's perfect."

Her face relaxed. "Then why are you trying to kill it?"

He glanced at his hand and relaxed his grip. She took the fabric from him and spread it across the workbench under the window, smoothing the creases with her hands. It wasn't half bad, considering what she'd had to work with.

Before her stretched a depiction of the Bingham farm, carefully embroidered in scavenged thread. The buildings were stitched in varying shades of brown, courtesy of Corrine's walnut dye. Ravelings from her dress fabrics had yielded varicolored greens for the trees and touches of red for accents. Due to the lack of proper embroidery floss or yarn, the variety of textures was unlike anything she'd ever seen, making the end result lively, satisfying, and unconventional. The farm itself looked different, too. Tidy and prosperous. The way she saw it in her mind and knew it could look in reality. Not a single building tilted. Not a board hung loose.

"I tried to think of the thing that meant the most to you, and finally decided it was this, your home. If you like the picture, you might want to hang it in your new cabin, but I'll understand if you don't."

Morgan blinked back a sheen of moisture so fast she wasn't sure she'd seen it. "I'll do that."

"Do you really like it?"

"Yes."

The suspicious gruffness in his voice told her more than his words. "I'm glad."

"Hellfire, Jessy!" He clenched his hands at his sides. "What are you trying to do to me?"

She cupped her hands around his fists. "I thought you'd figured it out by now. I'm trying to love you." Her softness surrounded and enclosed the quivering tension in his hands.

"You're tearing me apart," he groaned. "I don't know how much more I can take."

"Then stop fighting and give in."

As he searched her eyes, she sent him her message of love. He closed his eyes and groaned again. His hands burst from their gentle bonds, shooting out to grasp her shoulders and drag her into full contact with his hard body. He slid his fingers into her hair and clasped her head in a grip so tight it almost hurt.

A tiny gasp escaped her lips just before he smothered them with his. She felt as though he was trying to consume her whole, and at first, she recoiled from the unexpected intensity of his passion.

Almost immediately, she sensed a subtle shift. His fingers loosened their hold on her skull and wound through her hair, freeing the strands from their captivity. His lips never slowed their attack, but they gentled. His body still trembled, but with needs that went far beyond the physical.

She rose to meet those needs with all her heart.

He dragged his head away and stared at her with ravaged eyes. "You've given me so much, but I have nothing for you."

She gazed into his eyes, arms still wrapped around his waist, keeping their bodies close. "I only want one thing from you, and only when you're ready to give it."

"Oh, Jessy...I can't," he whispered, shaking his head. "I can't." His mouth came down hard on hers again, and she felt the struggle raging inside him.

She met his fevered assault head on, matching kiss for kiss, nip for nip. His hands slid from her hair to fondle the contours of her body, and she allowed herself the same freedom. Through his shirt she caressed the swells of his chest. Then her hands found their way around his sides to his back and down. When she squeezed the firm flesh, he jerked away.

"What do you think you're doing?"

She refused to be cowed. She was shameless where he was concerned and not the least bit repentant. "No more than you do to me. What's the matter? Don't you like it?"

He stared at her, his chest heaving. "No."

She raised her brows in disbelief. "You're trying to tell me you don't like the feeling of my hands on your body?"

"I swore I wouldn't do it, and I won't, no matter how much I want to." He sounded almost pained.

"Won't do what?"

"Haul you up that ladder and make love to you until neither of us can walk for a week."

A delicious shiver ran up her spine. A month ago, she'd vowed to make him wait, make them both wait, until he was ready to admit he loved her. Now she had trouble remembering why.

"Oh." Disappointment sounded in her voice.

"You want it too, don't you?" He paused for a moment, studying her face, then reached for her hand. "Come with me."

"Have you changed your mind?"

"No."

"Then why?"

"Come upstairs, and I'll show you." He half-dragged her to the ladder. When she hesitated, he placed one large hand under her bottom and gave her a boost to the second rung. "Go on. I'm right behind you."

She climbed the ladder and stepped onto the planks of the loft floor. He stepped up beside her.

"Now what?" she asked.

"Come over here." He took her hand and led her to the narrow bed.

She regarded him with a mixture of wariness and expectation. She wasn't sure what to make of his strange mood. He was visibly struggling for control, seething, yet not with anger.

"Take off your clothes" His voice was soft but laced with iron.

"W-what?"

He slid his hands to her upper arms. "I know what you're feeling." A shudder shook his frame, and his eyes closed for a second. "Believe me, I know. And I can help. But I don't want to ruin your dress, and what I want to show you will be much better without it."

She faltered, suddenly feeling shy. Disrobing in front of him was a far cry from both of them tearing each other's clothes off in the heat of mutual passion. He seemed fully in control after his brief lapse, and his control made her more uncomfortable than his anger.

"Let me help you." He turned her and unfastened the hooks down the back of her dress. In seconds, she stood shivering in her camisole and petticoats.

"These need to come off, too." He reached for the tapes at her waist. The petticoats sank to the floor, and she stepped out of them.

"Are you cold?"

She nodded and crossed her arms over her camisole.

"Come here." He pulled her into his arms. "I'll warm you up."

His mouth descended and caught hers in a hot, wet kiss that drove all thoughts of cold from her mind. Her lips parted the instant she felt the first probing of his tongue and welcomed him into her mouth. His tongue thrust and stroked against hers, and his hands began their conquest of the rest of her body. Her thin cotton camisole and drawers offered scant protection against the onslaught.

After what felt like an hour of sensual torture, her knees buckled, and she sagged against him. "Morgan, I can't stand it." Her voice was breathless and plaintive.

"I've barely started." He lowered his mouth to her straining breasts, sending fresh waves of desire rippling through her body.

When he eased her onto the bed but didn't touch her again, she opened her eyes and stared at him, standing in front of her. She reached out, wordlessly begging him to join her.

"No. This is for you."

He knelt before her and peeled her drawers down over her hips. What was he doing? Had he changed his mind about making love to her? He was still fully clothed.

Slowly, his head descended until his mouth touched her aching flesh.

She squirmed. "No...Morgan...what are you—?"

He raised his head. "Shh. Relax. Trust me." His head descended once more. The shocking actions of his lips and tongue drove all protest from her mind. All pretense of coherent thought dissolved like a spoonful of sugar in a cup of hot tea.

She quit fighting, and her hands moved to stroke his hair.

"That's right, just let it happen."

She couldn't stand it. She was going to die any second.

A series of tiny convulsions overtook her, leaving her limp but strangely wanting. She opened her eyes and saw him standing before her. His craggy features were tight and drawn, and his whole body shook.

"What about you?" she asked.

"No. This was just for you. Consider it a Christmas gift."

She sat up and dropped her gaze to his straining body. "I can't leave you like this."

"I'll live."

She reached for the buttons on his pants and began to pull them free.

He grabbed her wrist. "Jessy, no."

"Yes." She caressed him through the cloth. He released her hand, and she smiled an age-old smile of feminine satisfaction. "You want me."

While she spoke, she continued to work on his buttons. Her body clamored for his. Her earlier climax had been only a pale shadow of the powerful satisfaction she had experienced when they'd made love in the hunting cabin. She wanted that satisfaction again, and she wanted it now.

She lay back on the bed, drawing Morgan with her. "Come to me. Now."

"I shouldn't."

"Yes, you should."

He was too far gone to argue. "Feel what you do to me." He pressed against her. "I can't help myself."

She pushed back, and he groaned like a man stretched on the rack. One thrust joined masculine with feminine to complete the whole. She returned his passion with joy, and it was all he could bear. He stiffened, shuddered, and cried out, lost in the agony of ultimate ecstasy. With a soft cry of joy, she joined him in paradise.

Gradually, her thundering heart slowed. Jessy sighed. Morgan groaned and stirred. He rolled off and stared at her hard, his frown transforming into a scowl.

"Damnation, woman! Look what you made me do."

Chapter Fourteen

"What I made you do?" Jessy stared at him in disbelief. She levered herself onto her elbows and pushed a long strand of hair out of her face.

Morgan swung his legs over the side of the bed and sat up, raking his fingers through his hair. "I didn't want to do that. I swore it wouldn't happen again." He turned to her, his features angry and set. "You must be some kind of witch. All I have to do is touch you, and I forget everything else."

She felt as though he'd punched her in the stomach. It didn't matter that he was probably madder at himself than at her. How could he attack her that way? After the incredible intimacy of what he'd just done, of what she'd allowed him to do?

She mustered the shreds of her confidence and hid her hurt under a shell of outrage. "A witch! Don't try to tell me the attraction between us is all one-sided, that you're some poor, innocent boy, seduced against his will."

He stood with his back to her and buttoned his pants. "No, I'm not innocent, of anything. That's the point."

"What point? As usual, you're not making any sense."

Fully dressed, he turned back. She glared at him, ignoring that she wore nothing but her camisole.

"I'm not the man for you. You've got to face that fact and let this go. You'll only end up getting hurt."

Too late for that.

"And what about you?" she demanded. "How will you feel?"

"What I feel doesn't matter."

She rolled her eyes. "Will you stop trying to be so ridiculously noble?"

His bleak gaze hardened. "There's nothing noble about me. I'm the least noble man you'll ever meet."

"Of course. That's why you can't wait to get me alone at every possible opportunity, to take advantage of my naive infatuation to satisfy your own base desires without giving a thought to the consequences."

He tossed her drawers onto the bed. "Stop being melodramatic and get dressed."

She grabbed her undergarments but made no move to put them on. Her anger was real now, not just a cover-up for hurt feelings. She was so tired of his close-minded resistance to happiness she could scream. "You're serious, aren't you? You honestly believe we can never be happy together because you're not good enough for me."

"That's what I've been telling you for months."

"Well, guess what?" She thrust her feet into the legs of her drawers, stood, and shimmied them up her hips. "I'm tired of trying to convince you otherwise. You're so pigheaded you won't listen to anything I say. You won't even listen to your own heart." She jerked the drawstring at her waist. "I'm done. Finished." She stepped into her petticoats and tied them, too. "I'll write to my father to send someone for me as soon as you can take me into town."

"I don't know when that will be. I've got things to do."

"Well, if you're so all-fired anxious to get rid of me, you can make time." Her voice was muffled as she pulled her dress over her head. After shaking her skirts into place, she turned and lifted her bedraggled mass of hair. "If you'll be so kind as to help me with my hooks, I won't trouble you any further."

****

It was all Morgan could do to keep his touch impersonal when his fingers brushed the warm, bare skin of her back. He fumbled with the tiny hooks, trying to regain his concentration. Was this a ploy, or was she serious? Had he finally convinced her they could have no future together? More important—was she really planning to leave?

The words congealed in his brain, and a tight knot formed in his chest. The farm without Jessy—it was hard to imagine now. In the space of two short months, she had brought a sense of life and hope to the place unlike anything he could remember.

In his weaker moments, deep in the loneliest hours of the night, he allowed himself to dream of her. He dreamed of her standing on the front porch of the house he would build for her. He dreamed of her welcoming him with the teasing look in her emerald eyes that always set his blood boiling. He dreamed of her tending his fire, filling his bed, bearing his children.

But those were hopeless dreams. She couldn't stay. She had to leave. It was for her own good. He had no choice.

****

Jessy had mixed feelings about her decision to return to Weston, but Morgan had finally exhausted her patience. She was through waiting. Her leaving would either bring him to his senses, or she would have to accept that he had no senses.

Every day she asked when he would be free to take her to town and scoffed at his excuses. She made a point of reminding him of her intentions in front of the rest of the family. Sally looked hurt and Rachel seemed surprised, but they made no comment. Morgan just glowered. Corrine was the only one who said anything about her plans.

"Are you sure you want to go so soon?" she asked one night after supper. Jessy was drying the dishes, and Sally and Rachel sat by the fire mending. "We've all grown accustomed to having you here."

"It's time I was going." Jessy polished a cup with a flour-sack towel. "I no longer have any reason to stay." Morgan had left the cabin after the meal, depriving her of the opportunity for any more verbal salvos.

"I'm sorry you and Morgan couldn't come to an understanding." Corrine's brow furrowed, and she rubbed her swollen belly.

"Stubbornness and pride." Jessy shook her head. "That's all it is. Stubbornness and pride."

"I know what you mean." Corrine shifted in her chair. "Ooh."

Jessy set the cup down. "Is your back bothering you again? I'd be happy to rub it for you."

Corrine groaned. "That sounds lovely, but I don't think rubbing would solve the problem."

"Oh. Do you...that is..." Jessy's eyes widened. "Is it—"

"The baby? I think so. I've been having these pains in my back all afternoon. No matter what I do, they only seem to get worse."

Rachel had come to stand beside her daughter-in-law. She reached down with both hands and felt Corrine's hard belly. "Why didn't you say something earlier, child?"

Corrine shrugged. "I didn't want to worry anyone. Besides, it'll likely be hours yet. If you remember, Samuel took almost a full day."

Rachel glanced at her grandson, who stared at his mother's stomach, transfixed. "Samuel, you run and tell your daddy to get ready. The baby's coming."

His eyes widened. "For real? The baby?"

"Yes. You go tell him." She patted the boy to send him on his way and returned her attention to his mother. "Can you stand?"

"I think so, with a little help."

Jessy took one of Corrine's arms. Rachel held the other, and Sally watched with anxious anticipation. No sooner was Corrine on her feet than she doubled over, clutching her middle, and moaned louder. The floor at her feet turned dark, and a pool of liquid spread across the boards.

"My water..."

"Well, one thing's certain—this one won't take all day," Rachel said with brisk satisfaction. "Can you walk to your cabin, or shall I send for Morgan to carry you?"

"I...I think..."

"I'll take her." Morgan brushed his mother and Jessy aside and lifted Corrine gently.

Jessy had been so engrossed in the impending birth she hadn't noticed him come in.

"Samuel told me," he said by way of explanation, carrying Corrine toward the door.

Rachel, Jessy, and Sally followed him through the covered dogtrot to the cabin next door.

A big kettle of water hung over the blazing fire, and Ethan stood on his crutches beside the bed. His usual sneer had been replaced by a look of total concern concentrated on his wife, cradled in his brother's arms. "Everything's ready."

A hand-carved wooden cradle stood on the floor beside the big bed, ready to receive its new occupant. Jessy noticed the leather straps attached to the headboard, the pile of folded linens, and the sharp knife gleaming in the lamplight on the small table. She swallowed hard. The implements reminded her that birthing was a serious business, both momentous and perilous.

"The rest of you get on out of here now," Rachel said after Morgan laid Corrine on the bed. "Sally and I will take care of her. We'll call you as soon as there's any news."

Jessy was half-disappointed and half-relieved to be dismissed from the room.

Ethan's features took on a stubborn set. "I'm staying."

His mother shook her head. "You git, too. We'll call you when the baby comes."

"Corrine's my wife, and I'm staying with her." He didn't sound as much belligerent as determined.

Rachel glanced at Corrine, who nodded and reached for her husband's hand. "It's right for him to be here." Her eyes closed, and she squeezed Ethan's hand until it looked as if her knuckles would pop through the fragile layer of skin.

"All right. Now, out with the rest of you." Rachel shooed Jessy, Morgan, and Samuel out of the small cabin.

Evening dragged into night at a snail's pace. Jessy tried to ignore Morgan, who sat across from her staring into the fire, and concentrated her attention on Samuel. At first, he was so excited about the baby, he had trouble sitting still. But after an hour, then another, and then another passed, his excitement waned. Soon the little boy could no longer keep his eyes open. He fell asleep on Jessy's lap in the middle of a story about a princess and a frog.

Morgan stretched his legs, stood, and walked over to them. "I'll put him on the bed." He bent to lift the sleeping child.

Jessy shivered with a sudden chill when the boy's warm body left her lap. She stood and walked over to warm herself near the fire while Morgan laid the child on Rachel's bed and covered him with the quilt.

He joined her at the fireplace but was unable to keep still. He kept shifting his weight and rubbing his hands. "This is taking forever. Do you think it will be much longer?"

She frowned. She was concerned about Corrine, too, and his agitation wasn't helping. "How would I know?"

"Women are supposed to know about these things."

"Well, I don't." She turned and headed toward her chair. Morgan's hand on her shoulder spun her around.

"Jessy, that could be you in nine months. Don't you realize that?"

She had tried hard to keep the thought from her mind. The idea of giving birth was frightening, yet tempting at the same time. She opened her mouth to speak, but the door opened and Sally appeared. Her cheeks were flushed and her hair disarrayed, but her face glowed with happiness.

"It's here. The baby's born. It's a girl." She paused between words as if to catch her breath.

Morgan dropped his hand from Jessy's shoulder. "Thank God."

"Are they both all right?" Jessy asked. "Can we see them?"

Sally nodded. "Corrine's tired, and the baby's kind of little, but she's breathing. Ma says she's going to be fine. You can come in for a few minutes, if you want to."

Jessy glanced at the sleeping child on Rachel's bed. "I think we should wake Samuel to see his new sister."

Morgan walked to the bed, whispered something to the little boy, then lifted him, and they followed Sally to the cabin next door.

Corrine lay in bed, weak and pale, but smiling. Her long black hair had come unbound and curled damply away from her face.

Ethan sat next to her staring at the blanket-wrapped bundle in his arms. "A girl," he said in soft amazement. "I have a daughter."

Jessy leaned forward to peek at the newborn's red, wrinkled face and thick, black hair. "She's beautiful." And she was.

"Congratulations." Morgan's voice was oddly thick.

Ethan flinched when his brother's hand touched his shoulder, but all he said was, "Thank you."

"Samuel, honey, do you want to see your new sister?" Corrine beckoned to her son.

The little boy walked over and peered at the baby's sleeping face, studying it carefully. "She looks kind of puny."

His mother smiled. "So did you when you were born, but you grew and so will she."

"Do you have a name for her yet?" Jessy asked.

Corrine smiled at her new daughter. "Ella, after my grandma."

"That's lovely." Jessy straightened. "Now I think we should leave you to get some sleep. Will you be all right?"

"Ethan will see to us." Corrine glanced at her husband with love in her tired eyes.

Ethan handed the baby to her and rose. "That's right." A new pride rang in his voice, and he stood so straight Jessy almost didn't notice his crutches.

The days after Ella's arrival passed in a blur. Jessy was amazed at how one tiny scrap of humanity could keep so many people so busy. Ethan and Rachel insisted Corrine remain in bed to regain her strength. Ethan stayed with her most of the time, and Rachel and Sally saw to the household chores. Morgan took care of the livestock and hauled water from the springhouse. Jessy entertained Samuel and helped with the piles of laundry, which, thanks to Ella, could no longer wait for fair weather. She also took her turn walking the floor with the baby, who had developed a healthy set of lungs and an aversion to sleeping at night.

She'd never been close to a newborn before, and at first, the baby's fragility unnerved her. After a couple of weeks, however, she felt as comfortable with the infant as any experienced nurse. She loved Ella's whisper-soft skin and wide, unblinking blue gaze. She even loved the way the baby's silky black hair stood up on top of her head as if she'd just had a fright. In the small hours of the night, when the two of them were the only ones awake in the still house, it was not hard to think of the tiny girl as her own.

One afternoon, when a good stiff breeze and the threat of sun offered favorable drying conditions, she was behind the cabin wringing out sodden linens and pinning them to the clothesline with the wooden pins Ethan had whittled.

"You don't have to do that, you know."

She whipped around and hit Morgan square in the middle with a wet diaper. "You shouldn't sneak up on a person that way. You nearly scared me to death."

"I meant what I said. You don't have to work like this."

She turned and fastened the cloth to the line. "I'm glad to help. Your mother and Sally have too much work as it is, and it's getting harder for Sally every day."

In the past month, Sally's belly had blossomed. Now there was no mistaking her condition.

"What about you?"

She glanced at him in annoyance. "What about me?" She fished another diaper from the big washing kettle and wrung it out.

"You know what I mean."

"I do not."

"Are you going to look like Sally soon?"

She pinned the diaper next to its neighbor and turned to face him, hands resting on her hips. "Is that your delicate way of asking if I'm pregnant?"

He glanced away from her direct gaze. "Well, are you?"

Was she? Jessy didn't know. Her body had been acting a little strange lately, but sleep deprivation and hard work could do that to anyone. After getting to know little Ella, she half-hoped she was pregnant. However, her possible pregnancy wasn't the whole issue between them.

"What difference would it make to you?"

"Dammit, Jessy, I have a right to know if you're expecting my child."

"Maybe you do," she granted. "But what do you plan to do about it if I am?"

That stopped him. "I don't know."

"Well, you'd better think about that before you come asking questions you don't really want the answers to." She picked up the empty laundry basket and started back to the house.

Morgan stepped in front of her, blocking her path. "I want a straight answer from you, and I want it now. Are you, or are you not pregnant?"

She gave him a bland smile, but her eyes blazed. "I don't know. Is that straight enough?"

"You'll tell me as soon as you're sure." It was not a request.

"I'll do no such thing."

"You will."

"You can't make me."

He closed his eyes, drew a deep breath, and released it then opened his eyes. "Jessy, be reasonable. If you're pregnant, it's my responsibility to take care of you and the baby. You have to let me do it."

"I'm sorry, but that's not the way I see it. I won't marry you, baby or no, unless I'm convinced you want to marry me for myself, not just because you've decided I'm another of your responsibilities."

Morgan swore under his breath. "I'll never understand women. Here I am, offering to do the honorable thing, if necessary, and you won't let me."

If necessary. That made his feelings pretty clear.

"Don't do me any favors." She shot him an icy glare, hefted the willow laundry basket higher on her hip, and flounced around him into the house.

The next day, Morgan began work on his cabin.

Jessy was drying the breakfast dishes when she heard the rhythmic clanging echoing through the foggy morning air. She stopped and cocked her head. "Is Morgan chopping more wood?

That seemed unnecessary, given the enormous pile stacked against the side of the house.

Rachel continued stacking the clean plates on the shelf. "He said he was fixing to start his cabin today."

He'd mentioned he planned to build a home for himself several weeks ago. Jessy wondered if the timing was purely coincidental, or if his commencement of the project had anything to do with their conversation the day before.

A home of his own...maybe their own. She savored the tantalizing image for a moment before banishing it. She couldn't allow herself to indulge in such fantasy. Morgan had made himself clear. He would marry her for one reason and one reason only—to fulfill his responsibility as a father, should the need arise.

Well, she refused to sentence herself and any child she might bear to life with a hard, dour man who refused to acknowledge the basic human need to love and be loved. He could chop and hammer from now until doomsday, and it wouldn't change a thing.

All day long, the sounds of the axe bit into her consciousness, blow by blow. She busied her hands in an effort to distract her rebellious mind, but to no avail. She kept conjuring the image of a cabin, modest and tidy, but picturesque all the same, with a man and a woman inside, seated at a table, in front of the fire, sharing a bed. The man's features solidified into Morgan's, and the red-haired woman looked suspiciously familiar. The fact that the image was forbidden fueled its persistence. By the time dinner rolled around and Morgan appeared, damp and ready to eat, she was unable to force herself to remain silent and aloof.

"I hear you started your cabin today." She leaned over to set a plate of ham and grits in front of him. Her breast just missed his shoulder.

He lifted his chin, and mere inches separated their faces. "Umm-hmm. Figured it was time. Working alone, it'll take me several months to finish, and I might need it by then."

She glanced away from his probing gaze. "Perhaps you could find someone to help you, maybe one of your McTaggart cousins."

"I'd sooner ask a cottonmouth." Jabbing the ham with his fork, he missed the stricken look on his sister's face.

"Where did you decide to put your cabin?" Corrine asked, sensitive, as always, to tension in the family. She and Ella nestled in a pile of pillows in the big chair by the fire.

"Up the hill a piece," Morgan replied between bites. "When I clear a few more trees, you'll be able to see all the way to the river from the front porch."

"You're going to have a front porch? I hope you build a nice big one. When I was a little girl, I liked to play on the front porch with my brother and sisters." Corrine shifted Ella to her left arm and took a bite from the plate Jessy had set beside her on a small table.

"I'm going to make sure the place has plenty of room." Morgan's gaze followed Jessy as she sat across from him in Corrine's regular spot. "I plan to build two rooms on the first floor, with two more above."

"Sounds mighty grand for just one man," Rachel commented.

"Who knows?" Morgan shrugged. "The extra room might come in handy someday."

His mother glanced between Morgan and Jessy. "Do you two have something you want to tell us?"

"No," Jessy snapped.

She was furious at Morgan for turning the tables. It was one thing for her to needle him in front of the family about going home to Weston. It was another matter for him to make their lack of an understanding appear to be her fault. She wasn't sure what the exact distinction was, but she knew there was one.

Morgan's eyes danced, as if he were enjoying a private joke. "When I get the logs for the outer walls notched and hauled into place, I'll drive the wagon to the sawmill at Mack's Creek to get boards for the floors and inside walls. Maybe Ed'll have glass for the windows, too."

Jessy lifted her nose a fraction. She was too short to look down on him, but it gave her a shot of confidence. "Perhaps that would be a good opportunity for me to send the letter to my father."

A smile tickled the corners of Morgan's lips. "Maybe, but I'm not sure how you plan to get from Mack's Creek to Waynesville. It's nearly a hundred miles in the opposite direction."

"Oh."

"Your letter will have to wait—maybe until I get my cabin finished."

"But that could be months!"

"It could."

She couldn't stay here for several more months, not unless things between them changed drastically. "I don't know why you insist on trying to build the entire house by yourself."

"When I bought the cow from Newt Martin, he said he had a team of mules he might be persuaded to part with if he got a tempting offer. I plan to ride over to his place and tempt him."

"But it will still be just you and a team of mules, and they're just...well, mules."

"Sometimes there's a lot to be said for a strong back and a weak mind."

Her fingers tightened around the handle of her knife, and she sent Morgan a sweet smile dripping with poison. "Then the whole project should be a resounding success, with three strong backs and three weak minds working together."

His mouth opened but snapped shut when he saw the grins around the table. Jessy smiled. If nothing else, at least she had the satisfaction of the last word.

****

Ella's arrival seemed to energize Sally. Despite her growing awkwardness, she moved with purpose for the first time in months. She held the tiny baby as often as possible, cooing and smiling. She learned from Corrine how to bathe and dress the child and soon took over those chores to allow her sister-in-law to rest and regain her strength. Everything about the infant seemed to fascinate her. Even the hours of crying didn't seem to wear on her patience like they did everyone else's.

Ethan also appeared to have been deeply affected by his daughter's birth. Jessy was surprised by his supportive behavior toward Corrine during the delivery, and it hadn't ended there. While he hadn't quit drinking altogether, he had cut back a good deal. She never saw him in the morning, but he now spent most of the afternoon in front of the fire with his family, talking to his wife and whittling toys for the children. Jessy was so amazed by the transformation, she didn't mind sweeping the wood shavings from the floor around his feet.

One morning, when she and Samuel passed the barn on the way to the chicken coop, she heard a soft chopping sound coming through the open door. From up the hill, Morgan's voice shouted encouragement and curses at his new mules. Someone else must be in the barn. The women were occupied in the house, so that left only Ethan. She sent Samuel back to the house with the basket of eggs and poked her head through the open doorway of the barn.

She couldn't see anything in the dark building, but the sound was louder, a smooth, rhythmic scraping. She stepped inside and followed the sound. Behind the last stall, on a bench under a single small window, sat Ethan. Dust motes danced in the thin winter light, falling on his dark head bent in deep concentration. He held a flat piece of raw wood and shaved thin, fragrant curls from one side with a sharp chisel. Spread out on a length of old red flannel on the bench beside him was a set of chisels of varying sizes, obviously well-used and well-cared for.

She tiptoed around to the side to get a better look. It looked like…it had to be…it was. "Ethan, your violin!"

The sharp tool fell from his hand to the straw on the floor, and he twisted around. "Tarnation, woman! What are you trying to do? Make me cut off my fingers, too?"

"I'm sorry I startled you. I was just so surprised." She moved to stand in front of him. "You're working on the wood I gave you."

He bent to retrieve his chisel. "I was trying to. It's nothing. I just wanted to see if these were still sharp." He gestured to the neat row of chisels.

"Are they?"

"Seem to be."

"Where did you get them?"

"They were my grandpa's. He gave them to me before he died."

"The same man who made your violin?"

He nodded.

"Were you trying to make another one?"

"I told you, I just wanted to see if they were sharp." His sullen tone reminded her of the old Ethan, but when he raised his blue eyes to hers, their look was stark with pleading. "Don't tell anyone, please. I don't know if anything will come of this. I don't know if I can do it."

"Neither Morgan nor Corrine knows you've been working out here?"

He shook his head. "I don't want anyone to know, not yet."

"But Ethan, this is wonderful."

She had a sudden childish urge to march up to Morgan and thumb her nose. The thought brought a smile to her lips.

Ethan reached out and grabbed her wrist. "Promise me you won't tell anyone."

"I know they'd all be happy for you, but if you don't want me to tell anyone, I promise I won't."

"Good." He released her wrist.

"How much longer do you think it will take?"

He held the shell of the violin's face up to judge its thickness before shaving another smooth curl from the back. "I don't know. At least a couple of months. When this piece is done, I'll need to cut the back and the ribs and make a form to mold the ribs."

"Which parts are the ribs?"

"The sides." He ran his finger around the curved edges of the front. "They have to be very thin. I remember when I was little, watching Grandpa boil the strips of wood, then bend them around the mold until they dried and hardened. I wish I still had his mold."

"I'm sure Morgan would be glad to help you."

"No," Ethan snapped. "He has his own work. Besides, he thinks I'm just a worthless drunk, like Pa."

"Of course, he doesn't. You're his brother, and he loves you."

He ignored her comment. "The sorry part is, he's right."

She wanted to knock him in the head. What was it about these Bingham men that made them so blind to their own characters?

"You are no such thing, Ethan Bingham, and I won't hear any more talk like that. You were injured and you've suffered, but you have a fine family who loves and needs you, and you're working to find a way to take care of them."

He regarded the wood in his hand with skepticism. "I don't see how."

The kernel of an idea began to sprout in Jessy's mind. "You just worry about finishing that violin and leave the rest to me. If it works out, I think I have a plan to help you support Corrine and the children, no matter how many legs you have."

She whistled all the way back to the house. She had a good feeling about Ethan and his chances for the future. Even though he was only taking the first steps toward making a new life, she had every hope for his success. And she meant to do everything in her power to help him.

The minute she stepped into the house, she knew something was wrong. Corrine clutched Ella, who wailed piteously, and Samuel clung to her side. Before Jessy had a chance to ask any questions, Rachel pounced on her.

"Where have you been?"

Her accusatory question took Jessy aback. "Out in the barn."

"Did you see Sally?"

"No. What's the matter?"

Rachel turned away and rubbed her hands on her apron. "We've looked everywhere. She's gone."

Chapter Fifteen

"Are you sure?" Jessy didn't want to believe Sally had run away again, not nearly six months pregnant, not in the middle of February. "She was here when Samuel and I went out to gather eggs."

Rachel twisted the towel in her bony hands. "When I came back from helping Corrine take a bath, Sally was gone and all her clothes with her."

"She must have run to Will."

Rachael nodded. "I don't doubt it. I'd better send Samuel for Morgan."

"No, no. Don't do that. The last time Morgan went to the McTaggarts' place we were all lucky to get home in one piece. He and Mr. McTaggart don't have a very cordial relationship."

"No one could, with that crazy old coot."

"I'll go alone. I remember how to get there, and I don't think the boys will shoot an unarmed woman."

"Probably not, but you never can be too careful around Zeke. That boy never did have a lick of sense."

Jessy considered her previous encounter with Zeke in the cave. He was overgrown, strong as an ox, and not overly bright, but he didn't seem mean or violent, except in defense of his father.

"I'll be careful," she promised. "But I think I'd better change clothes first."

Sally might be familiar enough with the woods to make her way up the mountain to the McTaggarts' place in a dress, but Jessy needed her pants and boots on the slippery, winding path. A few minutes later, she stood before Rachel and Corrine, transformed into a slender, if somewhat curvy, boy.

"Now don't mention this to Morgan." She pulled on her jacket and tucked her hair under her battered brown hat. "I want a chance to talk to Mr. McTaggart alone. I'm sure I can make him see that Sally and Will belong together, and it's time to let go of the past. If I'm successful, Morgan need never know Sally and I were gone."

Rachel clucked her tongue. "As much as I hate to see my girl hooked up with that bunch, I suppose Will isn't such a bad boy, but I wouldn't count on reason where Dermott McTaggart is concerned. If you and Sally aren't back by suppertime, I'll have to tell Morgan."

"I know." Jessy opened the door.

"Good luck," Corrine called.

Jessy flashed a rueful smile. "Thank you. I have a feeling I'll need it."

She trudged through the woods, rustling the dried leaves on the path and generally making as much noise as she could. She figured she would be safer if the McTaggarts heard her coming. With luck, they wouldn't shoot first and investigate later. At any rate, she wasn't armed and she wasn't experienced enough to sneak up on them, so she would have to take her chances.

As she tramped along the narrow path leading to the clearing with the thong tree, she considered how to sway Dermott McTaggart on the subject of his youngest son marrying a Bingham. Any right-thinking man would take one look at Sally's condition and insist on an immediate wedding, but Dermott's long-standing hatred for the Binghams had clouded whatever reason he might possess.

The woods were quiet except for the crackling leaves beneath Jessy's boots. She was so far from the Bingham homestead, she no longer heard the sound of Morgan's axe or his voice shouting at the mules. Only the occasional call of a bird hidden in the trees reminded her she was not the only living thing for miles. As she neared the clearing, she noticed another sound.

Tap...tap...tap, tap...tap, tap, tap, tap.

Tiny pellets of ice fell from the sky and hit the leaves on the forest floor. She hunched her shoulders, trying to keep the sleet from going down the back of her neck.

She raced into the clearing and made a dash for the shelter of the thong tree. The sleet was coming down faster, and the little balls of ice stung her cheeks as she ran. Unfortunately, without its blanket of leaves, the big tree offered little protection from the elements. Shivering, she scanned the ring of trees surrounding the clearing. She needed to find the other path, the one leading to the McTaggart farm.

The sleet obscured her vision, so she followed her memory, searching the edge of the clearing until she stumbled across a narrow trail. When the path headed up the side of the mountain, she felt confident she was headed in the right direction.

The higher she climbed, the colder she got. The sleet that collected on her hat and in the folds of her jacket began to melt, and the damp chill seeped into her bones. Her cheeks were raw from the constant barrage of tiny stinging pellets. She wished the ice would change to snow. It might be just as wet, but at least it was softer.

She also wished she had a better idea of the distance to the McTaggart farm. The last time, she'd been scared half out of her wits and hadn't paid close attention. Her breath formed clouds of mist before her eyes, and each step felt like she was wearing lead boots.

"Stop right there."

Jessy let out a shriek, and her heart skipped a beat as Zeke materialized in front of her with his rifle pointed straight at her nose. He approached slowly, squinting from under the brim of his hat. He stopped and lowered the barrel of his rifle. "It's you."

She managed a shaky laugh. "Yes, Zeke, it's me. I'm looking for Sally."

"We knew someone would come, but Pap figured it would be Morgan."

"Morgan doesn't know she's gone yet."

Zeke tilted his head and regarded her, then nodded. "I 'spect you'd better come on up to the house."

"Thank you." Jessy was grateful both for a guide and the promise of warmth and shelter from the storm. Zeke surprised her by taking her arm to help her over the rough places. Unlike their first meeting in the cave, this time he handled her like a delicate porcelain figurine. When they reached the cabin, she was surprised again to discover that Jonah had fallen in behind her somewhere along the trail.

Zeke opened the door. "Guess who I brung, Pap."

Dermott McTaggart rose from his chair and glowered. "What are you doing with Morgan's woman?"

"Found her on the trail."

"Is she alone?"

"Says so, and I didn't see no one else."

Dermott eyed Jessy. "She looks near ruint. You'd better come over here by the fire, girl."

Jessy shivered. "Thank you, Mr. McTaggart." She walked to the fire and removed her sodden hat and coat. Rivulets of water ran onto the plank floor.

"I'll take those." Zeke stepped forward and relieved Jessy of her wet hat and coat. He draped them over the back of a chair next to the fire.

She smiled. Somewhere under all that dirt and hair lurked the heart of a gentleman. She rubbed her hands together, trying to get the feeling back.

"What have you got to say for yourself, girl?" Dermott McTaggart demanded.

"I came to see Sally, and to talk to you."

"She ain't here."

Jessy turned and narrowed her eyes. Was he lying and if so, why?

"She ain't been here, neither," Dermott continued, "and Will's gone. No one's seen him since breakfast."

The conclusion was obvious. They must be together somewhere, but where?

****

Morgan loped through the woods, his rifle poised in one hand. Once again, Jessy had rushed off without thinking. She wasn't stupid, but her impulses often led to situations where her sharp mind offered little protection. And now she had walked, alone and unarmed, straight into that den of wolves.

To be honest, the McTaggarts probably wouldn't hurt her, they'd have no call to, but he wouldn't relax until she was safe in his keeping again.

And Sally. He could only pray Will had the strength and good sense to take care of her.

Morgan had noticed Sally and Jessy were missing as soon as he came in, driven inside by the weather and the truculence of the mules. His mother was so worried she hadn't tried to hide the truth. Jessy and Sally were gone. Both of them. Gone to the McTaggarts.

Damnation.

The sleet made the path treacherous underfoot. He only hoped it would keep Zeke and Jonah inside. He was in no mood for a scuffle with his gun-toting cousins.

****

Jessy sat beside the fire sipping a cup of coffee provided by Zeke. Her jacket and hat hung from the posts of a ladderback chair nearby, drying in the heat radiating from the crackling flames. She glanced up when the hinges of the cabin door squeaked. A second later the door burst open, slamming against the wall. She let out a startled shriek and spilled the remnants of her coffee.

Morgan stood in the doorway, legs spread wide, rifle pointed at the occupants of the room. "Nobody move."

Everyone stared until Zeke and Jonah took a step toward him.

"Dammit! I said nobody move. I don't want to shoot, but I will."

Jessy set her empty cup down with a clatter. "Morgan Bingham, put that thing down right now. We have enough to worry about without you shooting someone."

Zeke's bearded face began to twitch. Soon his massive shoulders shook. If she didn't know better, she would swear the enormous man was giggling. "Zeke," she admonished in a sharp tone.

"Yes'm." He hung his head sheepishly but couldn't banish the lingering traces of a smile.

Morgan lowered his rifle. "Are you all right?"

She smiled inside. He'd come to rescue her. He cared for her, whether he wanted to admit it or not. "Of course, I'm all right. I was just discussing with your uncle and cousins how to begin the search for Will and Sally."

Morgan leaned his gun against the wall and took off his hat. "They're both missing?"

"Yes, and we assume they're together. We're just not sure where."

Morgan glanced at Jonah. "Did you check the barn?"

His cousin nodded. "All the horses and the wagon are still there."

"They must be on foot." Morgan paced in front of the fireplace. "They've been gone several hours, but in this weather, they couldn't get far, not with Sally in her condition."

"There's the hunting cabin," Jessy suggested. "She knows where that is, doesn't she?"

"Yes, but it's too far, and the climb would be too hard for her."

"Well, think." Jessy glanced from one man to the next. "Are there any neighbors they might have gone to, or any place closer where they might take shelter?"

Dermott shook his wooly head. "The Bingham place is the closest, and you know how far that is."

Zeke's eyes lit. His bulk quivered with the excitement of an idea. "The caves. They might be in the caves."

Morgan rubbed his jaw and regarded his ursine cousin. "You know, Zeke, you just might have something there."

"Do you mean the caves where we met you, Zeke?" Jessy asked.

Zeke's face reddened beneath his bushy beard. "That's a right polite way of putting it, Miss Jessy."

Morgan reached for his rifle. "Let's move. We've only got about an hour of daylight left."

Zeke and Jonah started toward the door. Jessy plucked her hat and coat off the back of the chair, but Morgan stopped her. "You stay here with Dermott. The weather's terrible, and I don't want to have to worry about two women."

She buttoned her coat and stuffed her hair under her hat. "Don't be silly. I'm coming. You want Sally and Will to come back with you, don't you?"

He frowned, and she let out an exaggerated sigh. "None of you is well known for his patience or powers of persuasion." She glanced sharply from man to man. No one argued.

She pulled on her gloves. "I'm coming to make sure Will and Sally know their families have their best interests at heart and are willing to compromise in order to ensure their future happiness."

"What?" Dermott McTaggart roared.

She whirled and fixed him with an angry glare. "Mr. McTaggart, Will and Sally are determined to be together. The only solution to this situation is for you to drop your opposition to their marriage. To do otherwise will only result in serious risk to them both, as well as your grandchild."

Dermott towered over her. "I'll never see my boy wed to a daughter of that—"

"That's quite enough, Mr. McTaggart." Jessy assumed her sternest schoolmarm voice and pointed an admonishing finger at his chest.

Dermott McTaggart stared at her, dumbstruck. She guessed no one had ever spoken to him in that tone—certainly not his sons, from what she'd seen.

"Fine." She gave a brisk nod. "Now, I suggest we leave before we find ourselves in complete darkness. You may come or not."

"I'll come," Dermott grumbled, but his expression simmered with outrage. He shoved his way past his sons and through the door. "Jonah, Zeke, get a couple of lanterns from the barn in case we don't find them before dark."

The boys returned, kerosene lanterns in hand, to join Morgan, Jessy, and Dermott at the head of the trail. Morgan settled his hat lower against the weather and set off in the lead before anyone could object.

The sleet had piled up nearly an inch and was still coming down. Where it fell on warmer surfaces, such as stone or wood, it melted and fused into a treacherous coating of ice. Several times, she would have crashed to the ground had it not been for Zeke's steadying grasp. Each time her footing slipped, he reached out a long arm and snared her until she regained her balance. For such a huge man, he had amazingly quick reflexes. She allowed herself a tiny smile at Zeke's actions. One might almost think the oaf liked her.

By the time they reached the thong tree clearing, she could barely make out the outline of the men ahead of her.

Morgan halted. "We'd better light those lanterns now. "Zeke, hand me yours and I'll lead. Jonah, you bring up the rear with the other."

The lanterns didn't put out much light. They did a wonderful job illuminating the falling sleet but obscured most everything else.

"It's going to be hard to see, even with the lanterns." Jessy peered ahead, remembering how much trouble she'd had on the same trail in broad daylight.

"You should have thought of that before you insisted on coming," Morgan replied. "I told you to stay in the cabin."

She set her jaw. She had nothing to gain by arguing with him. True, the conditions were miserable, but if the men could make it, so could she. Besides, Will and Sally would need someone on their side when the group caught up with them.

Morgan shot her a glance, then picked up his rifle and set off down the winding path to the caves overhanging the river.

The increasing slope and hazardous footing forced the members of the search party to concentrate their attention on the narrow path, lit only by the soft glow of the lanterns at either end of the line. Jessy followed Morgan, with Zeke behind her and his father and brother bringing up the rear. Because Zeke had to focus on keeping himself upright, he no longer offered his hand every time she slipped. She skidded down the slippery trail, nearly falling twice as she tried to match Morgan's pace.

The roaring of the river grew louder. They must be nearing the caves. She prayed they would find Will and Sally there, partly because she hated to think of them alone and unsheltered in the storm at night and partly because she doubted she could go much farther.

Morgan stopped on a flat limestone ledge, and the others slid to a halt behind him. He tucked his rifle under his arm, cupped his hand to his mouth, and called out, "Will…Sally… are you here? We've come to help!"

They listened. It was hard to hear anything over the rushing sound of the water. Jessy tried not to think about the sheer drop lurking just beyond the narrow circle of light cast by the lanterns.

Then they heard it. A small sound, difficult to distinguish. Morgan called again. "Will…Sally…it's Morgan. Are you there?"

The sound came again. Faint, but louder this time. "Help. Help me."

Jessy couldn't tell whose voice it was, but it had to be one of them. "We're coming!"

Her sudden exclamation startled Morgan, and the lantern slipped from his grasp. It crashed to the ground, extinguishing the light and splintering the glass into tiny pieces.

Jessy screamed and grabbed for him in the sudden darkness. She clung to him like moss on a rock.

He clutched her to his chest. "Are you all right? Not cut anyplace?"

"I-I don't think so."

He loosened his hold but kept one arm wrapped around her. "Jonah, I need the other lantern." He handed Jessy his rifle. "Here, hold this in your left hand and give me your right. The footing is treacherous up ahead."

She clasped his hand in gratitude. The footing ahead was bad? She'd barely made it this far without breaking a leg.

The group moved forward single file, and Morgan continued to call out to Will and Sally. The faint replies grew louder as the searchers inched their way along the sleet-slicked rock ledge above the river. Finally, they rounded a bend and saw Will standing outside the entrance to the big cave where Jessy and Morgan had first encountered Zeke.

He waved his arms. "Hurry! Sally's hurt."

Morgan dropped Jessy's hand and bounded forward, leaving the others to follow in the dark. He disappeared into the cave, and the light disappeared with him.

"Here, Miss Jessy, take my hand. I'll help you."

It was Zeke. Jessy couldn't see a thing. She pictured the narrow ledge and thought how easy it would be to stumble over the cliff to the river below. She raised her hand in front of her, and Zeke's big paw swallowed it up. His idea of guiding was to drag her behind as he marched into the inky blackness. It was her good fortune that he was strong and surefooted. In a matter of minutes, they stood at the mouth of the cave.

This time, she didn't hesitate to go in. She didn't stop to consider the confines of the space or the dank smell of the air. She didn't even notice the immediate reprieve from the sleet. She saw only Sally, lying on the dirt floor, pale and still.

She rushed in and knelt beside her. Morgan was already crouched down, checking his sister's slender throat for a pulse. Will stood beside her with a look of agony on his young face, and his father and brothers crowded around.

Morgan sat back on his heels.

"Is she...?" Jessy was unable to put her worst fears into words.

"She's alive, and she doesn't seem to have any fever." Emotion adding a rough edge to Morgan's voice. He glared at Will. "What happened?"

Will looked as though he were going to cry. "She came this morning...found me in the barn milking...said she'd run away to join me. I—I didn't have any place to take her. I couldn't take her into the house, not with Pap, not after what happened last time."

Jessy glared at Dermott McTaggart, who was staring, transfixed, at the body of the girl whose only transgression had been to love his son.

"How did she get here?" Morgan demanded.

"I thought she could wait here. I thought maybe I could get some things from the house and we could go away somewhere together. I don't know what I thought." Will covered his eyes with his hand.

Jessy's heart went out to him. He was so young. They were both so young. She stood and reached for his other hand, giving it a squeeze. "Don't worry. She's going to be all right. We'll take care of her."

Will sniffed.

Morgan stared at the slight rise and fall of Sally's chest as though it might stop if he glanced away. "What happened? Did she faint?"

Will rubbed his eyes and gazed back down. "She slipped on the trail and fell. She might have hit her head. I don't know. I carried her in here, and she's been like this ever since."

"When did it happen?"

"A couple of hours ago, maybe more. It seems like forever."

Morgan felt Sally's face, then her limp hands. "She's chilled. We'll be lucky if she doesn't end up with lung fever."

"What about the baby?" Will asked.

Morgan gave him a long, hard look. "That's the least of our worries now."

"We've got to get her out of this cave and back to the house," Jessy said. "Your mother will be worried sick."

Morgan stood, never taking his eyes off his sister. "It'll be dangerous as hell, trying to get back up the mountain carrying her, but we have to do it. We can't leave her here."

Dermott spoke for the first time. "The boys and I will make a litter. Come on." He turned and strode from the cave, followed by Zeke and Jonah.

Jessy stared into the darkness where the three men had disappeared. "They left us the lantern. How will they be able to do anything out there?"

"Don't worry about Pap and the boys," Will replied. "They know every inch of this mountain. They don't need to see."

He was right. Several minutes later, the men were back with a crude, but effective, stretcher fashioned from stout branches and vines. Three coats draped across the framework to form the body of the sling.

Jessy stared at the men, all coatless now. "You gave up your coats for her."

Zeke shrugged his hulking shoulders. "We don't want her to die."

She could have hugged him. "Of course, you don't." She glowed at the men standing around her. "Everything is going to work out fine."

"We haven't got her home yet," Morgan reminded her.

Morgan and Will lifted Sally as gently as possible, while Zeke and Jonah slid the litter under her.

"Just a minute." Jessy unbuttoned her coat. "Let me put this over her. She needs to be covered."

Morgan jerked her coat back over her shoulders. "You keep that on. One sick woman is enough. She can wear mine." He shrugged out of his coat and draped it over the unconscious form of his sister.

"Mine, too." Will quickly added his to the pile.

Now, all five men were coatless, but Sally looked as snug as a caterpillar in a cocoon. Morgan carried the lantern to the cave entrance, and Jessy followed. Will bent and picked up the front of the litter, while Zeke lifted the rear poles. Morgan nodded and led the way out of the cave.

With the falling temperatures of evening, the sleet had turned to snow. As soon as they stepped outside, crystals began to pile up on sleeves and hat brims and in the older McTaggarts' beards. Sally's pale face was exposed, so Jessy pulled Morgan's jacket up to protect her on the long trip home.

And it was a long trip. Long, cold, slippery, and miserable. Jessy had to hold onto the back waistband of Morgan's pants to keep her balance on the way back up the hill. Behind her, Will and Zeke plodded along, bearing their precious burden easily, with the sure steps of true mountain men. Jonah and Dermott brought up the rear.

All the way back, she fretted about Sally. No sound came from the stretcher behind her, not a moan, or even a sigh. With each step, she prayed Sally would be all right. Once, Morgan stopped to give Will and Zeke a chance to adjust their grip on the rough poles since both had refused Dermott's and Jonah's offers to spell them. As soon as the line halted, Jessy turned and lifted the coat to check on Sally. The girl lay as still as ever.

By the time they reached the clearing around the Bingham homestead, Jessy could barely stand. Her feet were numb, and her legs felt as limp as wet dishrags.

"You run on ahead and tell Ma we've got her," Morgan said.

The knowledge that Rachel had been waiting hours for news of her daughter spurred Jessy across the yard and up the front steps. She opened the door, and Rachel rushed toward her.

"We found her. They're coming with her." Jessy collapsed on the bench next to the table.

Rachel ran to the door as Morgan entered, followed by all four McTaggarts with Sally on the stretcher. She stared at the still, covered figure.

"Don't worry, Ma. She's alive." Morgan pulled his coat away from his sister's face.

Jessy held her breath and gazed at Sally. The girl had appeared pale in the cave and on the trail, but in the brighter light of the cabin, she looked much worse. Her skin was gray, and no sound of breath issued from her blue-tinged lips.

Jessy feared Sally had sacrificed her life and that of her unborn child to her family's stubborn refusal to heal old wounds.

Chapter Sixteen

"You killed her," Rachel whispered. She spun to face Dermott McTaggart. "You killed my baby!" Her voice rose to a wail, and she pounded the big man's chest with her fists, screaming her accusation. "You killed her! You killed her!"

"Ma, no." Morgan wrapped his arms around his mother, pulling her back. He held her until her struggles ceased and she collapsed against him.

"He did it because of me...because of how much he hates me." Rachel sobbed.

"Dermott didn't do anything, Ma. He helped us find Sally and bring her home."

Rachel tossed her head back and forth in denial. "She never would have run away if it hadn't been for him—him and his son."

"Mrs. Bingham," Jessy interrupted in an urgent voice. "Come here." She had thrown the coats off Sally's body and unbuttoned the top buttons on her dress. "Look. Look at her chest. I think it's moving."

Rachel shoved her way out of Morgan's arms and rushed to her daughter. Sure enough. The movement was slow and almost imperceptible, but it was there. Sally was alive.

The realization energized her. "Lay her over there on the bed. I need to get these damp clothes off her. And blankets. Morgan, get me all the extra blankets from the chest."

The men hurried to do her bidding. They transferred Sally from the litter to the bed, and Morgan placed her head on the pillow. "Will said she fell and hit her head, Ma. That might be why she's still unconscious."

"Hold the lamp closer." Rachel leaned over and examined Sally's head, moving the lustrous black hair aside to search for injuries. "Here it is." She pointed to a large purple swelling with a deep, oozing cut across it.

Will hovered over Sally. "Will she wake up and get better?"

"I don't know." Rachel shook her head. "I've seen better, and I've seen worse. I've seen some recover, and I've seen some die. Only time will tell."

"What about the baby?"

"It's too soon to say."

"I want to stay with her."

Rachel straightened and looked him square in the eye. "She's like this because of you, boy. I don't want you in my house."

"But I love her, and she's carrying my baby."

"And she may die because of it."

Morgan stepped forward, placing a hand on Will's shoulder. "I think you'd better leave, Will." He glanced at Dermott, Zeke, and Jonah. "You, too. Thanks for your help."

"I won't go." Will shrugged off Morgan's hand. "Not 'til she wakes up, and I know she's going to be all right."

"We'll let you know when she comes around. Now, go on home. There's nothing more you can do for her here."

"I won't." Will's young face was set in stubborn lines that mirrored his older cousin's.

"Sally tried to tell me you were different," Rachel said, "but I see you're just as mulish and ornery as the rest of the McTaggarts."

Dermott sputtered, and his face reddened beneath his beard. "I've taken all I'm going to take from you, you murdering jezebel!"

Morgan moved toward his uncle.

Jessy glanced from his hands to his face and threw herself between the two men. "Stop this right now, all of you!"

Rachel and the men stared at her.

She took advantage of their attention to say something that had been brewing in her brain for some time. "Do you think this will do Sally any good? She needs love and support right now. The best thing you can do for her is to end this ridiculous feud."

"Jessy," Morgan warned, "this is none of your business."

She refused to back down—there was too much at stake. "I will not stand by and watch Will and Sally's lives ruined by an argument so old I doubt anyone can remember what it's about."

"I remember well enough." Dermott waved his hand wildly toward Rachel. "She murdered my brother, David—her and that backshooting scum, Caleb Bingham."

Jessy straightened, and the fact that Dermott towered over her by at least a foot didn't dissuade her one whit. In her days as a teacher, she had cowed a room of rowdy teenage boys merely by using the proper tone of voice. For all his blustering, Dermott McTaggart didn't frighten her. "Mr. McTaggart, there will be no more name-calling. If you cannot control yourself, I will have to agree with Rachel and insist that you leave."

Dermott ignored her and pointed an accusing finger at Rachel. "She knows what she done! Just ask her."

All eyes turned to Rachel. She seemed to shrink before them.

"I never would have hurt David. Never. I loved him." Her voice was no more than a whisper.

"You lured him to the cliffs where Bingham was waiting to push him off," Dermott accused.

"No, no." Rachel shook her head, and tears welled in her eyes. "I asked him to meet me because I wanted to tell him we needed to marry soon, even if we had to run away. I wanted to tell him I was expecting his child."

Her words tapered to a choking sob, and long moments passed before she raised her gaze to her oldest son. "Caleb was pestering my pa something awful to let him marry me, but I kept putting him off. He had money in those days—Lord only knows where he got it—and David had nothing, so Pa favored Caleb."

Rachel straightened and faced her former lover's furious brother. "In all these years, I've never told anyone what happened that day. You can choose to believe me or not, but it's time you knew the truth."

Dermott scowled, but she continued, staring ahead as if in a trance. "Caleb must have followed me that day. I never knew he was there. When David came to meet me at our favorite place on the bluff, Caleb charged out of the brush like a wild razorback and pushed him over the edge of the cliff into the river. David and I were both so stunned, neither of us had time to fight back."

Her eyes closed, and tears slid from beneath her sparse lashes.

Dermott snorted. "You married his murderer quick enough."

She opened watery brown eyes filled with pain. "I was young and weak. I was afraid of Caleb's meanness. I was afraid of what Pa would do to me when he found out about the baby. David wasn't even cold in his grave when Caleb went to Pa again and got permission to wed me. I agreed because I didn't care anymore. David was gone, and I just didn't care." Rachel's thin frame shook with silent sobs.

Then she stiffened, and a flash of fire lit her eyes. "But I paid for my part in what happened, don't you think I didn't. Every day I spent as Caleb Bingham's wife, I paid."

Jessy shuddered, remembering Morgan's story of Caleb's death. For nearly twenty years the family suffered from the man's drunken violence, and probably no one more than Rachel. The time had come to end the legacy.

"Mrs. Bingham, Mr. McTaggart, can't you see what you're doing? By continuing the hatred between your families, you're forcing Will and Sally to repeat the tragedy you suffered all those years ago. Is that what you want for them?"

Dermott and Rachel remained silent, eyeing each other warily.

She tried again. "I know it will be hard to give up feelings you've held for so long, but it's the only way. Caleb Bingham is gone, and there's no reason to let his ghost ruin the lives of your children."

Rachel's shoulders slumped. "I suppose you're right, but it's really up to him." She gestured toward Dermott.

"Mr. McTaggart?" He was lucky she didn't have a ruler. If he continued his stubborn resistance, she'd like to rap his knuckles.

Dermott let out an explosive breath. "Maybe it weren't her fault, after all. Anyhow, nothing's going to bring my brother back."

"No," Jessy agreed, "but you still have his son. Perhaps if you let yourself get to know him, you might find some of your brother there."

Dermott peered at Morgan's face from beneath his bushy brows. "You always was his spittin' image."

"Maybe the resemblance is more than skin-deep," Jessy suggested. "You'll never know unless you try."

"You willing, boy?"

Morgan regarded his uncle. Finally, without a word, he stuck out his hand. Dermott clasped it in his huge grasp, and the two shook.

Jessy beamed. "Now, is everyone agreed that Will and Sally can marry as soon as she's able?" She refused to acknowledge the possibility that Sally might not recover.

"I'm willing," Rachel said. "When she's well."

Dermott nodded.

"Good." Jessy smiled at the McTaggart men. "Now why don't you gentlemen stay to supper so everyone can get to know each other better, and we can discuss plans for the wedding?"

Morgan frowned. "Jessy, you're pushing this too far. Don't you think you've done enough tonight?"

"Not at all. This family has twenty-seven years to make up for. I'll take care of supper while Rachel tends to Sally. You can help me." She turned back to Dermott and his sons. "Will you stay?"

"We'll not stay where we're not wanted," the old man grumbled.

"I'm sure you're welcome here." Jessy jabbed Morgan in the side with one sharp elbow. "Aren't they?"

He grunted. "Uh, sure." The creases between his brows deepened to furrows, but he acquiesced. "Stay for supper."

Dermott agreed, perhaps because Will was so reluctant to leave Sally while she was unconscious. After Rachel bundled her into a fresh nightdress and tucked her into bed, Will refused to leave her side, even to eat. Jessy set Morgan to work minding a large venison roast on the iron spit while she and Corrine prepared the rest of the meal.

Supper was civil enough, but she was amazed by the enormous quantity of food consumed by the McTaggart men, particularly Dermott and Zeke. Of course, they didn't get to be the size of small mountains by picking at their victuals. Sally remained unconscious, but as she warmed, her breathing and color improved, which Rachel pronounced to be an encouraging sign.

"When she's well, I can ride to Camdenton for the preacher," Zeke offered, shoveling another forkful of venison between grease-slicked lips.

Morgan glanced at his mother for her reaction. "Ma?"

Rachel nodded. "It's only right they should have a preacher. We'll have the wedding here."

Dermott eyed the large single room of the cabin. "Has anybody thought about where they're going to live after the wedding? There sure enough ain't no extra space here, and our place don't have privacy for a couple of newlyweds, especially not with a baby on the way."

Morgan set down his fork. "I've started work on another cabin up the hill a'ways. Only the walls are up, but if you boys are willing to help, we can finish it for Will and Sally in a month."

"I can't let you do that." Dermott pursed his lips. "Tell you what, I'd be willing to give Will ten acres of the meadow that runs between our properties down toward the river, if you'd do the same for Sally. That way they'd have a nice twenty-acre parcel to start on, right between both holdings. I'll send Zeke around with a call to the kinfolk, and we'll have enough men here to raise a cabin in one day." He rested his meaty elbows on the table and regarded his nephew. "What do you say?"

Jessy's heart lifted with every word. It was the perfect compromise. But would Morgan bend enough take it? She stared him, trying to read his thoughts, but his expression remained closed.

Finally, he nodded. "That sounds fair to me."

Dermott thrust his big hand forward, and Morgan shook it again to seal their bargain.

After two long days and even longer nights, Sally regained consciousness. Each member of the family had taken a turn in the vigil at her bedside, worrying more as every hour passed without change. Only Rachel remained confident her daughter would awaken from her unnatural sleep.

At Sally's first moans, Jessy abandoned her sewing and rushed to the bed where Rachel bent over her daughter. Corrine eased Ella onto her shoulder and pushed up from her chair to come, too, with Samuel in silent attendance.

"Is she awake?" Jessy asked.

Sally moaned again and tried to move her stiff, bruised limbs.

"She's trying," Rachel replied.

Sally's eyes fluttered open. She worked to focus on her mother's face. "Ma?" Her voice came out as a faint croak.

Rachel smoothed her daughter's tangled hair. "It's all right, child."

"Wh-what happened?"

Rachel glanced at Jessy and Corrine before answering. "You fell and hit your head, but you're going to be fine."

"Where's Will?" Sally's blue eyes searched the room. She tried to sit up but fell back. "I want Will." Tears pooled in her eyes and spilled over.

Jessy patted her pale, slender hand. "As soon as we tell him you're feeling better, he'll be here before you can blink. I'll fetch him myself." She squeezed Sally's hand. "Samuel, why don't you run and tell your pa and Uncle Morgan that Aunt Sally's awake."

Samuel raised questioning eyes to his mother. Corrine smiled and nodded. He raced across the room and out the door so fast he nearly knocked Jessy down. She laughed and followed him outside.

As she predicted, Will dropped everything the minute she told him about Sally and took off for the Bingham cabin, running as if the flames of hell were licking at his heels. Jessy took a few minutes to give his father and brothers the news, then followed at a more sedate pace.

When she returned to the cabin, Will was sitting beside Sally's bed, talking to her in low tones and holding her hand.

A few minutes later, he stood and faced the family. "I reckon it's time to send for the kin to get started on the house."

The following week, Zeke carried the word through the hills. Early one morning several days later, people began to arrive—some on foot, some on horseback, and some driving wagons—men alone and in groups, whole families with gaggles of children in tow. They looked like a ragtag army converging on the Bingham farm. Corrine and Sally stayed in the cabin, but Jessy followed Morgan and Rachel into the swarm of people in the yard.

She faced Morgan in wonderment. "Are all these people relatives of yours?"

He scanned the crowd. "I don't recognize many faces, but if they're kin to the McTaggarts, I guess they're kin to me."

"And soon they'll be kin to Sally and the rest of your family." Familial relationships in the hills might be tangled in a damaged web, but soon that web would be whole again, in all its intricate beauty.

Women and girls bustled into the house bearing cauldrons and kettles, wrapped baked goods, and lumpy burlap sacks filled with an astonishing variety of provisions. Under Dermott's supervision, the men loaded their tools and headed down the hill to the prospective home site.

The morning passed with dizzying speed. Jessy was drawn into the whirlwind of feminine activity necessary to prepare a huge noon meal for the workers. She noted with pleasure that the women each took time to congratulate Sally on her upcoming marriage. If any had negative thoughts about the bride's obvious pregnancy, she kept them to herself. Sally basked in the attention, probably for the first time in her life, and Jessy was happy for her. Every woman should get to enjoy the feeling of being special at least once.

Just before noon, the women loaded the food and trooped down the hill to where the men were working. They had made astounding progress in just a few hours, and when Jessy said as much to Rachel, she replied, "With this many hands, it won't take long. The men divide into teams and have contests to see who can fell the most trees or split the most shingles. You'll see, by nightfall they'll probably have the roof on."

The cabin was small, only about half the size of the one Morgan was building, but it had a lovely setting in a meadow overlooking the river. A number of large rocks would have to be hauled away before a field could be plowed, but at least there was no shortage of stone for the fireplace.

Jessy handed out tin plates filled with savory stew and light, fluffy biscuits and listened to the men talk. Morgan sat with his uncle and cousins and several other men. Between bites, Dermott gestured toward his nephew with his fork.

"Morgan here is building a house for himself, too, up the mountain a'ways."

A tall, lean man with scraggly black whiskers glanced up with interest. "You doing all the work yourself?"

Morgan nodded. "So far. I've got a pair of mules, but sometimes they're more hindrance than help."

The man chewed, swallowing before he spoke. "We could help you finish it when we come back for the wedding in two weeks."

Morgan shifted his hips on the log. "I couldn't ask you to do that. Everyone's done so much for the family already."

The man laughed, showing several missing teeth. "Son, it ain't like we're not all part of the same family. I'm your daddy's cousin, and after all, blood is blood."

It seemed the bad feelings that had poisoned relations between the McTaggarts and the Binghams for twenty-seven years didn't extend to the whole clan. Or perhaps they were grateful for the opportunity to mend fences. Either way, Jessy rejoiced. After struggling in isolation for so long, Morgan and his family deserved the comfort and support of a network of kin who felt blood was the strongest tie of all.

When he hesitated, she couldn't stop herself. "That's very generous of you. I know Morgan would appreciate the assistance."

"Jessy." Morgan looked as though he'd like to strangle her on the spot.

"Who's this pretty young thing?" the thin man asked.

Dermott chortled. "This here's Morgan's intended."

The man laughed and slapped Morgan on the back. "Hoo-eee! She's a looker, and anxious, too." He laughed again. "I can see you need help on that house, and quick. When's the big day?"

Jessy stared at a particularly fascinating cloud in the sky, and Morgan scowled. "We haven't decided yet."

"Well, I wouldn't waste no time if I was you." The man slapped his knee and guffawed. Morgan stood, thrust his plate into Jessy's hands and stalked off, muttering something about wasting the whole day when there was work to be done.

Rachel's prediction turned out to be true. By dusk, the sure-footed crew on the roof had nailed down the last shingle. To be sure, there was still work remaining before the cabin could be considered complete—doors and windows to be hung and interior details to be finished—but Jessy was amazed at how much had been accomplished in one day. Twilight stole across the land, and the army of helpers melted back into the woods, calling out their promises to return in two weeks for the wedding festivities.

"The McTaggarts certainly have a large family," Jessy remarked as she set the table for supper. Many of the women had left their remaining food with Rachel, so there was no need to cook.

"Yes." Rachel had a faraway look. "I'd almost forgotten. Some of those folks were my kin, too. I hadn't seen them in years."

"Then I'd say it was about time."

Rachel glanced at Jessy, and a faint light stole into her faded eyes. "You know, I think you're right."

During the next two weeks, Sally grew stronger every day. She was young and healthy, and for the first time in her life, she had something to look forward to. Soon she was walking down the hill every day to keep Will and his brothers company while they finished the cabin. Morgan didn't join them because he said he had other, more pressing, work in the barn.

Jessy wondered if Ethan had told him about the fiddle, or if he was still trying to keep the project secret from the rest of the family. At any rate, she didn't see much of either man in the days before the wedding, and in all the hustle of activity, her request to mail a letter to her father was forgotten.

One evening, Sally returned to the cabin just in time for supper. Jessy scarcely recognized the sad, pale girl of a month earlier. Sally's cheeks were flushed a lovely delicate shade of pink, and her eyes glowed with happiness.

"It's a wonderful house, don't you think?" She waddled across the room to the table.

"Lovely," Corrine agreed. Spring was in the air, and she could now take baby Ella out for regular airings. Like the rest of the family, she had made many trips down the hill to monitor the progress of the cabin.

"How many people do you think will come to the wedding?" Jessy asked.

"Forty or fifty, I expect," Rachel said. "It's a little early yet for plowing or planting, so most everyone who was here for the raising will likely be back, only with more children this time."

"How will we feed them? We only have a few days to prepare."

"Folks will bring their own. They'd never expect us to do for so many."

Jessy thought of another detail that had been overlooked. "What are you going to wear, Sally?"

The happiness drained from the girl's face. "I don't know. I hadn't thought of that. I guess I'll wear the red dress you gave me for Christmas. It's the best one I have, and the only one that fits me anymore."

Red for a bride, and a pregnant one at that, might be too much to overlook, even for family. "If we look through your dresses, I'm sure we can find another we could alter to fit."

"I have something," Rachel said.

She went to the large trunk at the foot of her bed and rummaged around until she pulled out an ivory dress of soft muslin in the style of a previous generation. She shook the fabric and held it up next to her daughter. "We can take it apart and re-make it. There's plenty of material."

"But, Ma, it's your wedding dress."

"And I'd like you to wear it. My memories of that day might not be happy, but I have no regrets. That marriage brought me you and your brother, so it was a blessing in its own way. If you wear this dress, maybe you can give it some happy memories."

Sally hugged her mother, and Jessy swallowed a lump in her throat, touched beyond words.

By the dawning of Sally and Will's wedding day, she was certain of two things—spring had come to the mountains, and she was carrying Morgan's child. There could be no other explanation for the changes in her body. Although she ate well and felt fine most of the time, she was so tired by mid-afternoon she was tempted to join Ella for her nap. Her breasts were tender and felt as though they had doubled in size. On top of that, she hadn't had her monthly since before Christmas, and it was now the middle of March. She could no longer fool herself. She was pregnant.

The realization both thrilled and sobered her. It also left her with one huge question—what should she do next? Morgan had a right to know, but he was sure to demand an immediate wedding solely out of his stubborn sense of responsibility. Even faced with the prospect of bearing and raising a child alone, she couldn't stand the thought of living with him for the rest of her life with nothing more between them than obligation. She might love him, but if he didn't love her in return, he would come to resent both her and the child before long.

She stewed about the problem all morning. By early afternoon, Zeke had arrived with the preacher, and wagonloads of kin started pouring in, hitching their rigs outside the barn and spilling noisy children into the yard. Soon, Jessy was swept up in the hubbub and had no time to think.

The ceremony was short, simple, and very moving. Her eyes misted when Morgan presented his sister to her groom and went to stand beside his mother. Sally looked radiant in her re-made gown, carrying branches of early-blooming dogwood and redbud. The was no disguising the bulge of her belly beneath the ivory muslin, but the love in her blue eyes when she looked at Will outshone every other aspect of her appearance and made her truly beautiful.

After the ceremony, everyone marched the newlyweds to their new home for the giving of gifts. Along with children, the guests had loaded their wagons with all manner of household goods—linens, dishes, utensils. There were even buckets and tools for Will. The gifts might not be new, but they were all useful and very welcome. Sally sniffed back tears as she fingered the sheets embroidered for her by Will's aunt's sister.

The most magnificent gift of all, however, was waiting in the cabin when they opened the front door. There stood a beautiful walnut bed with hand-carved oak leaf designs on the headboard. A plump mattress stuffed with cornhusks lay atop the grid of ropes strung between the side rails, and a pair of pillows in blue striped ticking rested against the headboard.

Samuel offered a shy smile. "The pillows are from me and Ella, Aunt Sally. They gots real feathers in 'em. I helped gather 'em myself."

Sally bent and kissed the top of his head. "Thank you, Samuel. They're lovely."

"Pa and Uncle Morgan made the bed. They're working on a table and some chairs, too, but they're not quite done."

Jessy glanced at Morgan. So that's what he'd been doing the past two weeks. She looked back at the bed. It was beautifully made with neat, tight joints and a soft finish of rubbed beeswax. He'd never given any hint he was such an experienced woodworker. Ethan had probably carved the design, but she was convinced the simple lines and satisfying proportions came from Morgan.

While the guests gathered to examine and comment on the gifts, Jessy went looking for Morgan. She found him standing in a corner of the room, away from the crowd.

"The bed is beautiful," she said above the noise of a dozen conversations. "I had no idea you were so talented."

"It's just a bed."

"No, it's not. It's lovely."

"Say, Morgan," someone called out, "When you goin' to make one of these for yourself?"

Jessy's face went hot, and she glanced around to identify the speaker. Then she saw him—the thin man with the scraggly black beard and gap-toothed grin.

When Morgan didn't answer, the man cackled. "You'd better get busy. That little lady ain't goin' to wait forever."

"Shut up, Clem," Morgan ordered without rancor.

Clem laughed again, pleased with his joke.

After the gifts had been presented and properly admired, the wedding party trooped back up the hill to eat. The women spread food on makeshift plank tables, and the real festivities commenced.

Knowing only Morgan's family, at first Jessy had assumed all hill people were silent, dour, and suspicious of strangers. She had since learned they could also be gregarious, fun loving, and even boisterous when they gathered to celebrate. As families mingled and ate, a couple of fiddlers took out their instruments and began to warm up. Soon they were joined by a concertina and a mandolin, and the music began.

She loved the lively music, and she smiled and tapped her toes as the dancers whirled by. She noticed Ethan watching the two fiddlers closely. When the musicians stopped for a rest, he hobbled over and engaged one of them in animated conversation. She wondered how he was coming with his own violin. Perhaps the fiddler would be able to offer some helpful advice.

She also noticed Morgan standing alone on the edge of the crowd, watching everyone else eat, laugh, and dance. His face was set in what she liked to call his granite look, showing no emotion and giving little hint as to his thoughts.

She strolled over. "It was a lovely wedding, wasn't it?"

He grunted and kept his eyes on the crowd.

She wondered why he was in such a foul mood on his sister's wedding day. She tried again. "Everyone seems to be having a good time dancing. Would you like to dance when the music starts again?"

"I can't dance, and you know it."

"No, I don't. The only time I took you to a dance in Weston, you wouldn't dance with me."

"That's because I can't."

The musicians struck a chord and then began a slow, mournful waltz.

"Even you can dance to this." She tugged his arm. "Come on." She dragged him out among the other couples.

"I can't do this."

"Yes, you can. Just relax."

Slowly but surely, he began to move his body to the lilting strains of the music. Soon, he could even take the necessary three steps without treading on her feet. Jessy relaxed in his arms and smiled in encouragement. "You're doing very well."

"I feel like a three-legged dog."

She smothered her laughter against his shoulder, and his arms tightened around her. Tingles rushed through her from head to foot. It had been so long since he'd held her or kissed her. Since Christmas he'd barely said a civil word to her. If he wasn't chastising her for interfering in his family's affairs, he was badgering her to tell him if she was pregnant.

Pregnant. She'd managed to forget for a few hours. She clutched him tighter. If she closed her eyes, she could almost pretend they were dancing at their own wedding and he was regarding her with the same unconditional love that glowed in Will's eyes when he looked at Sally.

"Jessy, was Clem right?" Morgan's voice rumbled just above her ear.

She jerked in his arms. Had he read her mind? "What?"

"About the bed. Was Clem right about the bed? Do I need to make another one?"

Their own bed. A beautiful bed like the one he'd made for Sally. A bed where future children would be conceived and brought into the world.

She plastered a brave smile on her lips. "Well, you have to sleep somewhere."

He scowled, and his brows hooded his mountain lion eyes. His hand tightened on her waist. "Stop it. You know what I'm asking. You have to know by now."

She stopped dancing, and the rest of the dancers swirled past them. She stared up at him, her eyes stinging with emotion. "Do you love me? Are you asking me to marry you?"

His frown deepened. "I said I'd marry you."

"If you have to! That's the whole sum of your interest in me, isn't it? Whether or not I'm carrying your child. Well, I'm sorry, but that isn't good enough." She spun out of his arms and dashed off through the crowd.

Chapter Seventeen

Desperate to escape the crush of relatives with their curious stares and well-meaning questions, Jessy ran until she found herself by the river. Winded and clutching a stitch in her side, she climbed up on a big, smooth rock and stared down into the turbulent water. It reminded her of her life, rushing headlong and out of control to who-knows-where. She had to regain control. She had more than just herself to consider now.

Random thoughts battered and buffeted her before they finally settled into a satisfactory plan. She would go home to Weston as soon as possible. She'd never make it back on her own without getting hopelessly lost, but if she wrote to her father, he would send someone right away. She would tell her parents Morgan had been killed in a tragic accident a few months after their marriage, and she wanted to come home. They would be so relieved to see her they wouldn't question her story too closely. There would be time enough to break the news about the baby later.

Each time Morgan's face intruded on her thoughts, she banished it. She'd done everything she could to show him how exciting and satisfying life could be if he opened himself to the power of love. But she wouldn't, and couldn't, do it for him.

Her mind made up, she followed the path back to the farm. Her eyes took in every detail, storing the memories to be savored later. She would miss the place. The signs of neglect had disappeared since Morgan's return. Even the woods, so stark in winter, looked fresh and promising, brightened by the pale green mist of new leaves and the flash of early-blooming wildflowers.

When she reached the house, she went straight to the loft to write her letter before her resolve weakened. Fighting back tears, she scribbled the note to her father. She wouldn't let herself think about it. She was doing the best thing for herself and her baby. She sealed the envelope and retrieved a coin from her reticule.

Had she really been here less than five months? It seemed like a lifetime since she'd left Weston.

She set out to find Zeke, knowing she could trust him to do her bidding without asking questions. She found him with a group of men behind the barn, swilling white lightning from a brown-glazed jug they passed from hand to hand. The minute they saw her, the jug disappeared.

"Zeke, may I speak to you for a moment?"

A couple of Zeke's companions hooted, but he silenced them with a grunt. "Sure, Miss Jessy." He followed her until they were far enough from the barn not to be overheard.

She handed him the envelope and coin. "Will you please take this letter to the stage office in Waynesville for me? This ought to more than cover the postage."

Zeke stared at the envelope, turning it over in his hand, as if he had never seen such a mystery before, but true to her prediction, he asked no questions. "Sure, Miss Jessy. I'll ride over there tomorrow."

"Thank you, Zeke."

She watched him stuff the letter and money into his pocket and amble off to rejoin his friends.

It was done. She was leaving Morgan. The knowledge left her sick and empty.

She didn't know how long it would take her father to send someone, but knowing her time with Morgan and his family was limited gave her days a new sense of urgency and purpose. She had so much left to accomplish in such a short time. She wouldn't have time to teach Corrine more than the bare rudiments of reading, but she wanted to make sure she knew enough to read Samuel's book to him. They spent the early afternoons while Ella napped, head to head, going over the simple words again and again.

Jessy also worried about Ethan. He seemed less sullen and withdrawn, but he still vanished for most of each day. She hoped he was working on his violin and the lure of easy money hadn't drawn him into the McTaggarts' moonshine enterprise.

After the wedding, Dermott had magnanimously offered to include the Bingham men in his family business. Jessy was relieved when Morgan declined. He'd put his outlaw days behind him and seemed determined to accept whatever life he could make for himself on the farm. However, for Ethan, unsure of his own ability to provide for his wife and children, the temptation to wink at the law might prove too great.

Spring also brought plowing time. Morgan had suspended work on his cabin, and he and his mules helped Will remove the large rocks from the meadow. Together, the men plowed more than twice as many acres as had ever been cultivated before, and the work kept them busy from dawn until dusk. By evening, the pain in Morgan's knee from his old war injury gave him a noticeable limp, but Will was young and strong and bursting with pride over his new adult status.

In early April, two weeks after she'd entrusted her letter to Zeke, Jessy was working in the garden with Rachel and Corrine. Sally sat in the sun minding baby Ella while Samuel amused himself building a fort with the rocks discarded from the garden.

She had just taken a break from the backbreaking labor of planting carrots and stood to stretch her cramped muscles when she saw a big man on a black horse riding toward them. Her first instinct was to rush the other women and children into the house and run for Morgan, but she hesitated, squinting in the early afternoon sun from beneath the brim of one of Rachel's old sunbonnets. Something about the man struck a familiar chord.

He traveled the path from the river without hesitating or speeding up, although she knew he could see them as clearly as she saw him. As he drew nearer, she narrowed her eyes. Slowly the broad shoulders and square jaw materialized into the face of her best friend's husband, Jared Tanner.

Jared Tanner, here? Then she realized her father must have sent him to bring her home. It made perfect sense. Who would make a safer, more competent escort than a former shotgun rider for the Overland Stage Company?

Jared pulled his horse to a halt and removed his hat. He peered at her with confusion in his black eyes. "Jessy Randall? Is that you?"

At his incredulous tone, she glanced at her dress and realized what a different picture she presented from the last time he'd seen her. Gone were the embellished gowns, voluminous petticoats, and delicate slippers of her former life. In their place she wore a plain, straight skirt of brown homespun with a matching blouse she'd borrowed from Corrine, a wide-brimmed sun bonnet, and heavy work boots.

Jared might not be able to tell by looking at her, but her clothes weren't the only things that had changed. She was no longer the naive girl who had set off five months earlier in pursuit of the man she loved. In less than six months, she would be a mother.

Jessy knew she had yet to learn the true meaning of selflessness. When she watched Corrine with Samuel and Ella, she began to understand what lay ahead. And like Sally, she would soon have a child to consider. Her own wants and needs could never come first again.

At that sobering thought, she gazed into Jared's face. "Yes, it's me."

Taking in her ragged appearance and subdued demeanor, he frowned. "Not that I ever approved, but I was sorry to hear about your loss. Your father asked me to bring you home."

She nodded. "Thank you."

The Bingham women had stopped working and regarded him with suspicion.

Jessy motioned to them. "Rachel, Sally, Corrine, I'd like to introduce Mr. Jared Tanner, the husband of my oldest friend. He's come to escort me home. Jared, this is Rachel Bingham, Morgan's mother; Sally McTaggart, his sister; and Corrine Bingham, his brother's wife."

Jared nodded and doffed his hat. "Ladies." He glanced back at Jessy.

"I didn't know when anyone would arrive." She brushed the dirt that clung to her apron. "I'm not quite ready to go. Besides, I'm sure you need to rest after your long journey. If you'll follow me to the house, I'll show you where to put your horse and fix you something to eat. We can leave first thing in the morning."

"Jessy, you're not going so soon!" Corrine dropped her hoe in the muddy furrows.

The sadness in Corrine's eyes stabbed her heart. Aside from Morgan, she would miss Corrine most of all. Before she broke down, she gathered her resolution. "We knew this day had to come." Her voice was firm. "There's no point putting it off any longer. It's for the best." She faced Rachel. "I'd be obliged if you could put Jared up for the night. After tomorrow, I'll place no more demands on your hospitality."

"Of course," the older woman replied, "but you've been no trouble."

That comment brought a reluctant smile to Jessy's face. "I know at times I've been a great deal of trouble, but it's kind of you not to say so."

"Hmph." Rachel stared at the ground, suddenly fascinated by a rock at her feet.

Jessy turned back to Jared. "If you'll follow me, I'll take you to the house."

He waited for her to lead the way, then followed behind at a slow, steady pace. When they reached the barn, he dismounted and led his horse inside.

"You can put him in here." Jessy pointed to an empty stall.

"Jessy, is that you?" a voice called from the back of the barn.

Morgan. What was he doing here in the middle of the day?

"Um…yes. It's me." She struggled to think of a way to explain the situation to Jared. Before inspiration struck, Morgan walked around from behind the end stall with a small keg in his hands.

"I needed some more nails." He saw Jared and stopped dead. "What the…Tanner, is that you?"

"Morgan? Morgan Bingham?"

"What are you doing here?"

"I came to take Jessy home. What are you doing here?"

Morgan set the nails down. "I live here. And what's this about Jessy going home?" He glanced at Jessy, but she remained silent

"You're alive."

"I am. What's this all about?"

Jared's gaze darted between the two of them in confusion. "But she said..."

Morgan stepped closer to Jessy. "Jessy, what's going on here?"

She bit her lip.

Jared advanced, too. "I did not come all this way to take a woman from her husband."

"Did you tell him we were married?" Morgan demanded.

Jared's black brows lifted. "Married's the least of it. She told her parents you were dead."

Morgan stepped closer. "Jessy..."

"That's enough." She straightened to her full height and lifted her chin. "I don't have to explain anything to you. The important thing is that Jared has come to take me home. I'm leaving in the morning."

"The hell you are."

"You can't make me stay. Besides, you don't want me here, and you know it." They stood nose to nose shouting at each other.

"You two calm down," Jared ordered.

Jessy fell silent and glared at both men.

"Look, I don't know what's going on, and I'm not sure I want to," Jared continued in a lower voice, "but I'm leaving at first light. If you're not married and Jessy wants to come with me, she can. Is that understood?"

"Absolutely." Jessy gave a vigorous nod.

"Damnation! If she wants to go so bad, take her." Morgan bent, picked up his nails, and stalked out of the barn.

Jared pinned Jessy with a hard gaze. "You're not married, are you?"

Her heart fluttered, and she grasped his hands. "You've got to promise you won't tell anyone—not even Lisa."

"Jessy, your parents—"

"Will never speak to me again if they learn the truth. My father will explode, literally, and you know my mother. She'll take to her bed and never leave the house again. I can't do that to them."

"You should have considered that before you left on this foolhardy adventure. What were you thinking?"

She dropped his hands and stared at the ground. "I didn't think, or at least not beyond myself and what I wanted at the moment." She raised her gaze. "I've learned a lot since then. I don't want to hurt them further. Will you help me? Will you keep my secret?"

He hesitated. "I won't lie."

"I wouldn't ask you to. Just don't volunteer anything."

"That's a form of lying."

"Help me spare them pain. That's all I ask."

Conflicting emotions warred across his handsome face.

"Please," she begged.

"All right. But if anyone asks me a direct question, I'm telling the truth."

It was the most she could hope for. "Thank you."

At supper that night, Jessy could barely swallow around the lump in her throat. Everyone in the family wore the same hangdog expression except Morgan, who glowered. No one spoke except when necessary, and much of the food went untouched. Samuel clutched his book and snuffled back tears.

When she'd pictured her departure, she'd only imagined how Morgan might react. As usual, he refused to cooperate with her fantasy. The rest of the family was another matter. She'd failed to consider their response or how their unhappiness might affect her. Even though she'd been an outsider at first, the trials of the past months had forged bonds that defied separation.

Finally, Jessy could make no further pretense of eating and rose to help Rachel and Corrine clear the table. The depth of her pain surprised her. It was much worse than when she'd left her parents to follow Morgan. That had been a lark, an adventure, and she hadn't planned to be gone more than a few days. This would be forever.

Ethan reached for his crutches and stood, too. "Before you leave, Jessy, I have something I want to show you." He hobbled to the door, and returned moments later, clutching a violin by the neck and struggling to balance on his crutches.

"Oh, Ethan!" She rushed to his side. "You finished the violin. It's beautiful!" She kissed his cheek.

He flushed. "You haven't heard it yet."

"Come, sit down. Play for us." She urged him toward a chair. "I'll carry it for you."

She took the violin and followed him. While Ethan eased himself down, she examined the instrument. It glowed with life and light. The workmanship was exquisite, from the gleaming finish on the deeply grained maple top to the delicately carved "S" holes. When Ethan was seated, she handed it back with reverence.

He settled the violin beneath his chin and drew the bow across the strings a couple of times. Tiny beads of sweat popped up across his brow. Jessy understood his nerves. It was one thing to make a fiddle that looked beautiful but quite another to make one that sounded as good as it looked. He glanced at the expectant faces of his family, took a deep breath, closed his eyes, and began.

A haunting melody curled into the air, twining around each listener. It was sweet and sad and familiar. Jessy closed her eyes, remembering where she'd heard the music before. It was the same song he'd been playing the day she surprised him by the river, the day he destroyed his first instrument. It was only fitting that the same melancholy tune should inaugurate the new violin.

When he finished, she clapped and the rest of the family joined in. Ethan struggled to keep his pleasure from showing, but it seeped through his stern expression.

"That was wonderful," she exclaimed.

He regarded the instrument critically, stroking his fingers across the silky finish. "If I could do it again, I'd do some things different. I got some ideas from one of the fellows who played at Sally and Will's wedding."

Jessy pursed her lips. "Do you think you could make more violins?"

He paused to consider. "I guess so, if I could get the strings somewhere. But what would I do with the fiddles when they were done? There aren't that many folks around here who can play, and those who do, have their own."

The idea that had been forming in her mind for weeks came into sharp focus. "My uncle in Philadelphia is a music teacher and runs a shop selling instruments. I know he would be delighted to carry violins of such fine quality as yours. He would also be able to supply you with the strings you need."

Ethan regarded her with skepticism, but she plunged on before he could object. "You'd be surprised how much people would pay for a violin like this in the city. You would be able to make quite a bit of money." She waited and watched while he digested the idea. If he were willing to work hard, it offered a way to support his family that didn't require two legs.

"But how would I be able to handle the business of orders and such with your uncle if you're gone? No one here can read or write."

Jessy caught Morgan's eye. She couldn't tell what he was thinking, but she knew he would do this for his brother. "Morgan can. I'll write to my uncle and make the arrangements as soon as I get home. In the meantime, you can start on a new violin."

"I don't know." Ethan hesitated. "It took me a couple of months to make this one."

She let out a puff of exasperation. "Ethan, even if you only made and sold a half dozen a year, you'd be far ahead of where you'll be if you don't."

He half smiled. "You've got a point there."

"So, you'll try it?"

"I'll try it."

"Wonderful. Now, this is cause for a real celebration. Do you know any livelier tunes?"

He grinned and lit into a spirited number that had everyone tapping their toes and humming along. By the time he exhausted his repertoire, the mood in the cabin had lightened. Ella dozed on her mother's shoulder, and Samuel nodded against her side.

"I think we'd better get these children to bed," Corrine said.

Will rose to help Sally from her seat. "We need to be going, too."

Jared left with them because Will had invited him to bed down in the loft in their cabin. Morgan followed Ethan and Corrine, carrying Samuel snuggled against his chest, leaving Jessy alone with Rachel.

The older woman regarded her with an inscrutable expression. "Well, girl, we'd best get to bed, too. You'll be wanting to get an early start in the morning."

"Yes, that's true." She didn't know what to say to Morgan's mother. She had truly come to care for Rachel in the months she'd spent in her home, but she didn't want to embarrass the woman with a sentimental display. Rachel frowned on overt expressions of emotion. "I want to thank you, Mrs. Bingham, for making me welcome in your home."

"Hmph." Rachel turned away to fold down the quilt on her bed, as if she were reluctant to speak her mind to Jessy's face. "It's a sorry thing, you leaving, that's all I can say. If that fool son of mine had any sense, he'd have married you long ago."

Jessy smiled sadly for the vote of confidence that came too late. "Morgan has to do what he thinks is right for himself."

Another *hmph* was Rachel's only response.

Hours later, Jessy lay in bed, still awake. She was going home. Her bags stood packed and ready. She was really leaving. It seemed strange to think of Weston as home. The Ozarks, with their rounded, tree-covered peaks, rugged bluffs, and deep ravines felt more like home now. It was almost as if the past five months had blotted out the twenty-one years that preceded them. She had always considered herself an active person who lived life to the fullest, but she'd felt more alive since coming to these hills than at any other time in her life.

She couldn't help but be satisfied with the outcome of Sally and Will's dilemma, and Ethan teetered on the brink of salvation. She could leave feeling she had accomplished something on both counts. Rachel's life revolved around her family—if they were happy, she was happy. That left only Morgan.

Was he any happier, any more at ease, than when they arrived? She couldn't honestly answer yes. Now that she understood him better, she loved him more than ever. He'd been half right when he accused her of following him out of childish infatuation. But that infatuation had grown into an abiding love as she'd watched him sacrifice time and again for the people he loved. She might even count herself among that group—she knew he cared about her deeply despite his denials—but she wanted his love to be a joyous thing, freely admitted and freely shared, not a burden to drag them both down for the remainder of their days. That was why she had to go.

But she couldn't leave without seeing him alone one last time. With the family around, they hadn't spoken more than a few words in weeks. She needed to see him, to fill her eyes and senses with him. She wanted to be able to call up his image and feel him with her during the long, lonely days ahead. A specter might not keep her warm on cold winter nights or lift her spirits at the end of a tiring day, but it was the best she could hope for, and she meant to have it.

Her mind made up, she slid out of bed, tiptoed across the attic floor, and climbed down the ladder, taking care not to trip on her long nightdress. At the door, she paused to grab a shawl from one of the pegs. Wrapping it around herself, she slipped outside into the darkness.

The dewy grass froze her bare feet as she scooted across the yard to the barn. Shoving the heavy door aside, she squeezed through. The warm air smelled of animals and hay. She had to stop for a moment to get her bearings in the pitch-black building. Rustlings greeted her from the stalls as she felt her way to the ladder. Gathering the front of her nightdress in one hand to keep from stepping on it, she climbed until she reached the top rung and stepped onto the platform.

A faint light shone through the window next to the bed—just enough to illuminate Morgan's dark shape. She crept across the floor to the bed.

"Morgan, wake up." She touched his shoulder. "Morgan."

He mumbled something and rolled onto his back.

"Morgan, wake up. I want to talk to you."

"Hmmm?"

"I came to say good-bye."

He squinted at her then opened his eyes. "Jessy? What are you doing out here at this hour dressed like that?"

"I came to say good-bye."

"Just a minute." He reached over and lit the lantern next to the bed.

The golden flame flared, and he slid the glass globe back down. She allowed her eyes to feast on him in the warm glow. His sandy hair was rumpled and whiskers darkened his jaw, but the muscles of his smooth, bare back and shoulders bunched and flexed, creating highlights and shadows that beckoned her fingers. She couldn't help herself; she reached out and touched. After all, it would be the last time.

He grabbed her hand as if her fingers had burned him. "What do you think you're doing?"

"I'm leaving in a few hours." Her voice caught. "I just wanted to see you again...to say good-bye...to remember."

He slid his hand up her arm. "You're freezing."

"It doesn't matter." She felt as if she were in a trance, immune to cold or pain, transfixed by the sight of him.

He glanced down at her feet. "Good God, woman! You're barefoot! Get in here." He threw back the covers and pulled her down beside him.

Once inside the snug cocoon, her limbs gravitated to his warmth and draped themselves across him. In response, his arms tightened around her.

"Why did you come, Jessy?" His words vibrated against her ear.

"I told you. I had to see you again, one more time."

"Why?"

She pushed herself up until she could see his face. "I won't tell you it's because I love you, because you don't want to hear that, although it's the truth."

His expression hardened, but she read the pain in his eyes.

"Go back to the house."

"You're holding me."

He was. His words might tell her to go, but his arms begged her to stay.

He released her. "Go."

She leaned forward and pressed a soft kiss to his lips then pulled back a sigh's breadth. "Why? Why should I go?"

Pain twisted his features, pain like a knife in her heart. His eyes squeezed shut in agony. When they reopened, his heart lay bare before her.

"Because if you stay here one more second, I can't be responsible for my actions. I can't hold back any longer. And I can't take the risk."

"There is no risk."

"How can you say that?"

She smoothed his brow with her fingers. She knew what she wanted—what she had to have—and she would only be telling the truth. "No matter what we do tonight, I can guarantee it won't make me pregnant." He hesitated, and she kissed him again. "Love me tonight," she whispered. "Please love me. For the last time."

That did it

He groaned and rolled her over until she lay pinned beneath him. He devoured her mouth like a starving man. "Oh, Jessy. It's been so long, too long."

All over her lips and cheeks, neck and ears, he licked and tasted, sucked and nipped, as if trying to extract the essence of her. She tossed and turned, thrusting against him and calling his name. This was her last chance for the ecstasy of his touch, and she meant to take all he was willing to give.

They had held themselves apart so long that when they came together it was a desperate thing, fast and furious, until they cried out their pleasure and collapsed, sweat-slicked, in exhaustion. After their breathing calmed and their hearts ceased pounding, they loved again—slowly, gently, exquisitely, making every touch count. When it was over, she cried softly from the sheer beauty of it.

Finally, she lay quiet, listening to the soft, even sounds of his breathing, knowing he slept and cherishing the moment. When she could delay the inevitable no longer, she slipped out from under the quilts and retrieved her nightdress and shawl. Wiping the remnants of tears from her cheeks, she pressed a featherlight kiss on his hair then turned out the lantern and made her way down the ladder and back to the house.

At first light, she was dry-eyed and ready to leave when Jared arrived at the cabin. Their horses waited outside the barn, saddled and ready to go, but there was no sign of Morgan. The rest of the family stood on the front porch to bid her farewell, but still he didn't come. Jessy sat tall in her saddle, gave a bright smile and a jaunty wave to the rest of the Binghams, then turned to follow Jared, never looking back.

Chapter Eighteen

Jessy sat on the wide veranda of her parents' elegant brick home enjoying the early May sunshine with her closest friend, Lisa Tanner. Lisa's sixteen-month-old son, Andrew, toddled between them, babbling happily and showing them the wooden horse Dada had carved for him. Jessy felt a pang of jealousy whenever she saw Jared with the little boy. He might not be the child's biological father, but he fit the bill perfectly in every other way.

Her own baby would never be so lucky. Unlike Lisa, whose first husband had died before she had a chance to really know him, Jessy was still passionately in love with the father of her unborn child and always would be. She was glad her friend had found the love she deserved with Jared, but Jessy knew she would never want another man to touch her the way Morgan had.

She'd been home for nearly a month, and each day seemed more difficult than the last. Her mother hovered and fluttered, dressed in black, and suffered Jessy's bereavement as if it were her own. She was, however, thrilled about the impending arrival of her first grandchild. She had ordered Jessy's old nursery furniture brought down from the attic and cleaned and had embroidered several delicate little gowns for the layette. Jessy's baby might never know its father, but with Annabelle Randall around, the child would never want for material comforts.

The air was warm and humid for so early in the year, and Lisa and Jessy fanned themselves as they rocked.

"How have you been feeling?" Lisa removed a lilac leaf from Andrew's fist before he stuffed it in his mouth.

"Better. I think the worst is over. Now I mostly feel fat."

"You? Ha!" Lisa laughed, rubbing her own stomach. "Now this is fat." She was a month farther along in her second pregnancy than Jessy and had a much more noticeable bulge beneath her skirt.

"Well, what do you expect, since you and Jared are both giants?" Jessy teased.

She'd been thrilled when Jared told her about her friend's pregnancy on the trip back to Weston. She'd felt so bereft without Morgan those first few days and was nervous about her reception at home. Knowing she would be able to share the experience of motherhood with Lisa helped lighten the load.

"Are you planning to stay with your parents after the baby is born?"

"Mama wouldn't have it any other way. You should see what she's done with the old nursery."

Lisa grinned and nodded. "Your mother always likes to do things up right."

"She certainly does." What would Mama say if she ever found out her precious only daughter—her precious *pregnant* only daughter—had never been married at all? It didn't bear contemplation.

"Do you miss him all the time?"

"Hmm?" Jessy glanced at Lisa. "Oh,...yes...all the time."

It was true. Morgan might not be dead, as everyone assumed, but not a day passed, not a minute, that she didn't think of him.

As soon as she returned home, she wrote to her uncle in Philadelphia about selling Ethan's violins and found him most receptive to the idea. But when she picked up her pen and tried to write to Morgan to explain the arrangements she'd made, she froze. She didn't want to write to him about shipping schedules and money transfers, she wanted to know if he was happy, if he missed her. Finally, she forced herself to write a brief, business-like letter, containing only the essential information. She hadn't received a reply, so she didn't know if he'd even read it.

She opened the top two buttons of the mourning gown her mother insisted on and fanned her throat. "It's warm for May."

"Yes." Lisa made a grab for Andrew before he tumbled down the steps. "You should see the apple trees in the orchard. They're covered with blossoms. Why don't you come out to the farm after church tomorrow?"

Jessy stared down the road without seeing. "I don't like to intrude on you and Jared."

"Intrude?" Lisa laughed. "Except for my mother and her husband, Ben, we hardly ever have visitors. I'm sure Jared would be as happy to see you as I would."

"Maybe. We'll see."

"Jessy, I know you're grieving, but you have to get out and do things. You've hardly left the house in the past month. It isn't healthy for you or the baby to stay cooped up here by yourself."

Jessy arched one brow. "I'm never alone. I have Mama, remember?"

"Maybe you could use a break from all that love."

Jessy laughed, and they drifted into a companionable silence in the afternoon heat. Andrew toddled over to sit on his mother's lap and nodded off with his face against her breast. Soon his dark hair formed damp little points around his rosy face. Lisa shifted him to lie across her lap and raised one hand to shade her eyes. She squinted and peered down the road.

"What is it?" Jessy asked.

"I'm not sure. My eyes must be playing tricks on me."

Jessy glanced in the direction of her friend's attention. A lone man on horseback approached.

"Jessy. Oh, my stars, Jessy!"

She didn't respond. She couldn't.

"I know it can't be, but—"

Jessy stared. She tried to stand, but her knees gave way, and she clutched the porch railing. "Morgan," she whispered, never taking her eyes from him. "Morgan."

There was no doubt. The man with the grim face beneath the dusty black hat was the late Morgan Bingham.

Jessy and Lisa watched, transfixed, while he dismounted and tied his horse to the railing. He climbed the stairs, never taking his eyes off Jessy.

Lisa shrank back and raised one hand to her throat. "B-but you're supposed to be—"

"Dead? I've heard that before." He reached Jessy's side. "Are you still telling that story?"

She was, and she'd never expected to be found out. Certainly not this way. Jared had kept his promise, and not even Lisa knew the truth.

"What are you doing here?" Jessy barely heard her own voice above the buzz of the bees in the honeysuckle bush beside the porch.

"I came to get you."

Struggling against the weight of her sleeping child, Lisa stood. She shifted Andrew's limp body to her shoulder and he slumbered on, undisturbed. "What's going on here? Jessy, if Morgan's still alive, why did you come home?"

Jessy winced at her friend's sharp tone and felt a stab of guilt. "It's a long story."

"And a very interesting one, I'm sure." Lisa turned her sharp gaze to Morgan.

Jessy allowed herself to follow suit. Her eyes caressed every feature of his face. It seemed like a year since she'd seen him instead of a month. He looked wonderful—angry, but wonderful.

His frown deepened. "How soon can you be ready to leave?"

Leave? Had he come to take her back? She scanned his tawny eyes, trying to read his thoughts. Had he learned about the baby somehow? She had to find out what had really brought him here before she agreed to anything. "Have you changed your mind?"

"I'm willing to marry you, baby or not."

Lisa's brow furrowed. "But Jessy, if Morgan's not dead, doesn't he know about the—"

At that moment, Annabelle Randall opened the front door. "Jessy, dear, have you asked Lisa...?" She stared at the three faces turned in her direction. She gaped at Morgan, and her round blue eyes grew rounder. "But...but you're—"

He doffed his hat. "Supposed to be dead. I know. It's a pleasure to see you again, Mrs. Randall."

At that, Annabelle let out a tiny squeak. Her eyes rolled up into her head, and she sank to the floor. Morgan bounded up the steps and caught her before her head hit the hard boards. He slid his arms beneath the unconscious woman's shoulders and knees and lifted her carefully.

"Where should I take her?"

Jessy rushed to hold the door. "Bring her into the parlor. This way." She led the way to the ornate red parlor and pointed to a carved rosewood sofa. "Lay her down there. I'll get some water." She hurried toward the kitchen calling, "Clara, would you please fetch Mama's smelling salts?"

The maid returned with the small bottle, and Jessy unscrewed the lid and waved the bottle beneath her mother's nose.

Annabelle's eyes fluttered open, and she struggled to focus on her daughter's face. She raised one hand to her forehead. "Oh, Jessamine, dear. I know it must be the heat, but the strangest thing just happened. I don't want to upset you, but I thought I saw your Morgan standing on the porch."

Morgan leaned over Jessy's shoulder. "Are you feeling better, Mrs. Randall?"

Her eyes widened and she let out another little shriek. "Aah! It is you!"

He smiled like a big cat. "Yes, ma'am. I've come to take Jessy home."

Annabelle tried to raise herself up on her elbows. "Home? But—"

Jessy put her hands on her mother's shoulders and pushed her back against the cushions. "Don't distress yourself, Mama. You've had quite a shock."

"A shock. Yes." Annabelle's confused glance darted between Morgan and Jessy. "I-I'm sure there must be some explanation." She closed her eyes, as if that might make the whole problem disappear, and sighed. "We'll send for your father. Amos will know what to do. He always does."

Jessy glanced uneasily at Morgan. She didn't trust his smile.

"That's a good idea," he said. "I'd like to hear you explain this situation to your father."

A sudden panic seized her throat and threatened to strangle her. Morgan might or might not know about the baby, but her father certainly did, and he was bound to mention it to her *late husband.*

What Papa didn't know was that she and Morgan had never been married at all. She wondered how she could persuade Morgan to keep that information secret. It probably didn't matter. Either way, disaster loomed. By suppertime, Morgan was likely to find himself on the business end of Papa's shotgun, headed either to church or to jail, depending on her father's frame of mind.

Before she could think of a way to forestall the inevitable, her mother called out weakly to the maid hovering in the background. "Clara, run down to the courthouse and fetch Judge Randall right away. Tell him it's an emergency."

"Yes, ma'am." Clara headed toward the back door.

Lisa shifted her son's limp weight on her shoulder. "Morgan, perhaps you could hitch my horse to the wagon and help me get Andrew settled. I need to go home."

"I'd be glad to."

Jessy turned pleading eyes to her friend. "Must you go now? Papa will be home soon, and I need you."

"This is a family matter." Lisa's voice was gentle but firm. "I'd just be in the way. Besides, I need to start supper."

"But—"

"The invitation to visit the orchard still stands." Lisa glanced from Jessy to Morgan and back. "Why don't you come together? I'm sure you'll both need a respite by tomorrow afternoon."

Jessy didn't answer. Her busy mind was already conjuring up a multitude of possibilities for the next twenty-four hours. She had never considered herself a coward, but at that moment, she wanted nothing more than to run away, as fast and as far as she could.

By the time her father stormed up the front steps, her mother had recovered and ordered Clara to serve lemonade and cookies in the parlor. She was entertaining Jessy and Morgan as if they were visiting dignitaries, steadfastly refusing to listen to Jessy's attempts to explain her bizarre situation. "That's a matter for your father, dear." She dismissed Jessy with a wave of her hand.

The front door slammed, and Morgan stood. Jessy and her mother froze.

"Annabelle, what's the meaning of this?" her father roared from the front hall. "I was right in the middle of an important meeting when Clara—" He stepped into the parlor and stared. "What in...? Thunderation! Bingham, is that you?"

"Yes, sir." Morgan set his glass on a table.

Papa's face reddened, and he switched his glare to Jessy. "Jessamine!"

Jessy stared in fascination at the color rising up her father's forehead until even the smooth dome of his head glowed. His bushy white moustache stood out against his red skin and quivered in outrage.

"Well, young lady? What is this man doing here?"

She didn't reply.

"I came to take Jessy home."

"Silence!" Judge Randall ordered, as if he were quieting an unruly courtroom. "I'll deal with you in a moment." He returned his attention to his daughter. "I'll have the truth, and I'll have it now."

She swallowed nervously. Nothing was going the way she'd planned.

"Well, I'm waiting. Did this man beat you or abuse you in any way? Is that why you came home? Because if it is, I'll—"

Morgan scowled. "Now, wait—"

"No, Papa." Jessy rushed forward and placed a placating hand on her father's chest. "It's nothing like that."

"Did he chase after other women, or fail to provide for you? By Jove, I always knew—"

"No, Papa. That's not it either."

Her father's bushy white brows drew together even tighter. "Then what is the problem? You know I don't condone married women abandoning their husbands and running home every time they have a little tiff."

She couldn't meet his eyes. "That's just it."

"What's just it?" Her father appeared to be approaching the end of his judicial patience.

She fiddled with a piece of black braid on her dress. She'd reached the moment of truth. There was no putting it off any longer. "We're not married." She had intended to speak the words bravely, but they came out in a pitiful whisper.

"What's that? Did I understand you to say you're not married to this man?" His red face grew mottled.

Jessy nodded. Her mother gasped and fell back against the pillow on the sofa.

"Then what about the baby?"

"Baby?"

Jessy turned. Morgan was advancing on her with fury written across his countenance. "Jessy—"

Her father stepped between them. "Bingham, do you mean to tell me you didn't know Jessamine was expecting your child?"

Morgan squared his shoulders and looked the angry man in the eye. "Judge Randall, if Jessy's going to have a baby, it's mine. But I didn't know about it, and that's the truth."

Her father regarded Morgan as though trying to assess his honesty. "Well, now you know. What do you intend to do about it?"

"I offered to marry her before, and she refused. Now I don't see she has much choice."

"Neither do I. I can perform the ceremony myself, right here, with Mrs. Randall and Clara as witnesses."

"Wait!" Jessy shoved her father aside. "Stop it, both of you. There isn't going to be any wedding."

Her father frowned. "What do you mean? This man's willing to do the right thing by you, and I insist on it."

"Morgan knows my conditions. He can't meet them, so there won't be a wedding."

"Jessy, you're going too far," Morgan growled.

"Why did you come here?" she demanded. "Until you can tell me honestly, from your heart, there will be no wedding." With that she turned and fled.

Upstairs, she locked herself in her room. She left her dinner tray untouched outside her door and refused to speak to anyone. When Morgan pounded on her door and shouted at her to let him in, she met his demands with resounding silence. Only her mother's soft entreaties brought any response, and then only a request to go away and leave her alone.

****

Morgan spent a sleepless night in the guestroom, tossing and turning, trying to figure out the woman across the hall. He thought he knew what she wanted, but his coming here should be enough to prove his feelings. He came for her without even knowing about the baby. While she was still in the Ozarks, he'd hoped she might be pregnant. That would have kept her in the hills for good. But when she left with Jared, he was sure there was no baby. He never believed her threat to raise their child alone without telling him. The thought made him mad enough to spit nails.

All the way to Weston, he'd wrestled with his decision to follow Jessy and persuade her to return home with him. He would never be good enough for her, but the last month hadn't been worth living. He'd snapped at everyone and generally been as prickly as a riled porcupine. The rest of the family moped around acting like he'd stolen the sun. And, of course, that was before he knew about the baby. Now, there was no way he'd leave without her.

By the time a neighboring rooster announced the coming of dawn, he had settled on a plan. He had to get her alone, out of the house, someplace he could talk to her without a locked door between them. Lisa Tanner's orchard sounded perfect.

He had no trouble persuading Annabelle Randall to let him take a breakfast tray up to her stubborn daughter. Balancing the tray on one hand, he knocked on the door, hoping Jessy would think it was Clara or her mother and open the door without a fight.

"Who is it?"

He grimaced. He wasn't going to be so lucky. "It's me. Open the door."

"Go away."

"Dammit, Jessy, are you trying to starve the baby? Do you hate me that much?"

The door opened, and his heart tightened. Her bewitching green eyes were red and swollen, with deep purple circles underneath, and her glorious hair hung down on her shoulders in a tangled red mass.

He shouldered the door open and pushed past her. Setting the tray on a low table at the foot of the bed, he turned to face her. "I hate to say it, Jessy, but you look awful."

She twisted her mouth in a ghost of a smile. "Thank you."

"I'm not joking. You've got to take care of yourself, for the baby's sake."

"Yes...the baby."

He marched over to her and placed his hands on her shoulders. "Sit down." He gently forced her onto a rose-colored velvet settee. He dragged the table with the tray close to her, hunkered down, and picked up the fork. "You are going to eat this food, every bite. Then you are going to climb into that bed and sleep until your parents get back from church."

"I can't."

"You can, and you will. I'm going to stay here to make sure you do."

Jessy just stared at him.

"When you wake up," he continued, "you are going to take a bath, brush your hair, and put on something pretty. Then I am going to drive you to the Tanner's farm. Do you understand?"

She nodded blankly.

"Good. Now eat."

In the end, he fed her. When she had eaten everything, he slid his arms beneath her knees and shoulders and carried her to the bed.

"Now sleep." He drew the covers over her. With tender fingers, he brushed the tangled curls away from her face.

"I can't." Her voice was weak, and tears seeped from the corners of her eyes.

He reached over and dried her tears with a corner of the sheet. He stroked one finger down her cheek. "It's all right. I'll be here beside you the whole time. Now sleep."

She sighed and closed her eyes. Within seconds, she was asleep. He pulled up a chair to wait and watch.

Chapter Nineteen

Jessy awoke to sunlight streaming through the windows. She blinked to allow her eyes to adjust then stared. Morgan was fast asleep in the chair beside her bed. His head lolled to one side and bristly stubble coated his jaw, but he looked wonderful.

She vaguely remembered that he had come into her room, fed her, and put her to bed, but the memory was fuzzy, like a half-forgotten dream. She'd been too distressed and exhausted to think clearly, but the hot food and few hours' sleep had worked wonders to restore her strength. She would still have to deal with him when he woke, but at least now she had most of her wits about her.

She slipped out of bed and tiptoed across the room to her wardrobe. The door creaked, and she held her breath. She had been far too vulnerable when he came to her room earlier. A bath and change of clothes were just what she needed to restore her confidence before facing him again.

"Feeling better?"

She shot up from the drawer with an armful of undergarments.

Morgan stretched lazily in the chair and yawned. Unfolding his long legs, he rose and ambled over to her. "Don't wear black."

"It's all I have. Mama insisted."

"Well, find something else. I'm not dead yet." His voice was deep and scratchy from sleep. "Besides, no bride of mine is going to wear black on her wedding day."

Her heart skipped a beat. He was offering the very thing she'd wanted for nearly a year. But she didn't want him to marry her because of his overactive sense of duty. It had to be for the right reasons or not at all.

She forced a light smile. "Then that should pose no problem, since no one is getting married today that I know of."

"We'll see. Find something else." He began rifling through the dresses in the wardrobe.

"I can't fit into anything else." She was unable to keep the touch of accusation out of her voice.

His gaze slid to her stomach. "You look as tiny as ever to me."

She flushed and glanced away. "There's no need to be gallant. I'm as plump as a pumpkin. I haven't even worn stays since you cut them off outside Independence."

He reached out and encircled her waist with his hands. He let his fingers glide up her ribs in a touch as light as a lamb's kiss. "Like I told you at the time, you never needed one of those contraptions. You're perfect."

Flustered, she sought his eyes. They burned with a promise she was afraid to acknowledge.

He dropped his hands. "Find something else to wear. Please. I don't have the energy to fight you."

She nodded. She didn't want to fight either. She was too confused by the novelty of his words and attitude.

Morgan rubbed his rough jaw. "I've got to get cleaned up. I'll be back in half an hour."

True to his word, he knocked on her door thirty minutes later. Jessy was ready—for what, she wasn't sure. She wore a white summer gown sprinkled with little nosegays of violets and hoped no one would notice she'd moved the hooks at the waist to accommodate her expanded girth. She felt dumpy and awkward, but at least the dress wasn't black.

"You look beautiful."

She opened her mouth to protest, then stopped and stared at him. "Do you realize that's the first time you've ever said that to me?"

Morgan gave her a half smile. "I've thought it plenty of times, though. Shall we go?" He offered his arm like the finest city-bred gallant and swept her down the stairs and out to the waiting carriage.

"Where are you taking me?"

"I promised your friend Lisa I'd bring you over to visit before I left town."

Left town? Was he giving up so quickly and going back to the hills?

Neither of them spoke during the drive to the Tanner's farm. Jessy cast swift side-glances at Morgan's profile. He was different since he'd come back to Weston. She couldn't put her finger on the change, but it was there, pricking at her, teasing her.

They pulled into the drive of Lisa's comfortable old brick farmhouse, and Jessy was surprised at how orderly and prosperous the place looked. The white trim gleamed with a fresh coat of paint, the overgrown bushes had been pruned into new vigor, and colorful flowers bordered the front porch. As long as she could remember, the farm had been in a state of shabby decline. The changes must be Jared's doing. Lisa had resisted Jared's attentions long and hard, but his persistence had finally won out, and now they were awaiting the birth of their first child.

Lisa answered Morgan's knock with a smile of delight. "You came! I wasn't sure you would."

"Morgan insisted," Jessy replied.

Lisa's smile widened, and she nodded in approval. "Good. Why don't you come in for some lemonade and cookies before you go to see the orchard? Jared built the loveliest bench under the trees. I'm sure you'll enjoy it."

Nervous anticipation fluttered in Jessy's stomach. She wished she could read Morgan's mind. He was better at hiding his feelings than anyone she had ever known. From his comments to her father yesterday, she suspected he might try to bully her into marriage.

Well, she would have none of it. The worst was over now. Her parents knew the truth, so he had no leverage on her. She refused to bind herself for the rest of her life to a man who didn't love her. Her resolve strengthened, she made polite small talk with Lisa and Jared.

Morgan downed his lemonade and stood, setting his empty glass on the table. "That was very good, Mrs. Tanner. Now, if you'll excuse us, Jessy and I will go see that orchard of yours." He grabbed Jessy's hand and hauled her to her feet.

Lisa's smile betrayed her amusement. "Yes, of course."

He half dragged her across the yard and past the barn to the neat rows of apple trees. Thick clouds of sweet-scented blossoms swathed their gnarled black limbs. "Now where's that damned bench?" He spotted the bench in the center of the orchard and marched toward it with single-purposed determination. "Sit down."

She pulled her hand from his grasp. "I prefer to stand."

He closed his eyes and let out a sigh. "Jessy, please sit down. This is hard enough for me as it is. I've practiced over and over in my head, and if I don't get it out now, I'm bound to forget every word."

Part of her wanted desperately to hear what he had to say, and part of her was terrified. Withdrawing behind a protective veil of imperiousness, she sank onto the bench as gracefully as her figure would allow. "Very well, since you asked so politely."

"Jessy, you have to marry me."

She bristled. "If it's because—"

"Hold it right there," he interrupted. "I've got something important to say. The least you can do is hear me out."

She snapped her mouth shut.

"Good." He turned and paced in front of the bench. "Now, as I was saying, you have to marry me. I know I can't offer you the kind of life you deserve, but my life's been as worthless as last week's coffee grounds since you left." He stopped and waved a hand in the air. "Ma will barely speak to me. Corrine and Sally leave the room whenever I come in. Even Samuel glares at me all the time."

"They'll get over it."

He threw her a sharp glance. "I don't know about that." His gaze softened. "You brought new life to the whole farm and everyone on it."

Her eyes stung at the tenderness in his tone, but she shook her head. "If any changes were made, your family did the work themselves."

"Don't make light of it. You know what you did."

She took a deep breath and folded her hands in her lap before lifting her gaze to meet his. "If my visit improved life on the farm in some small ways, I'm gratified. However, that is not sufficient reason for me to return."

"They need you to come back."

She shook her head.

He clenched his jaws and released them, flexing the muscles in his cheek. His brows drew together. Jessy steeled herself.

"I need you to come back."

His voice was so soft and so completely at odds with his ferocious countenance that it rendered her speechless while the meaning of his words soaked in.

He ran his fingers through his tawny hair then resumed pacing. "This isn't going right at all." He spun to face her. "When I brought you here, I intended to tell you everything I told your father last night after you went to your room."

Jessy tried to picture Morgan in the role of earnest suitor, but the image refused to come. He was too self-contained, too proud. And he was struggling. She reached out and touched his wrist.

He grasped her hand like a lifeline and sank to one knee in front of her. "So help me, I'm going to do this right." He raised his gold-flecked hazel eyes to hers. "Jessy, I'm asking you to marry me." She opened her mouth, but he shushed her. "No, don't say anything yet. I told your father about my prospects and intentions, and I'm going to tell you, too."

He looked so fierce, she almost laughed.

"Except for the parcel I gave Will and Sally, I own the farm. It's not much, but it's free and clear. Zeke and Jonah and some of the others helped me finish the house. I know it's not what you're used to, but it's got two stone fireplaces, glass in the windows, and real plaster on the walls."

"I'm sure it's beautiful."

He maintained his grip on her hand. "Besides the fiddles, Ethan and I have started a furniture business in the barn. A lot of the kinfolk who came to Will and Sally's wedding saw the bed and asked about one for themselves. We've even talked to Hiram Boone about carrying a few smaller pieces in his store."

He paused, and a fleeting frown crossed his face. "I'll never be able to give you everything you deserve, but I'll always provide for you and our children. I swear it."

"I never doubted it."

He dropped her hand and rose to his feet. "Then why won't you marry me?"

She rose to face him. "You have told me all the things you can do for me, all the things you can give me, if I marry you. But you've left out the most important thing, the only thing I really need." Her voice wavered. "The only thing that matters."

He regarded her with confusion and impatience. "And what is that?"

"A husband who loves me." Defiance flared amid her glittering tears.

"That goes without saying."

"It does not."

"I rode all the way back here to fetch you. That alone should tell you how I feel."

She stood her ground. "I expect you to tell me, in words and out loud. I refuse to accept any declaration I have to bully out of you."

He stared at her. Then a glimmer of amusement twinkled in his eyes. His mouth began to twitch.

Jessy set her lips. This was no laughing matter.

He reached out and pulled her into his arms. "You've been trying to bully me since the day I first laid eyes on you."

She wriggled against his embrace. "I have—"

"—and I expect you to keep it up every day for the rest of our lives." His lips came down on hers, silencing her protest. They lingered and caressed, promised and enticed.

"I love you, Jessy," he whispered next to her ear. "I fought it, but you've known all along, haven't you?"

"I was afraid I might be wrong." Her response was breathless because he was kissing the soft skin of her neck beneath her ear.

"You were wrong, wrong to fall in love with a worthless, no-good outlaw like me. But you were never wrong about my feelings for you. Never." One large hand slid into her hair to hold her head, and the other pressed her hips through layers of petticoats while his lips plundered hers again.

She shoved at his chest, hard, until he lifted his head. "Don't ever say that again. Do you hear me?"

"What?"

"You are a brave, selfless, hard-working man. The father of my child. The man I love. You are not worthless, and I will never allow you to say that again. Do you understand?"

He laughed out loud. "And you claim you're not a bully."

She refused to be deterred. "Stop it. This is serious."

His smile disappeared. "You're right. This is serious." His thumb outlined the soft curve of her cheek. "Jessy, I was nothing before I met you. I was less than nothing. If there's any good in me at all, it's because of you. You make me want to be more than I've ever been. I want to be good, good enough for you."

Tears started in her eyes. She reached up to reciprocate his touch with loving fingers. "I love you," she whispered.

"And I'll thank the good Lord every second of every day of my life."

He kissed her again with all the passion in his being, pouring his love into her. "Say you'll marry me," he urged against her lips. "Today."

Her heart rose and soared like a hawk riding an updraft. She had waited so long for that declaration, she almost believed it would never come. "Yes." Her breath mingled with his. "Today."

He set her back and searched her eyes. Then he groaned and crushed her to him once more. "Oh, God, Jessy! I love you so much! I'll never stop loving you."

Two hours later, they were married in front of the fireplace in her parents' parlor by her solemn-faced father, with Lisa and Jared Tanner standing up for them, just as she had planned months earlier.

Jessy was surprised when Morgan declined to consummate their marriage vows that night, but the thought of being so near her parents made her a little nervous, too. When he also refused in the hotel in Kansas City and again camped out along the trail, she grew concerned. He was attentive and loving in every other respect, but when she snuggled against him at night, he kissed her forehead and said, "Wait. Just wait."

On the evening of the fourth day, they crossed the Osage River onto Bingham land and began the final ascent to the homestead. Her anticipation rose with every foot they climbed. She hadn't realized how much she'd missed his family until it was almost time to see them again.

When Morgan rode past the cabin, she called out to him in consternation, "Why aren't we stopping? Where are we going?"

"Home."

Then she realized he was taking her to her new home—their home—the home he'd built for her and their children with his own hands. The house came into view, and her breath caught in her throat. Like the main cabin, it was built of hewn logs, but it was nearly twice as big, with a covered front porch running across the entire length and a massive stone fireplace at each end.

"It's beautiful."

"It's yours."

She turned and smiled at her new husband. "No, it's ours."

He didn't return her smile, but a look of intense satisfaction swept his face. "Yes." He dismounted and reached up to help her. "Come inside."

They climbed the steps hand in hand. When they reached the front door, he pushed it open and ushered her inside. In the dusky light of early evening, she could barely make out a few dark shapes.

"I'll light a lamp." He stepped away and struck a light. A bright glow fared, illuminating a gleaming trestle table flanked by two chairs.

"Oh, Morgan, it's lovely."

He picked up the lamp and reached for her hand. "Come with me."

He led her to a staircase—a real staircase, not a rickety ladder—and steered her up, lighting the way with the lamp. At the top of the stairs was a hall with two doors.

"This way." He guided her to the room on the left.

They stepped into the room, and he held the lamp high. In the center stood the most beautiful bed Jessy had ever seen. It was similar to the one Morgan and Ethan had made for Sally and Will, but the carving was finer and the hand-rubbed finish shone with a life of its own. An intricate blue and yellow quilt covered the plump mattress.

She stared at the bed, her hands pressed to her cheeks. "I don't know what to say. I'm speechless."

He relaxed and smiled. "That's a first."

She was too happy to take offense. She beamed with sheer joy.

"It's yours, your marriage bed."

"This is why you wanted to wait, isn't it?"

He nodded.

She threw herself onto the quilt and sank into the soft mattress. She rolled over and flashed him a grin. "It's very comfortable." She patted the bed. "Why don't you join me, Mr. Bingham?"

Morgan tossed his hat onto the post at the corner of the headboard. "Don't mind if I do." He climbed onto the bed and pulled his new bride into his arms.

Jessy kissed him before he had a chance to kiss her first. "I love you, Mr. Bingham."

He kissed her thoroughly in return. "And I love you, Mrs. Bingham. Welcome home."

The rightness of his words sank into her heart, healing the hurts and making her whole. She was wanted. She was loved. She was indeed home.

ABOUT THE AUTHOR

I haven't always been a writer, but I have always embraced creativity and relished new experiences. Seeking to expand my horizons beyond Kansas City, I chose a college in upstate New York. By the time I was twenty-one I had traveled the world from Tunisia to Japan. Little did I suspect I was collecting material for future characters and stories along the way.

I began writing when my daughter entered preschool (she's now a full-fledged adult) and became addicted to the challenge of translating the living, breathing images in my mind into words. I write romance because that's what I like to read. The world provides more than enough drama and tragedy. I want to give my readers the happily-ever-after we all crave.

I've been married to my personal hero for more than thirty years. After decades of living in the Midwest, we heeded the siren call of sun and sea and moved to the most breathtakingly beautiful place imaginable - the gorgeous central coast of California. I look forward to bringing you all the new stories this place inspires.

Alison

Made in the USA
Coppell, TX
28 May 2021

56456602R00177